KRIEG

KRIEG

STEVE LYONS

BLACK LIBRARY

A BLACK LIBRARY PUBLICATION

First published in 2021.
This edition published in Great Britain in 2022 by
Black Library, Games Workshop Ltd., Willow Road,
Nottingham, NG7 2WS, UK.

Represented by: Games Workshop Limited – Irish branch,
Unit 3, Lower Liffey Street, Dublin 1,
D01 K199, Ireland.

10 9 8 7 6 5 4 3 2

Produced by Games Workshop in Nottingham.
Cover illustration by Miklós Ligeti.

A CIP record for this book is available from the British Library.

ISBN 13: 978-1-80026-204-1

See Black Library on the internet at

blacklibrary.com

Find out more about Games Workshop
and the world of Warhammer 40,000 at

games-workshop.com

Printed and bound by CPI Group (UK) Ltd, Croydon, CR0 4YY

---

*For Annie and Arthur, my parents, without whose love and support I could
never have pursued my dreams.*

For more than a hundred centuries the Emperor has sat immobile on the Golden Throne of Earth. He is the Master of Mankind. By the might of His inexhaustible armies a million worlds stand against the dark.

Yet, He is a rotting carcass, the Carrion Lord of the Imperium held in life by marvels from the Dark Age of Technology and the thousand souls sacrificed each day so that His may continue to burn.

To be a man in such times is to be one amongst untold billions. It is to live in the cruellest and most bloody regime imaginable. It is to suffer an eternity of carnage and slaughter. It is to have cries of anguish and sorrow drowned by the thirsting laughter of dark gods.

This is a dark and terrible era where you will find little comfort or hope. Forget the power of technology and science. Forget the promise of progress and advancement. Forget any notion of common humanity or compassion.

There is no peace amongst the stars, for in the grim darkness of the far future,
there is only war.

949.M40

THE ASHES

The planet was dead. Every reading confirmed it.

The augurs' findings scrolled across viewscreens and hololithic displays on the bridge. The planet's stratosphere was choked with soot. It was too cold to sustain human life. No plants could grow in the ash that smothered its surface. Its oceans were a frozen soup of toxic chemicals. The augurs probed for man-made energy sources in vain.

The planet, every inch of it, was lethally radioactive. The medical cogitators screamed a warning that to tread its ground would be to suffer a certain, lingering death.

The planet was dead. How could it be, then, that a ship had just taken off from it?

Nothing had been heard of Krieg in half a millennium. The planet, to its name, had been all but forgotten, not only through time's passage but also in part by Imperial edict.

That had changed two months ago. A number of astropaths, passing through the Segmentum Tempestus, had picked up fragments of a message. It had taken time and effort to put those fragments together before their source was revealed.

Krieg's civil war, begun five hundred years ago, was over. Its loyalists had triumphed over the secessionist traitors. They stood ready to serve the Emperor once more. They wished to wipe the stain of sin from their planet's history. They wished to atone.

The message was debated at the Administratum's highest levels. Some feared it might be a deception, a lure set by their enemies. They opined that a world like Krieg could only be a drain on their resources. After all this time, what could they have to offer? Others pointed out that, in these days, one world – any world that could raise a single regiment for the Emperor's armies – could not be overlooked.

And so, a delegation was despatched. An Imperial grand cruiser dropped into orbit around Krieg. It announced its arrival over a range of frequencies, though the vox-operators felt sure no one would hear them, that they were chasing astropathic echoes. To their surprise, they received a reply.

The ship that rose from Krieg's surface was an Arvus lighter: an Imperial Naval shuttle, though its markings had been burnt away. The image of a leering skull had been painted crudely in their place. The ship showed its age in every dent and blister on its hull, and in the black smoke that belched from its starboard rocket engine. It seemed miraculous that it could fly at all. The voice from the planet, however, had advised against sending a lander – much to the relief of the ratings who would have had to crew one.

The airlock door groaned open, and there they stood, revealed by its circular aperture. Six in number, as agreed, in strict formation. The ash of the blasted planet below clung to their clothing. Each of them wore a dark, buttoned-up greatcoat, through which the lines of flak armour could just be discerned. Spiked helmets, scuffed and dented, crowned their heads. They were booted and gloved, every inch of their bodies protected – including their faces. The men of Krieg wore gas masks. Their eyes were concealed behind opaque circular lenses. Hoses linked the masks' distended snouts to rebreathers: cumbersome chest-mounted boxes. They ticked and whirred, analysing the ship's recycled air.

Larreth stood apart from the welcoming committee, flanked by her personal retinue, eyes narrowed. She detected no deformities in the Krieg men's postures. Still, something about them, something in the combination of their concealing ensembles and their rigid discipline, plucked at her nerves. The masks reminded her of nothing more than hollow-eyed skulls, like the one daubed on their shuttle.

Ambassador Strack paused to swallow before he smiled and introduced himself. A Krieg colonel – he displayed Imperial rank insignia on his helmet – looked at his outstretched hand. Then he stepped forward, through the aperture, and took it.

En route to the conference chamber, Strack attempted to make small talk. He told his guests how surprising it had been, though a pleasure, to hear from them after all this time. He prompted the colonel for a name, which the man hadn't yet offered, and the Krieg colonel spoke for the first time, his voice low and rough like gravel.

'We,' he said, 'are the Death Korps of Krieg. We are soldiers of the Emperor.'

The Krieg colonel sat at the conference table, only at Strack's urging.

His soldiers stood sentry behind him, though they were unarmed by agreement. They stared blankly over the heads of the assembled dignitaries of the Departmento Munitorum. The colonel sat stiffly, arms straight by his sides, and only spoke in his husky voice when a direct question was put to him.

He confirmed that the war on his planet had ended, with the faction he commanded – the Death Korps of Krieg – victorious. 'Then you are Krieg's military governor?' a much-decorated lord general militant asked him. The colonel had spied him upon entering the chamber and had saluted the image of the Imperial aquila upon his cap.

'Yes, sir,' he said.

'And yet you only hold the rank of colonel?'

'Yes, sir,' he repeated, offering no explanation.

'What is the current fighting strength of your… "Death Korps"?'

'At present, we can offer the Emperor sixty thousand soldiers, trained, equipped and organised into twenty regiments.'

The statement was met by a brief stunned silence. Then the lord general militant leaned forward in his seat. 'You did say sixty thousand? *Twenty* regiments?'

'Standing by for immediate deployment, sir.'

'But how? Where on the planet are they stationed? How do you survive in those conditions, let alone…?'

'Eighty-three Krieg regiments once served in the Astra Militarum,' the Krieg colonel intoned. 'Our goal – our duty – is to equal that number, and better it.'

'What is Krieg's current population?' asked the lord general militant.

'As I said, sir, we can offer sixty thousand–'

'I mean, your total population. Not just soldiers, but civilians.'

'There are no civilians on Krieg,' the colonel stated. Larreth noted that he had sidestepped the question, not for the first time. He gave only the information he wanted to give. She sensed the eagerness around the table, however. The colonel was offering a prize far greater than any they could have imagined.

It was time she interceded. She cleared her throat and the room fell silent again. When a witch hunter spoke, loyal citizens, whatever their stations, knew well to listen. A faulty servo-motor in her ancient power armour whined as she adjusted her position.

'You may remove the face mask, colonel.' Ambassador Strack had made the same suggestion, but he had lacked Larreth's accusing tone.

'The rebreather units are part of our uniforms, sir.'

'Out of necessity, I'm sure. You have no need of them aboard this ship, nor will your soldiers on the worlds to which they are assigned.'

'On the contrary. We expect to be assigned to the most hazardous warzones available. Worlds upon which the atmosphere is toxic. We are well used to such conditions and thrive in them. This is where we are best equipped to serve.'

The Imperial dignitaries looked as if they couldn't believe their fortune.

'The, ah, the conditions on your world…' the lord general militant ventured. 'I imagine you must wear the masks, the rebreathers, even off duty. If the Krieg are used to breathing filtered oxygen, then even the air in this room may be poisonous to them. It may contain pathogens to which they possess no immunity.'

The colonel inclined his head in tacit agreement.

'Or might you have a graver reason to hide your faces from us?' Inquisitor Larreth persisted. 'Might you be afraid that we would disapprove of them?' She raised a hand to silence the general before he could answer for the Krieg officer again.

'Our world paid a high price for its treachery,' the colonel conceded. 'The war took a heavy toll upon us. Nevertheless, we stand before you now, made stronger by our trials and ready to resume our rightful service.'

'What is your name?' asked Larreth.

He didn't answer her. She wished she could see his expression or glare into his eyes. What manner of being, she wondered, must a world so tainted as his breed? And who could survive upon that world, without becoming tainted too? 'The rest of us have introduced ourselves,' she prompted. 'What is your name?'

The Krieg colonel cocked his head a little.

He looked as if he didn't understand the question.

AFTER THE GREAT RIFT

THE LINE

Hive Arathron was lost. In truth, it had been lost from the moment the voidship had crashed into it.

Arathron's doom had come screaming from the heavens without warning, in a ball of vengeful flame. The impact had sundered the hive's walls, collapsing fifty residential levels into one. It had touched off a chain of explosions, ripping through the industrial blocks. Millions had perished, unaware, in those first few fateful seconds.

The ship itself – a ramshackle assembly of armour plates, bolted to the frame of a junked Imperial cruiser – was all but disintegrated. Nothing aboard could have survived; but then, somehow, orks always did.

The planetary governor assumed the crash to be accidental, rather than a deliberate attack: fallout from the war raging through the Octarius System. She may have been right. Where orks were concerned, it was often hard to tell the difference. The result, either way, was the same. The local militia, expecting to find only broken bodies in the wreckage, were taken by surprise and overwhelmed.

A Cadian regiment, diverted from another battlefield, fared better. They fought with their customary skill and precision, in contrast to the feral and disorganised invaders. They kept the orks pinned down for several days.

Just one more, and they might have stood a chance.

Ven Bruin was on the lowest level when he heard the news. He was herding three hundred hopeless stragglers through narrow thoroughfares, towards the exit.

Down here, the hive was more or less structurally sound but creaking under the weight of the devastation above. The greatest threat was other hopeless citizens, driven to panic by the loss of all they knew. Many had allowed the Ruinous Powers into their hearts. They had joined up with the street gangs, whose only aims were to vandalise and terrorise, to satisfy their own gratuitous urges.

For two days, Ven Bruin had fought a running battle with the gangs. His greatest asset in this was his distinctive garb. His black cloak and capotain hat, with the skull motif on their buckles, announced his rank as clearly as did the Inquisitorial seal, which he wore clasped above his heart.

His appearance struck shame and dread into the newly faithless. It reminded them that the Emperor's reach exceeded that of the godless xenos, even now, even still. Many of them melted into the shadows, to cower and weep and regret their impulsive actions. For others, the sight of a witch hunter provoked unreasoning fury. These were the truly damned, and they had had enough of running.

The attack was launched from the steps of a half-demolished church. The gangers used its cracked and crumbling pillars for cover. Perhaps they enjoyed the twisted symbolism. A garbage fire sputtered in the doorway behind them. A few had laid their hands on rusted old percussion rifles. They spat out bullets indiscriminately, into the screaming crowd.

'Everyone, down on the ground!' Ven Bruin yelled, but few of the would-be evacuees obeyed him, and those who did were trampled by the rest. He shouldered his way through them, inferno pistol drawn, looking for a clear shot. He unsheathed his sword and thumbed the activation rune in its hilt, bathing its blade in a field of fierce, bright energy. This had the desired effect of clearing his path somewhat.

Ven Bruin was an old man. Rejuvenat treatments had kept him lean and vital, strong of limb – he took pride in the image he presented, eyes blazing in the shadow of his hat's lowered brim, gritted teeth framed by a silver-streaked beard – but he *felt* old. He would not be around forever, and had begun his search for a successor long ago.

He gained sight of one of the gunners: a straggly haired youth in a ripped vest, bare arms crazed with illiterate tattoos. He steadied his target in his sights as he advanced upon him. The inferno pistol had only a short range, which normally suited Ven Bruin. He did most of his fighting eye to eye.

The youth saw him coming, one old man striding against the tide, and almost dropped his weapon in fright. He loosed off another burst of badly directed fire. Ven Bruin didn't flinch as three civilians were cut down around him. He trusted his body armour – more so, the armour of his faith – to keep him safe. He squeezed his pistol's trigger, and fried a stream of air before him.

The youth's hair erupted into flame and his face blistered. His smouldering corpse broke on the stone steps. What the inferno pistol lacked in range, it gained in power – too much power for so weak a foe, but it made a salutary point.

Three more foes came at Ven Bruin from his left. Three more tattooed heretics, whirling chains above their heads. Immediately, he discerned the weeping pustules on one's neck, the unnatural curvature of another's spine. They were mutants, vermin washed up from the underhive to revel in Arathron's woes.

He holstered his pistol and gripped his sword two-handed. The first mutant leapt at him, screeching, and impaled itself upon the interposed blade. The second accidentally wrapped its chain about its own head. It crumpled with a groan and was stamped to death by a crowd now more disgusted than scared by it.

The third mutant, seeing its fellows' fates, was cautious. Its chain struck like a venomous snake from six feet away, glancing off Ven Bruin's chestplate. He yanked his blade out of the first dead mutant, feeling minimal resistance. The crowd around him had finally thinned out, giving him much-needed elbow room.

The chain lashed out again and he ducked under it, at the same time propelling himself forward. His blade described a brilliant arc of purifying light. It struck the mutant's left side, beneath its ribs, and emerged from its right. The stink of mutant blood assailed his nostrils, but it swiftly boiled away. The blade also cleansed itself.

The sounds of gunfire ceased. The crowd calmed down a little, though some still wailed in fear or mourning. Two of Ven Bruin's acolytes caught up with him. They flanked him, scanning their surroundings for renewed threats, their pistols readied. It was their duty to protect him, their inquisitor. He was well aware how hard he made this for them.

He had brought six with him, just his warriors. The others had been busy too. A second ganger lay dead, slumped against her pillar. The third was on his knees, fumbling with a jammed rifle, as Interrogator Ferran attained the church steps and bore down on him. The ganger, in panic, cast the rifle away and began to raise his hands, tears streaking his crudely inked cheeks. Ferran executed him with a bolt to the temple.

'Keep moving!' Ven Bruin bellowed. He hauled a cringing civilian to his feet, flashed him a contemptuous glare and sent him on his way with a shove. 'No time to lick our wounds or count our dead. Keep heading east – that way – in an orderly fashion. Anyone judged to be impeding others will be shot.'

He reached the steps and marched up them. Someone pressed a laudhailer into his hand, which he raised to his lips. He repeated the instructions, adding directions to the exit. It was likely that no one here had left the hive before. He sent his acolytes back out to guide, protect and motivate them, but signalled to Ferran to hang back.

'There are more of them out there,' said Ferran, once they had a measure of privacy. 'Heretics. Mutants. I saw a shadow behind the church windows. It feels wrong to turn our backs on them, to allow them to profane that holy place.'

'You heard the vox reports?' Ven Bruin asked him.

'I did. The Cadians are pulling out of Arathron today, ceding it to the xenos, Emperor damn them.' The curl of Ferran's lips and the beetling of his dark, bushy eyebrows underlined his disgust at this development.

'It was to be expected,' said Ven Bruin, with greater equanimity. 'Their forces are depleted from their previous engagement. They held out longer than we expected they would.' He allowed himself a sigh. 'Not as long as we had prayed they might.'

'And our mission here, inquisitor? Are we to proceed?'

'If only we were closer, perhaps.'

'It may be days yet before the xenos reach these levels.'

'It may be sooner than we think. If not before we reach our

goal, then certainly before we could do anything about it. We could even lead them there ourselves. No, best I feel if Hive Arathron's secrets remain hidden. For as long as they can be.'

'If the xenos don't stumble upon them, the heretics might.'

'If the Emperor is with us, they'll be kept too busy tearing each other apart.'

'We can only pray, again,' the interrogator grumbled.

They spilled out of a broad opening at the hive's base. They were met by the glare of the sun, sitting high in the eastern sky before them. Few of Ven Bruin's charges had seen a light so bright and they flinched from it, complaining that it burnt their eyes.

They joined thousands more evacuees, milling about in confusion. Reservist militiamen, identified by armbands, fought in vain to herd them northwards. Another hive squatted on the distant horizon – at least a hundred miles away, Ven Bruin reckoned.

The barren ground was churned with recent vehicle tracks, but few vehicles were left in evidence. Fights had broken out around a couple of trucks. People clung to their chassis and hammered on their windscreens, imploring, so that while their engines growled and their exhaust pipes spluttered, their tyres could gain no traction.

To their backs, Hive Arathron marinated in a self-created smog. Thicker smoke billowed from its upper levels, miles above, as flyers circled like disoriented insects. Its outer roadways teemed with insects too: the vehicles of the withdrawing Cadians. According to vox chatter, they had pulled back to the bottom hundred levels, collapsing strategic access points to slow down their pursuers.

Ven Bruin took to the hailer again. He ordered the crowd to disperse, to make room for others adding to the crush behind them. He promised that vehicles were being sent back for them, though he knew there would never be enough.

The xenos in the hive had found a cannon. It had only been a matter of time. The Cadians had destroyed artillery emplacements as they left, but orks had a reputation for making the most broken weapons function. Breathless reports squawked over each other in Ven Bruin's earpiece. Explosive shells were landing at the base of the hive to the west, obliterating victims by the hundred.

He knew now that most of the people around him were doomed.

He called for transport, which arrived in less than a minute. Hope swept through the crowd as a shuttle dropped down among them. With some prodding from the reservists, they cleared a space for it to land, almost at Ven Bruin's feet. Hope turned to resentment as they saw that it hadn't come for them. Their objections were swiftly quelled, however, by the witch hunter's fiery glare, along with his warriors' warning shots.

He paused with a foot on the landing ramp. Something drew his gaze upwards, and he saw streaks of light across the cloudless sky. An instant later, the drone of rocket engines reached him. The crowd had seen and heard it too, and wondered what it meant. Ven Bruin knew, as did Ferran. 'Our reinforcements,' murmured the latter, as the streaks converged upon the hive to the north.

'Dead on schedule,' Ven Bruin noted.

Ferran's brow furrowed. 'Already too late,' he added bleakly.

A new command headquarters had been established out on the plain.

It was ten miles east of Arathron, beyond its cannons' range. The Cadians' support staff and fresh-faced, untrained conscripts assembled the last of its prefabricated huts. The first Centaurs and Chimeras rolled up on their tracks, disgorging weary soldiers. Some were helped to the medicae hut. Others headed for the mess hall, where slab was already being served. Tents began to spring up everywhere.

Colonel Drakon, commander of the Cadian 432nd, settled at his new desk. A servitor poured amasec for him and his guests. The colonel expressed surprise at Ven Bruin's request for quarters for himself and his retinue. 'Am I to infer that you have further business here?' he asked.

'You may infer it, yes,' said Ven Bruin, tight-lipped.

'I heard there was an… issue with the former governor, before he passed away. My people could know nothing of that, of course, but if we can assist in any way…?'

'Not at this present moment.'

Drakon sat back and took a long sip from his glass. Ven Bruin's presence worried him, but he knew better than to push too hard for information. It might have been different had Ven Bruin served the Ordo Xenos. The Ordo Hereticus existed to seek out *human* treachery – and the only humans here now were the colonel's own shock troops.

Ven Bruin could have reassured him, but chose not to. It did no one any harm to be reminded that the Emperor's eyes were always upon them.

'We are to be joined by a Krieg regiment, I hear,' said Interrogator Ferran.

'I believe so,' said Drakon.

'The infamous Death Korps.'

'Exceptional fighters,' Ven Bruin commented, approvingly. 'I have encountered them often. Their world exists on a permanent war footing. Soldiers are their only export, so they are trained from birth, instilled with the highest possible level of commitment.'

'The same was once true of my world,' the Cadian colonel said, a little stiffly.

'You have new orders, presumably,' said Ferran. 'To retake the hive?'

Drakon shook his head. 'To eradicate all trace of xenos from this world – even if it means Hive Arathron is razed in the process.'

Ven Bruin inclined his head, so his eyes fell back into his capotain's shadow.

'This world is a crucial link in the cordon about this system,' the colonel explained. 'It cannot – it must not – fall. The line must be held here.'

Ven Bruin was not surprised to hear it. The Octarius War had been raging for several years. Imperial machinations had set a burgeoning ork empire against a tyranid hive fleet. The hope had been for it to end in mutual destruction. Instead, both sides had thrived on the conflict. The hive fleet had engorged itself on the biomass of billions of foes. The orks had multiplied and grown stronger too, while billions more had flocked to join them from all corners of the galaxy. The war was expanding, the fallout felt on many bordering worlds like this one. Some had already suffered the ultimate sanction.

Those worlds had been destroyed for the sake of keeping the xenos hordes contained.

The approach of the Krieg was first evidenced by a dust cloud on the horizon.

Sergeant Renick saw it as she sat in the dirt outside the medicae hut, waiting for her turn to be seen. Her injuries were less severe than many, just cuts and bruises, but she had taken her last dose of stimm. She had had no choice, after sixteen hours defending a makeshift barricade from wave after wave of ork attacks with no prospect of relief. According to regulations, now she had to be examined for side effects.

She also wanted to replenish her stimms, of course.

At present, all she felt was tired. She lost the battle to keep her eyelids raised, and next she knew, she was woken by a sound like the drone of a million bees. She shook her head and clambered to her feet, reproaching herself for her weakness. She brushed down her khaki fatigues and donned her helmet over her spiky black hair. She fastened the chinstrap so tightly that it cut into her flesh.

The queue ahead of her had dissipated, the temperature had dropped and that dust cloud had drawn closer. Squat, angular shapes were becoming discernible within it, and the insect drone had grown into a roar of heavy-duty engines.

She was in and out of the hut in under three minutes. She gathered with her Cadian fellows outside their tents, beneath the blood-red sky of sunset, as the first armoured vehicles reached the encampment and juddered to a halt.

The rest of the convoy, a mile long and almost as wide, dispersed in search of plots of land to claim. Scores of Gorgon transports were interspersed with smaller Trojans, laden with supplies and towing Earthshaker cannons on platforms. The Leman Russ tank was ubiquitous as always, mainly in its Demolisher siege variant. Renick also saw a pair of massive Baneblades and some vehicles she couldn't identify.

Most of the tanks were customised with trench rails, dozer blades and air filter units, for the harsh environments in which they commonly operated. Their hulls were decorated with cracked and fading decals, depicting grinning skulls with spiked helmets and identifying the Krieg 43rd Siege Regiment.

The most surprising sight of all – the one that had troopers nudging each other and pointing in astonishment – was a phalanx of horses, masked and armoured the same as their straight-backed riders. They had matched the convoy's pace from the northern hive's space port and hardly seemed tired; Renick marvelled at their stamina.

Krieg soldiers poured from the transports and climbed down from their mounts. They set straight to work, unpacking equipment. The sounds of engines died down to be replaced by a clatter of purposeful activity. Amid this, the near absence of voices was eerily noticeable. Krieg soldiers, it seemed, required only minimal instruction, and only conversed with each other when they absolutely had to.

Nor were the onlookers keen to break the silence. Sergeant Renick imagined that most felt the same way she did: a confusing mixture of relief that reinforcements were finally here and shame that they were so badly needed. Since their home world's fall, this Cadian regiment had felt like they had more to prove than ever.

An Aquila lander swooped from the darkening firmament, wings spread proudly like the eagle for which it was named. Colonel Drakon emerged from his quarters in olive-green dress uniform, and a retinue fell in about him. Renick noticed that the witch hunter – she didn't know his name, but everyone was only too aware of his presence – attached himself to it.

The commander of the Krieg 43rd strode down the landing ramp, his own aides formed up behind him. He regarded Drakon's outstretched hand as if puzzled, before taking it. Drakon introduced himself, but the Krieg colonel didn't give a name.

His mask and greatcoat were the same as those worn by his soldiers, if less dusty. His braided shoulders and the winged skull engraved upon his helmet were his only trappings of rank – apart from a bronze breastplate and sabre-blade of superior craftsmanship. The former left no room on his chest for a rebreather unit. The hose from the colonel's mask snaked over his shoulder, to a cylinder peeking out from the top of his backpack.

'If you'd care to see the war room,' said Colonel Drakon, 'I can bring you up to date on the situation here and brief you on the tactics we intend to employ against–'

'I have been briefed,' the Krieg colonel interrupted him gruffly, 'and have drawn up the plan that we will follow.'

Drakon frowned. 'With all due respect,' he began, 'I know the ground here and I–'

'Perhaps you have not been contacted by command. I have been given operational control of all military forces on this world, effective immediately.'

'I was *not* informed of that,' said Drakon, pointedly.

'I understand you have surrendered Arathron.'

There was no accusation in the Krieg colonel's tone, but still the watching Renick bristled. Drakon wasn't happy either. 'No other unit could have held on longer than we did,' he pointed out, quite rightly, 'against such odds.'

'This changes the mission parameters. The orks control the hive's defences,' the Krieg colonel continued as if his counterpart had not spoken. Pre-empting the protest forming in Drakon's throat, he added, 'Compromised though they may be. We are now in a siege situation. My regiment are siege specialists. I also command the greater number of men, five thousand to your… What is your current strength?'

'In the region of eighteen hundred,' Drakon conceded, reluctantly. 'The ordinates are still counting casualties. Let me show you to the war room.'

He turned on his heel and both colonels marched away, pursued by their respective entourages. In their wake, the Cadian rank and file dispersed. Most settled into their tents for the night, though Renick's impression was that few of them slept, but rather lay awake discussing the new arrivals in resentful whispers.

She sank into her own bedroll, letting it cradle her aching

bones and muscles. She woke only once, before dawn, to hear the Krieg still working outside. An odd feeling crept over her as she realised that she had dreamt not of rampaging xenos but of those blank-eyed masks with their rebreather hoses. She suppressed a shiver.

By morning, the encampment had more than doubled in size.

The Krieg had erected more huts and tents of their own, though relatively few of the latter. The Korpsmen, their equivalent of troopers, had done most of the work. Support staff were few in number, and tended to hail from other worlds. Those that did were easy to tell from the Krieg natives. The air this far from the hives had a thin smog film but was relatively fresh, so they kept their respirator masks slung about their necks.

The Krieg and Cadian soldiers kept a distance from each other. Each faction had its own mess hall and latrine facilities, so they had little cause to mingle. 'A few of us went over there to introduce ourselves,' a Cadian lieutenant confided in Renick, 'but it was impossible. They answered our questions, they were perfectly polite, but we could barely draw more than a few syllables out of them.'

An argument flared between one of the newcomers and a member of Renick's own squad. In fact, it was largely one-sided: Trooper Rask was yelling, red-faced, as the Krieg man regarded him impassively. As Rask gave the Korpsman a belligerent shove, Renick waded into the fray. 'They think they're better than us, sergeant,' Rask complained. 'Too good to return a simple greeting.' Renick put him in his place, assigning him punishment duties. She would not have strangers thinking that her people were lacking in discipline.

She drove home the point by drilling her squad for the rest of the morning. Other sergeants soon followed her lead. As always, the Cadians took pride in their manoeuvres, especially as they had an audience and felt they had something to prove. Still, she knew it would take far more than that to repair their fractured morale.

Ven Bruin took a pensive stroll about the camp, inviting Ferran to join him.

They paused to admire the two Baneblades, which towered over them. They were more like mobile fortresses than vehicles, resplendent in khaki and black. Two Korpsmen clambered over each hull with oilcans and wrenches, servicing their arsenals of heavy weapons. They paid the witch hunters little heed, but betrayed no fear of them either.

'These men of Krieg unnerve me,' said Interrogator Ferran.

'How so?' Ven Bruin asked him.

'I stopped four of them at random and questioned them.'

'And their answers were unsatisfactory?'

'On the contrary. Their answers were succinct, saying no more than they needed to say. They professed their faith in the Emperor and their shame at their people's past transgressions. Each of them chose almost the very same words, as if they had learned them by rote. You said you knew the Krieg, inquisitor?'

'As well as anybody can, perhaps,' Ven Bruin demurred.

'I pride myself on my ability to read a heretic's guilt,' said Ferran. 'I can see it in his eyes, in the tics of his facial expression, in the tilt of his head and the way he holds his hands. I can't read these men at all, and not only because of the masks they wear.'

Ven Bruin regarded his subordinate, eyes narrowed in thought. Ferran was squat and muscular. His round, bald, dark-skinned head looked small, cradled by his high collar of office. He was an unimaginative man, single-minded, insensitive, inflexible – the very qualities that the Ordo Hereticus most valued. He had been part of Ven Bruin's retinue for years and was his current candidate to succeed him. The Death Korps of Krieg would be a test for him.

Ven Bruin hailed a passing unmasked commissar, who had spotted him an instant too late to change his course without making his intentions obvious. 'How long have you served with the Krieg?' he asked him, politely.

'Six and a half years,' said the commissar.

'Quite long enough to form an opinion of them. In general, I mean.'

'They…' The commissar paused to consider his words. 'The regiments raised on their world, I believe, have the lowest combined desertion rate in the Astra Militarum.'

'I have heard that said,' agreed Ven Bruin.

'Morale is unstintingly high – and, in my time attached to this regiment, I have recorded few disciplinary offences. I would hazard to suggest that the Krieg have no need of a commissar, not in the traditional sense. If anything, my role here is to rein in their fervour at times. That, and to act as a liaison officer for them – if you will, their human face.'

'Do you ever see *their* faces?' Ferran asked him.

'Never yet.'

The interrogator raised a bushy eyebrow. 'Not a one of them?'

'They are soldiers. The face mask is their uniform, and they are never off duty.'

'Thank you,' said Ven Bruin. 'That is all.'

The commissar tried not to look too relieved as he hurried away.

The inquisitor took in another armoured vehicle: an unwieldy, ancient-looking monster, barely more than a cannon jammed atop a pair of tracks. He knew that, during its centuries-long war, cut off from the rest of the Imperium, Krieg had been forced to improvise.

'The Krieg are famed for their utmost devotion to duty,' he remarked to Ferran. 'Entrust them with a mission, and they will pursue it relentlessly. I am not quite old enough to have witnessed the campaign on Vraks Prime, but a Death Korps army laid siege to that world for seventeen Terran years, at a cost of some fourteen million lives.'

'We don't have nearly that long, sir, nor so many lives to spare.'

'No,' agreed Ven Bruin, gravely, 'we do not.'

'Once the orks gain a foothold upon fresh soil…'

Ferran needed to say no more. Both witch hunters knew the nature of the orks too well. They knew how quickly an infestation of the fecund brutes could spread. They also knew the Departmento Munitorum was preparing for exactly this contingency. Despatches had alluded to evacuation plans, not just for a hive but for a world.

The planetary governor had taken office three weeks ago, and already she was drawing up lists of her most valuable citizens, the few that might be saved.

Krieg officers emerged from the hut that housed the war room. They gathered their troops and moved them out across the plain in platoons, consulting maps on data-slates. The Korpsmen marched until they were almost out of sight. Then they produced entrenching tools from their backpacks and began to dig.

The thunder began about an hour later. The orks had looked out of their captured hive, seen the plain swarming with busy figures and acted as their kind instinctively did when they saw beings unlike themselves. They tried to destroy them.

It began with the faltering bark of a single cannon. A second joined in only minutes later, followed swiftly by a third and then a fourth. Within the hour, a pyrotechnic display of muzzle flashes lit up the distant edifice. Most shells fell short of their targets. They kicked up violent dirt storms across the plain and made the earth tremble. The Krieg disappeared into their half-dug trenches, heads down but still working away.

In the meantime, six Cadian Centaurs scuttled back from the area now known as no-man's-land. They had been out collecting refugees. An ork shell blew one off its tracks and forced its crew and shell-shocked passengers to abandon the vehicle.

More refugees had drifted into the camp throughout the morning. A stockade kept them safely out of the way. They would be conveyed to another hive, but only with the next supplies run. The Krieg quartermasters wouldn't hear of wasting fuel on an extra round trip.

'We lack the numbers to surround the hive effectively,' the Krieg colonel explained in the war room, 'and time is of the essence. We shall focus our assault upon one side – this side, the eastern side, where the voidship hit and the structure is weakened.'

Colonel Drakon frowned at a tactical hololith. 'You intend to leave the western perimeter unwatched? Leave the xenos an escape route?'

'Orks don't retreat from battle,' said the Krieg colonel.

'No, but they're easily bored, and may well scamper off seeking fresh opportunities for mayhem. Should a single pack reach another hive...'

'Then we must be careful not to bore them. Let them know we're here, that we're strong and ready for a fight, and that ought to hold their attention.'

'I'll keep a pair of Vultures in the air,' Drakon decided, 'to strafe any escapees that attempt to cross the plain.'

The Krieg colonel nodded. 'As you wish.'

* * *

Ferran dined with a fellow acolyte in a quiet corner of the Cadian mess hall. Majellus was a dour-faced crusader, trained by the Adeptus Ministorum. He was quiet but observant, a man with few words to say for himself, and Ferran trusted in his discretion.

'I requested sight of Inquisitor Larreth's report into the Death Korps,' he said in a conspiratorial tone. He could see that Majellus knew the name. 'She was with the delegation that visited Krieg upon the conclusion of its war. It was she who sanctioned its readmittance into the Imperium. Hers were the first feet – perhaps to date, the only non-Krieg feet – to tread upon its blasted surface.'

Majellus raised an enquiring eyebrow.

'Her report, at least the version shown to me, has been redacted.' Ferran scowled. 'It speaks far more of Krieg's past than it does of its present. Ven Bruin tells me what he thinks I need to know, diverting me from deeper truths. He tells me he trusts me. He says that, one day soon, I shall inherit his duty, but he treats me like a novice.'

Majellus grunted sympathetically.

Ferran sighed, frustrated, and sat back in his seat. He recalled the words he had heard from the lips of Larreth's hololithic image, just hours before. 'Did you know that Krieg's name, in some ancient language, means "war"? No one is sure why. It was one of the few worlds in the galaxy untouched by war.'

'A warning, perhaps?' Majellus mumbled.

'If so, it went unheeded. Krieg was a hive world, with vast industrial capabilities. Of course, it was appropriately tithed. Many Astra Militarum regiments were raised from it. The Departmento Munitorum requested more, but Krieg's rulers resisted. They imagined their peace would last forever. The height of hubris.'

'How was this not detected and acted upon?'

'Even our eyes can't be everywhere at once,' said Ferran, sagely, 'as much as we might profess to the contrary – and it was among those rulers, rather than among Krieg's citizenry, that the seeds of heresy took root. They were nurtured by its governor, whose name I couldn't tell you if I knew it.'

He saw the surprise in his comrade's eyes, and nodded. 'An Edict of Obliteration. All records of his very existence were expunged by Imperial decree.'

Majellus gave a grunt of emphatic approval.

'Still, we can discern the shape of his deeds in his planet's unfortunate history. They're reflected in the actions of the heroes who rose to defy him – and in those of one true soldier in particular. *His* name is known well, for the Krieg venerate it to this day.'

'Who was he?' asked Majellus.

'Larreth's delegation was met by Krieg's new governor. A colonel. There *are* Krieg generals now and a select few higher-ranking officers, but only at high command's insistence. I suspect that on their own world a colonel still presides. The saviour of Krieg earned that rank in the Astra Militarum and claimed none higher.'

'Who was he?' Majellus asked again.

'The commander of the 83rd Krieg Regiment,' said Ferran, betraying a rare hint of admiration, 'even then renowned as one of our most disciplined, effective fighting forces. A man who refused to bow down when his whole world turned against him. A man who made the greatest sacrifice imaginable, in the name of his unbending faith.

'His name was Jurten.'

433.M40

BEFORE THE FALL

'Confess!'

Colonel Jurten looked out across the lush, green fields of Krieg.

'They say this is the best view on the planet,' said the woman at his shoulder.

Jurten didn't doubt the statement. He was standing on the balcony of the Chairman's palace. The sun was setting on the western horizon ahead of him, painting the sky in shades of scarlet and gold. The irregular shape of Hive Auros rose up behind him, but cast its shadows elsewhere at this time of the evening. A bright blue river snaked its way towards the reservoir and, when the breeze blew in his direction, its soft chuckling reached his ears.

'Canapés are being served, sir, if you'd care to come back inside?'

'I would not,' growled Jurten.

The woman chose not to press the point, wisely.

The colonel sighed. 'I was stifled in that room, with all those puffed-up bureaucrats, obsessed with feathering their already comfortable nests, avenging imaginary slights and briefing against their political opponents.'

'I understand, sir,' said the woman, diplomatically.

'I stepped outside for a breath of air.'

She ventured a suggestion. 'Perhaps to remember what you've been fighting to protect?'

Jurten rounded on the woman. Their uniforms had similar colour schemes of blue and gold, but hers bore the flashes of the Krieg Home Guard and a captain's pips. Her decorations were also more modest. Barely an inch of Jurten's tunic was not covered by a medal or a ribbon, worn for formality's sake. He had always felt such tokens weighed him down.

'On the contrary,' he said, 'here, it is easy to forget.'

'For some of us, colonel, not all. We are all too aware of the horrors lurking out there in the dark. That is why the council invested in–'

'In their own protection,' Jurten snorted.

'They've fortified our cities and assembled a fleet of battle cruisers to–'

'Those horrors you cower from,' he said, speaking over her, 'the monsters and mutations – they would tear through your defences like parchment paper were they to reach you. You enjoy your peace for the sole reason that other worlds stand as bulwarks for you, because we meet the horrors on those worlds and beat them back.'

'And Krieg must play its part in that struggle,' the woman accepted.

'Not only for its own sake,' said the colonel in a dangerous voice, 'but because the Emperor demands it.'

A short silence brought the river's chuckling to his ears again.

He took a breath. 'Tell the Chairman I had to leave,' he said. 'Tell him I couldn't tolerate his whining voice and his petty, self-interested complaints a second longer.'

'Sir?'

'Tell him what you like.' He stepped past the woman, towards the ornate doors leading back into the palace. A sharp twinge in his left hip, the ghost of an old war wound, told him he had stood still for too long.

'You'll be shipping out soon, then,' said the woman.

Her voice brought Jurten up short. He turned to regard her, framed now by the darkening sky. She was slight of stature, but her muscles were well toned. She could have been proving her worth on a battlefield, but instead she languished here. She was in her mid-twenties – she was twenty-four, he *knew* her age – so must have worked to earn her rank. Her high cheekbones and bobbed, flame-red hair reminded Jurten of her mother.

He responded to her question with a non-committal grunt.

'Goodbye…' said Captain Sabella Jurten, hesitantly adding, 'father.' She snapped to attention and saluted.

He returned the gesture, adding an awkward nod and a twitch of approval at the corners of his lips. Then he turned and marched away, growling instructions into his comm-bead for his aides, waiting elsewhere in the building, to rejoin him.

'Pardon me, Colonel Jurten.'

They were waiting for him on the roof: a five-strong Home Guard squad led by a broad-shouldered, square-jawed sergeant. He was surprised, but not unprepared for them. He couldn't make out their faces clearly as the shuttle pad's glaring lumens had just snapped on behind them. He wondered if Sabella had known about them.

'I need you to come back inside with us, sir,' the sergeant said.

'For what reason, and on whose authority?'

'On that of the Chairman of the Council of Autocrats.'

'I am no longer a citizen of this planet, sergeant. I am an officer in the Astra Militarum, and' – Jurten spoke the Chairman's name with a sneer – 'has no authority over me.'

'All the same, colonel, I'm afraid I must insist. I have my orders.'

'Am I under military arrest?' asked Jurten.

'No, sir, but–'

'Then I intend to board that shuttle, along with my staff here.' He nodded past the sergeant, to where an Imperial lander was easing itself down onto the rooftop pad. 'I would advise you not to try to stop me. If the Chairman wishes–'

Jurten started forward as he spoke. The Home Guard sergeant stepped to bar his way, drawing a gun. Jurten had been prepared for this too and drew his laspistol simultaneously, as did three of his four aides, including Lieutenant Ionas, his adjutant.

Jurten's bloodless lips peeled back from his teeth as he fixed his antagonist with a deathly glare. 'As I was saying, the Chairman can contact me any time he likes, at the Ferrograd barracks. Now step aside, sergeant. *That* is an order.'

The sergeant blanched but held his ground. 'I need to vox my commander for further–'

'I told you, sergeant,' Jurten roared in his face, 'I do not answer to your authority, but as a subject of the Holy Emperor, you certainly answer to mine. Now, *step aside!*' And with that, he bulled his way past the conflicted militiaman, his aides in lock-step with him.

He heard the sergeant voxing for instructions as he marched aboard the shuttle. Its hatch closed behind him with a thunk. Its pilot had served with Jurten's regiment for several years, and the colonel trusted him.

'You spoke to the Chairman, sir?' asked Jurten's adjutant, as the engines fired and they strapped themselves into their seats. Ionas was a young officer, slim and tanned with dark hair and a trimmed moustache. Jurten valued his quiet efficiency, while suspecting that he felt more at home with data-slates than on the battlefield.

'As briefly as I could,' he grunted. 'He didn't like my answers to his questions.'

'Evidently not, for him to tip his hand so boldly.'

Jurten nodded thoughtfully. 'It seems he plans to make his move sooner than we expected.'

'Confess!'

When Jurten closed his eyes, his mind was jolted back to the prison cell again.

He recalled the pain as his every nerve tightened and his spine arched involuntarily. His wrists were manacled, heavy chains splaying out his arms behind him. His knees ached from kneeling on the cold stone floor, and his left hip throbbed.

The greatest indignity was that he had been stripped of his uniform. Grubby hands had pawed every inch of his body, feeling for a hint of mutation. They had found only bruises and old scars, a map of Jurten's faithful service.

'I have committed no sin,' he declared for the thousandth time. His throat was raw, but he would repeat it as many more times as he had to.

His interrogator stood over him, features hidden by a hood. In a gloved hand, she held a black box, bristling with wires and needles. A torture device, and far more. She pressed the box against his upper arm, a wire sparked blue, and Jurten burnt with pain again.

'You have plotted against the Holy Emperor. Confess it.'

'I have always strived to honour Him.'

'But your heart harbours doubts. Confess it.'

'I am an officer in His Imperial Guard. I have stood against the xenos and the mutant. I know the darkness that seeks to extinguish His light.'

'You have consorted with and given succour to heretics. Confess it.'

'I have seen how the merest thought of heresy twists body and mind.'

'*Confess!*'

She thrust the box into Jurten's ribs. He clenched his teeth against a scream, but it rattled in his throat. 'I have… committed no… sin!' Water stung his eyes, from sweat or tears he couldn't tell. He glared up at his accuser defiantly. *I have nothing to hide,* he told himself, *and so nothing to fear, and those deserving of my wrath are far from here.*

His head swam, and the walls seemed far away but closing in on him at the same time. The box had injected him with chemicals – truth serum, he suspected. Words tumbled off his tongue before he knew what they would be. 'But if… if the charge against me is complicity in the treachery of others…'

His interrogator eased away from him, listening eagerly.

'…the rulers of my world, perhaps, then I deny that too… although…' He couldn't help himself. 'I cannot claim to be especially surprised to hear of it.'

The cell door opened with a wrench. Weak candlelight spilled in from the passageway without, forcing him to squint. Fresh bodies milled about him, and a voice he had heard before but couldn't place in that moment asked if he had incriminated himself. The interrogator replied that he had not, in a disappointed tone.

A cushioned chair was set down reverently before him. A cloaked figure, stooped by age, lowered himself stiffly onto it.

The scent of incense, clinging to him, triggered recognition. Jurten blinked to bring Inquisitor Rectilus' grey face into focus.

'I wrote a report,' Jurten said hoarsely. The pain had subsided now, clearing his mind a little. His exposed flesh was drenched in sweat, and he felt cold. 'I wrote several reports and sent copies to your ordo. I reported my observations of the Chairman and his council, everything I had heard from my contacts back on Krieg and from new recruits to my regiment. I warned you of the dangers as I saw them.'

An eternity of portentous silence ticked by before, at last, Rectilus spoke. A simple, three-word proclamation – but one that rarely passed a witch hunter's lips, and always with the utmost reluctance.

'I believe you,' he said softly.

He had not been surprised when the witch hunters came for him. Disappointed, perhaps, but he had known for months by then that something was amiss.

Jurten had been posted to an undeveloped world upon which an outcast cult had gathered. Their profane rituals could have unleashed who knew what horrors. The Krieg 83rd had been assigned to root the cultists out of their boltholes in the mountains. It had all been over in days, but no troop ships had arrived to pick them up again.

This was not unprecedented in itself. Wires were often crossed within the Imperium's ponderous bureaucracy. This time, however, no excuses nor promises were offered. Jurten's messages to the Departmento Munitorum had become increasingly terse, but all had been swallowed by silence.

When the Inquisition's ships had blazed down from the sky, he had almost been relieved, for at least now his questions might be answered.

He had formed his regiment up in the base of a valley. He had allowed himself a rare moment of pride as he surveyed their polished ranks, not a hair or a foot out of place. When the soldiers of the Adepta Sororitas had arrived, he had put up no resistance. He had made only one statement to them: 'In the Emperor we trust.'

Rectilus had made his headquarters in an ancient castle, a relic of a bygone age. Above ground its stone walls were crumbling, but its dungeons still served their purpose. Jurten had made the four-hour climb to it in chains, along with his senior officers. He had held his head high and demanded that the others did too.

Now the chains were removed from him at last, at a gesture from his captor. His muscles groaned, relieved, as the iron weight sloughed from him. They protested anew as Jurten levered himself to his feet. The aged inquisitor had stood too, and turned to leave. Jurten feared that, were the inquisitor to let him go, he might never see him again. Most in his position would have welcomed that prospect; not he.

An acolyte handed him his cleaned and folded uniform. His peaked cap sat atop the bundle, and he noted the rank insignia gleaming upon it. He mustered every ounce of his restored authority. He barked at the back of the departing figure: 'Wait.'

His tone was enough to make Rectilus turn in surprise. 'What happens now?' demanded Jurten.

The interrogator brandished her black box, making it spark. The inquisitor dismissed her with a wave. He took a step back towards the colonel. 'I find the charge of heresy against you unproven. You and your officers will be released without a stain on your records.'

'That isn't what I meant.' Blood had rushed to Jurten's head, making him dizzy. He willed his legs to hold fast, not to buckle underneath him. He closed his eyes for a second, bit his lip and took a rasping breath.

'I thought we might discuss the matter in more congenial sur-roundings, once you have had a chance to–'

'I'd rather talk about it now,' he interrupted. 'I would know the reason I've been beaten, sleep deprived and starved these past three days. I have answered every question put to me, honestly and fully. Now I have questions for you.' At a shade over six feet tall, Colonel Jurten loomed over the stooped witch hunter and, even half-naked, was possessed of the more imposing physical presence.

Inquisitor Rectilus retook his cushioned seat. He leaned back, steepling fingertips beneath his chin. He regarded the colonel with a cool but still somehow probing gaze. 'Your regiment, I'm told, is at less than half-strength currently.'

'Some recent engagements have exacted a toll from us,' admitted Jurten, 'but our achievements more than vindicate my strategies. On Actilon Prime alone, we took on an army more than four times our size. Had we not risked–'

'You need no longer justify yourself to me, Colonel Jurten. Having studied your actions on Actilon Prime and other worlds, I consider you to be an exemplary officer and the soldiers you command a credit to you.'

'I… Thank you, inquisitor,' said Jurten, slightly wrong-footed. 'I should add that I have requested, demanded, new recruits from the home world many times.'

'That,' said Rectilus, 'is part of the problem.'

'Am I to understand that Krieg… that its rulers have earned the Emperor's displeasure? That they have… defied Him?' Jurten had to force the question out. Part of him didn't want to hear the answer, didn't want to face that shame.

'Not openly. Not yet.'

'But?'

'Some of the Chairman's recent proclamations do give us cause to be concerned.'

'Sufficient cause to cast suspicion upon all Krieg personnel out in the field? Including those who have not seen our home world since we left it over twenty years ago?'

'My ordo has fewer eyes on Krieg than we would like. We cannot be sure when this particular rot took hold, nor yet how deeply it might run. You, as a case in point, had contact with the Chairman only weeks ago.'

'I did.' He could see that the inquisitor was waiting for an explanation. 'As I'm sure you've already ascertained, I tackled him directly about my troop shortage.'

'And how did that conversation go?'

'He said he could offer no more conscripts than he'd already sent. He said the harvest was especially poor this year and that he needed hands to maintain his manufactoria.' The colonel scowled as he recalled the Chairman's mewling, self-serving communiqué. 'He implied that the Emperor asked too much of His subjects.'

'The very height of hubris.'

'He also spoke of the need to defend Krieg against threats from without. He was set upon creating a "ring of steel" about the planet, though it was already under the Emperor's protection. I have no proof of this, inquisitor, but I felt strongly that the Chairman was building defences against more than just the xenos.'

Rectilus nodded grimly. 'My ordo is liaising with the Departmento Munitorum. If all goes well, you should soon receive new orders.'

'Which will be?' prompted Jurten, already suspecting the answer.

'You will return to Krieg, ostensibly to replenish your depleted regiment. You will inspect its recruitment and training centres and remind its autocrats of their obligations to pay the modest tithe requested of them. You will also assess the situation on the planet and report your findings directly to the Ordo Hereticus.'

'With respect, inquisitor, should the ordo not send its own–'

Rectilus cut off the question with a shake of his head. 'The Chairman's orbital blockade is already in place. Were we to send an Inquisitorial army, and were he to panic and refuse it permission to land…'

'Then war would be unavoidable,' Jurten concluded.

'Quite so. He may, on the other hand, let a single Krieg regiment with a plausible motive through, rather than reveal his intentions before he is ready to. Your very presence – that of an Imperial force upon his soil – may even deter him from his heretical path.'

'Failing which,' Jurten swore, his fists clenching by his sides, 'his true motives will reveal themselves – whereupon I will take great pleasure in leading my army through the gates of his opulent palace and slitting that bloated slug's stomach with my own knife.'

The Chairman looked out across the lush, green fields of Krieg.

This balcony was his favourite spot in the world. He came out here when the chains of office grew too heavy for him. He pouted, then, when General Krause cleared his throat behind him and he felt the tug of those heavy chains again.

'Your magnificence,' said the general, gruffly. The Chairman had been experimenting with that form of address. He was likely an ugly man, with a nose too big and yet eyes too small for his face. He must have been overweight; no doubt his jowls trembled when he spoke.

'Never disturb me out here,' he snapped. 'For any reason.'

'Begging your leave, sir, they're waiting for you in the broadcast chamber. You did ask to be informed.' Krause was a short, thickset, cruel-looking man. Formerly the commander of the 41st Krieg Regiment, he had been invalided out of Imperial service after an enemy's bullet had nicked his heart. He had been granted a transfer back to his home world, where he now served as the Chairman's military adviser.

'Are you sure we're doing the right thing, general?' asked the Chairman.

'You had no such doubts yesterday.'

'I don't feel… ready.'

'Under normal circumstances, we might delay – again,' said Krause with the hint of a sardonic edge. 'But after last night's botched attempt to detain Colonel Jurten–'

The Chairman winced. 'I know.'

'Had he not guessed the truth before, he knows it now and won't hesitate to act. Serving alongside Jurten, I found him to be an unyielding individual – and the character of military units is shaped by their commander. He ruled his regiment with an iron fist, and had their utmost dedication in return.'

From his few encounters with the man in question, the Chairman knew what the general meant. 'How many…?' he asked, hesitantly.

'He has assembled, by my estimate, a force over three thousand strong at the Ferrograd barracks, having arrived with half as many soldiers. Some, he took fresh from our academies. Others he commandeered from local Home Guard chapters.'

'To which, I presume, that craven fool Dremond consented.'

'Add to that the usual quota of low-hive trash, sir. Gangers and the like – anyone with the wit to point a lasgun in the right direction and keep firing until they are shot.'

'I should never have allowed his drop-ships to land,' the Chairman muttered darkly.

'I did advise against it at the time,' Krause reminded him.

'I expected him to have his say, to muster his army, then to leave.'

'Taking hundreds, thousands of our young, strong workers with him,' Krause pointed out. 'It may be better this way, your magnificence. Jurten has a single regiment, that's all. A regiment of unseasoned youngsters, bullied by him into joining his hopeless cause because for now they see no other option.'

'Yes,' breathed the Chairman, feeling hope building in his chest. 'Yes. Yes.'

'Give them that option, sir,' suggested Krause, 'but do it now. Today. Make your announcement as we planned – before Jurten worms his way into their hearts and minds and turns another generation of our young people against us.'

The Chairman turned his back and stared out at the fields again. His heart beat at twice its normal pace, but the general was right. He had put off this moment long enough.

'Take me to the broadcast chamber, General Krause,' he instructed, in a voice slightly higher and less steady than he had intended. 'It is time we made our stand.'

'My people. My countrymen. My friends...'

The Chairman's voice crackled from vox-speakers all across the planet, in workplaces and public squares. His image was projected to low-resolution screens in well-appointed offices and banqueting chambers. Had the latter been clearer, then his military officers and government officials might have seen sweat dribbling down his neck.

'I have an announcement of some import to make to you.'

He glanced back at Krause, standing stiffly to attention, his back to the wall, his stolid, granite presence like an anchor. He wrenched his eyes back to the words on the prompter, being held up by a nervous scribe behind the pict-caster's dispassionate eye. He didn't need the words. He had rehearsed this speech a thousand times in his head.

'I have spoken to you often about our… relationship with the Imperium of Man. I am the first to acknowledge that we have enjoyed their protection, and free trade with many other civilised, prosperous worlds. I know you share my concern, however, about the price exacted from us in return.

'Many of us – most of you – know well the pain of having our sons and daughters torn from us by remote bureaucrats who have never set foot upon our soil nor breathed our air. The High Lords of Terra have taken generations of Krieg's children, forcing them to fight and often die in a war that feels less like our war each day. I weep when I think of what those lost generations could have accomplished, right here on Krieg. I mourn for the joy they could have brought us, as I do for the world they could have built.

'So, it is with regret but also with hope for the future – and after consultation and much discussion with my council – that Krieg declares its secession from Imperial rule. No longer are we prepared to pay punitive tithes, nor tolerate the ever-increasing burden of unreasonable rules imposed upon us. From this moment forth, we are an independent world, sufficient unto ourselves and more than capable of defending ourselves against external threats.

'All non-Krieg citizens, therefore, must leave this world immediately. This applies to the bureaucratic minions of the Adeptus Administratum. It applies to importers and exporters, and to the ambassadors who are no doubt clamouring for an audience with me as I speak. It especially applies to the Inquisitorial spies who haunt the shadows around us in the hope of overhearing secrets that can be used against us, or detecting thoughts of which they disapprove.

'I give these people three days to make suitable arrangements, after which our borders will be closed. To the rest of you – those born and bred upon this world, who take pride in its name and its history – I make this pronouncement. Our long years of vassalage are over. From now on, we shall keep our families close to us, and enjoy the fruits of our own labours. From this day, this moment, forth, we are finally free.'

The Chairman's words reverberated through the palace's deep-carpeted corridors.

Captain Sabella Jurten had a sick feeling in the pit of her stomach. It had been there all day, since General Krause had called her into his office. 'I thought it was time we talked,' he had said. 'About your father.'

'As you wish, sir. But you should know that I have spoken to Colonel Jurten only four times in my life. He left Krieg while I was in the womb. I would venture that you have exchanged more words with him than I have.'

'Does that include your conversation at last night's reception?'

'It does,' she had responded without hesitation. 'I informed the Chairman of it at the time.'

'And what did Colonel Jurten say to you last night?'

'As I understand it,' said Sabella, 'little that he didn't also say to the Chairman's face. I tried to persuade him to stay, to discuss the matter. I suggested to him gently that the Chairman had a point, that the Emperor does ask much of us, but he didn't want to hear it.'

'No,' said Krause with a sneer, 'I'm sure he didn't. Jurten would never hear an opinion other than his own. The mark of a fanatic, wouldn't you agree? A mindset that the self-styled "Emperor of Mankind" seems to breed.'

He looked at Sabella sharply. She just managed not to wince

at his casual blasphemy. The general, seeming to approve, had changed the subject. 'I want you to carry out a security sweep of this building. I want our defensive weaknesses identified and eliminated. The guard on the Chairman's personal quarters will be doubled and approach roads kept under close surveillance at all times. I want your report on my desk by eighteen hundred hours.'

'Yes, sir. Of course, sir. But, may I ask, is there some–'

'Eighteen hundred hours, captain,' Krause had dismissed her icily.

She had paused on her way out of the room. 'You know, sir, that I've commanded the Chairman's personal guard for three years now. I believe I have proven myself a loyal and effective officer.' The general had grunted a response but hadn't looked up at her, already engrossed in the contents of a data-slate, and her sick feeling had begun to grow.

She knew now that her instincts had been right.

The import of the Chairman's declaration, the consequences for her world, was only just beginning to sink in. She knew what it meant for her, though. Krause had just been making work for her, keeping her out of the way, keeping her in the dark. He didn't trust her. Did that mean the Chairman didn't trust her either? She felt a hot flush of resentment. Her family name alone had damned her. She thought about running, but that would only prove her guilt in their eyes; and suddenly it was too late to run.

'Pardon me, Captain Jurten.'

They rounded a corner in front of her: a five-strong Home Guard squad led by a broad-shouldered, square-jawed sergeant. She greeted them as if they were here on a routine matter, as if she suspected nothing more. 'Is there a problem, sergeant?'

'I need you to come with us, ma'am, on the general's orders.'

'The general could have voxed me,' said Sabella, but the sergeant made no comment. She sighed. 'I was on my way to see him, anyway. I have a report to take to him.'

Colonel Jurten ground his back teeth as he watched the Chairman's speech.

He had brought only two aides into the committee room with him. Its esteemed occupants were in no doubt, however, that he had many more without. He had declined a seat, but had removed his cap and tucked it under his armpit, exposing his shaved head.

His glare swept the room as if he owned it, and everybody in it.

'We...' breathed High Autocrat Dremond, 'we had no idea.' The colonel raised a disbelieving eyebrow.

It was one of the others, Marelle, who answered the implicit accusation. 'That is to say, the Chairman has been pushing for secession for some time – it has been an item on many a council agenda – but, speaking for myself now, I was firmly opposed to it. And certainly no formal proposal was ever presented to, let alone approved by, anybody here.'

'Then the Chairman is acting without his government's consent?'

Dremond shook his grey head, dolefully. His liver-spotted hands trembled on the table before him. 'He has the full support of hives Auros and Argentus, and a majority among the smaller territories. Were it to be put to a vote–'

'There *was* no vote, that is my point,' Marelle insisted. Her straight-backed posture and dark hair piled up and pinned atop her head gave her the illusion of loftiness over her fellow autocrats. Her neck and wrists were draped with gold; a gleaming red gem clasped her velvet robes. 'A move like this can only stir up trouble. Especially here.'

'Hive Ferrograd houses Krieg's largest manufactoria,' Dremond explained.

'Quite so,' agreed Marelle. 'We are not farmers like Argentus, nor bureaucrats like Auros. Our people toil hard in uncomfortable, often dangerous conditions – their lives are short and brutal – but they accept their burden gladly, in the service of a higher cause.'

'We have more cathedrals per head of population than anywhere else.'

'And that is your only concern?' Jurten snorted with contempt.

'I would say that is reason enough to–'

He spoke over the bristling Marelle. 'You oppose the Chairman's heresy, not out of moral indignation, not because you condemn his affront to our glorious God-Emperor, but because the unrest of His loyal subjects might cause you some minor inconvenience.'

'We can debate morality later,' said Marelle primly. 'Right now, our priority as this hive's ruling autocrats is to ensure that order is maintained within its walls.'

'Agreed,' growled Jurten.

'Then your soldiers will assist our Home Guard forces in suppressing any–'

He interrupted the autocrat again. 'Our first priority must be to make a hive-wide announcement. It must be made clear that Hive Ferrograd stands with the Emperor and against the Chairman's treachery.'

'That… that would be unthinkable,' wheezed Dremond. 'It would mean…'

He was silenced by a withering glare from Jurten. Marelle was not so easily cowed, however. 'The high autocrat is right. The Chairman would not stand for it, nor would it solve our immediate problem. Some citizens, even here, would surely take his side – and what about our Home Guard troops, torn between our orders and his?'

Jurten loomed over her, baring his teeth. 'Then thank the Emperor that you have a regiment of His Astra Militarum on hand, fully staffed and trained, equipped and prepared to deal with any hint of insurrection – just as you requested of us, *ma'am.*'

Marelle forced a tight smile to her lips, accepting her defeat.

Jurten turned back to Dremond. 'You should make that announcement straight away.'

The old man nodded and pushed himself to his feet with a world-weary grunt. A pair of aides flanked him as he shuffled out of the room.

'*Colonel Jurten?*' Ionas' familiar voice came through his earpiece.

'Speak,' he instructed.

'*Sir, Lieutenant Voigt reports that his team has secured the astropathic tower.*'

'Did they encounter much resistance?'

'*No more than we anticipated, sir. It sounds as if the Home Guard officer in charge there was… conflicted as to where his duty lay.*'

'Tell Voigt to ensure that the astropaths are not likewise "conflicted",' Jurten growled, 'and have them transmit my report at once. Word for word, as we agreed – and let me know as soon as there is a response.'

He turned his attention back to the table in front of him. The pale-faced autocrats around it avoided his eyes, except for one. 'I hope you know what you are doing, Colonel Jurten,' Marelle hissed coldly, 'what you are forcing High Autocrat Dremond to do.'

'I am doing my duty,' he said flatly, 'as are we all, is that not so?'

'You are declaring war,' Marelle accused him.

'No. Your Chairman has done that.'

'The Chairman only severed ties with–'

'He declared war on the Emperor,' Jurten roared, his sudden fierceness making even Marelle shrink from him, 'by an act of sedition that he knew could not be ignored.'

'You may be right,' she conceded, 'but you… this… this is different. The Chairman might still have listened to reason. This could have been settled without bloodshed. Not now that you have instigated this act of rebellion against him. You are setting Krieg against Krieg, Colonel Jurten. You are bringing *civil* war to a world that has only known peace. A war that can bring nobody any good. A war that will tear this world apart.'

Jurten spoke into his comm-bead. 'Ionas.'

'Yes, sir?'

'I want another message sending. Only to the Auros tower, but use the psykers even so. For the Chairman's personal attention. Message comprises one word only: *"Confess!"'*

AFTER THE GREAT RIFT

THE SIEGE

Colonel Drakon had been right about the orks. By midday, they had tired of shelling no-man's-land. Their cannons had produced much satisfying noise, but little in the way of actual carnage.

A scant few continued to take potshots at the distant trenches, or at the Vulture gunships circling just out of reach. The rest fell silent one by one. The hive offered other, more visceral distractions for the cannons' operators.

Hundreds of thousands, if not millions, of citizens must have failed to get out in time. The weak and the faithless. The former would cower behind barricaded doors, while the latter would loot and pillage and imagine some kind of kinship with the invaders. The orks would paint themselves in both groups' blood; Ven Bruin had no sympathy for either.

The Krieg trenches had spread rapidly, and deepened. They joined up to form the beginnings of a network. Small alcoves were dug into their sides, and furnished with blankets and bedrolls by the Korpsmen. 'Good to know they have to sleep sometimes,' Interrogator Ferran remarked dryly.

Finally, the Krieg re-emerged from their underground holes in their hundreds, and some returned to the encampment. Ven Bruin was keeping an ear on all vox-channels, but had heard no order given. As if the Korpsmen were following some preprogrammed timetable. As if they were not human at all, but mindless automata.

They crewed their armoured vehicles and started them up. The small but dogged Trojans wheezed as they dragged their heavy burdens out onto the plain. Each was met by a veritable swarm of Korpsmen, who detached the Earthshakers from their trailers, wrapped them in rope and lowered them laboriously into the trenches.

Both Cadian and Krieg colonels came out to oversee the operation. Drakon offered his troopers' assistance, but his counterpart declined it. 'They aren't needed and would likely get in the way,' he stated flatly. 'Let them rest a little longer.'

'They've rested long enough,' protested Drakon, but the Krieg man had already walked away. Ven Bruin was standing in his path, and the colonel appeared to see him for the first time. He looked directly at him, and they exchanged nods of acknowledgement.

It was rare, in the inquisitor's experience, for anyone – from the lowliest citizen to the highest-ranking officer – to make eye contact with him unbidden. 'The mark of a clear conscience?' suggested Ferran, appearing beside him.

Of course, he hadn't *seen* the colonel's eyes...

And then there was thunder again.

The long noses of the Krieg cannons poked out of their underground emplacements. They spat out black iron shells with staggering force, enough to propel them all the way to Hive

Arathron's walls. They did so with deafening blasts, which had swiftly numbed Sergeant Renick's ears. She had stuffed cotton gauze from her first aid kit into her eardrums, but it didn't help much.

Colonel Drakon had got his way, and four Earthshakers had been assigned to his shock troops. Renick's squad was among the first to tackle one. She had some gunnery experience, but with far lighter weapons. The first recoil had almost knocked her off her feet, though the cannon was firmly tied down. She made sure to stand as far back as she could now, as she tugged at the frayed firing lanyard.

As soon as each shell was discharged, her squadmates lowered the next into the breech. They worked in two teams of two, hefting the casings between them. Still, the Krieg-manned cannons to each side of them fired off three shots to every two of theirs. 'Pick up the pace!' Renick bellowed at her troopers, though she could see the strain on their faces already.

She hoped they were doing some good. She squinted along the Earthshaker's sights uncertainly. Explosive shells burst against the hive in fiery blossoms, but she couldn't tell if any were *her* shells. The journey of each took several seconds, during which time she was too busy with the next to follow its progress.

A Krieg lieutenant had preset her sights before her arrival, telling her not to tamper with them unless otherwise instructed. Renick knew there were spotters in the trenches, equipped with magnoculars. They would vox her if her shots were falling short – though she feared she might not hear them if they did – and if they weren't, then the hive was surely too big a target to miss.

She was just about to pull the lanyard again when something whistled over her head. She ducked instinctively, before she knew what it had to be. The orks in the hive were firing back – of course they were! She couldn't tell how close the shell had landed – she couldn't separate its blast from all the others – but it was close enough to feel through the soles of her feet. Trooper Creed – her squad's most experienced member, more so than her, but more suited to following orders than giving them – muttered a familiar refrain. 'The ones you see coming aren't the ones you need to worry about...'

The siege had been in full swing for several hours.

Hive Arathron was barely visible from the encampment now, through cannon smoke and under the starless night sky. When Ven Bruin glimpsed it through his magnoculars, however, it seemed as huge and obdurate an object as ever.

The beating of the cannons must surely have had an effect. Iron structures must have buckled as rockcrete roadways crumbled away. The damage, viewed from close up, must have been devastating. Still, from this distance, when weighed against the hive's colossal size, it seemed like almost nothing.

Ven Bruin decided to turn in for the night and pray for a breakthrough by morning. He froze with one foot on the steps to his private quarters as vox chatter flared in his ear.

Orks had been sighted, by multiple spotters at once. It seemed that, as before, they had had enough of long-range combat. A mob of two or three hundred poured out of the hive, wielding massive guns and axes, clearly hoping to take the fight to their unseen attackers. They surged across the plain, heedless of the shells plummeting about them, tearing knots of them apart. Behind them, a dozen hulking mechanical contraptions came ploughing through the hive's wrecked outer walls. Reports likened these to the Krieg's own tanks, but lacking their robust elegance. They might have been cobbled together from spare parts in mere hours by lumbering brutes, but they would doubtless be no less effective for it.

The ork tanks advanced at little more than walking pace. Heavy green brutes clung to their protrusions, howling at them to make more speed, pounding them with green fists when they faltered. The impatient ones leapt from the tanks to dash ahead of them, before remembering how far they still had to go. They waited for the tanks to catch them up and leapt aboard again. In this manner, they made steady progress, but gave the Imperial forces ample warning of their coming.

Two hundred Cadian shock troops were roused from their tents. They dressed hurriedly, drew their weapons and double-timed out towards the trenches.

Meanwhile, ten Korpsmen clambered into each of the two Krieg Baneblades. Powerful headlumens blazed, and the gears of the behemoths crunched as they inched their ways between the Cadian huts, as if straining against some instinct to bulldoze such flimsy obstructions. They led the way out across no-man's-land, followed by a string of smaller Demolishers, and even the Cadian soldiers whom they passed turned to watch these palpable symbols of the Emperor's might, chests swelling with pride.

Against such a small and badly organised xenos force, it almost seemed like overkill.

For Sergeant Renick, the timing could hardly have been worse.

Her squad had been relieved of gunnery duty. They had started to make their way back to camp, through the trenches. Her every muscle ached. She looked forward to a hot drink and sleep. When fresh orders buzzed in her ear, she let out a muttered curse.

She looked around, guiltily. She half expected the silver-bearded witch hunter to step from the shadows and condemn her careless blasphemy.

She turned her squad back the way they had come. 'A mob of orks is on its way,' she explained, 'and we're to help defend against them.' A chaotic half-hour ensued, as Krieg Korpsmen emerged from their dugouts in their hundreds, and the trenches became extremely crowded. Renick couldn't navigate the maze, so went with the flow.

A massive shadow slid over her, with an engine roar so loud that it penetrated even her deadened ears. She looked up, startled, to see the underside of a Baneblade tank poised above her head. She winced as its front end slammed down, for a half-second sure that the trench's sides would collapse beneath its weight and the juggernaut would crush her.

Its scrabbling tracks found purchase, however, and it hauled itself away. As its shadow passed, she realised that none of the Korpsmen pressed around her had broken their strides. *Siege specialists*, she reminded herself. Trench warfare was nothing new to them. Still, blood rushed to her cheeks at the thought that they must have seen her fleeting fear.

The Baneblade's passage gave her a bearing to follow. She eventually found space on a narrow fire step in what must have been the forward trench, and she elbowed her way into it. Rask and Creed squeezed in to her left, while her other two troopers were swept out of her sight. She raised her head gingerly above the sandbagged parapet to check she was facing in the right direction. She couldn't tell for sure, but a coil of barbed wire a hundred yards in front of her nose seemed like a good sign. As did the Korpsmen stretched out to each side of her, making hollows in the sandbags for their rifle barrels.

She followed their lead. She wriggled into a comfortable position, knowing she could be facing a long wait. She kept an ear out for vox updates, or fresh instructions via her regiment's command channel. The trench cannons kept blasting at the distant hive, so the approaching xenos now had to be safely under their arc of fire.

She knew they were close when the cannon fire intensified. If she twisted her head, she could make out the shapes of the Krieg tanks spread out behind her. They let rip with all guns at once, from the powerful Demolishers and chattering bolters of the smaller vehicles to the devastating mega battle cannons of the Baneblades.

'Hardly seems worth our being here, does it?' Creed remarked.

Renick's lasgun too felt light in her hands and, against the other weapons' shattering power, almost redundant. 'Every shot counts,' she asserted. 'Some greenskins will make it into our range. They always do.'

Even as she voiced the words, Trooper Rask barked a heads-up. A dark shape slowly formed inside a curtain of thick smoke. A dozen orks clung to the sides of a junk heap on caterpillar tracks. Their eyes alighted upon the spiked helmets of the Krieg, protruding above the lip of the trench, and they whooped and bellowed in delight. They abandoned their ride and galloped towards their quarry. They whirled axes above their heads and fired crude, oil-leaking guns in every direction, including straight into the ground.

Renick's squad, the Krieg and the other Cadians present returned fire. The brutes were riddled with tiny bursts of flame, which made them jerk and thrash and howl in umbrage. Some were bowled onto their backs, while the arm of one was severed at the shoulder. It gaped at the limb, still convulsing in the dirt, with slack-jawed incomprehension. Then it shrugged, prised its axe handle out of dead fingers and, gripping it with its remaining hand, resumed its advance.

Another ork tore through the barbed wire, which snagged in its hide and ripped its flesh. It loomed in Renick's sights, blood streaming down its face, merging into the drool on its chin. Las-beams scorched its exposed chest, and it finally succumbed and toppled forwards; but a dozen more like it were already trampling over it. Behind them, the junk heap whirled from side to side. Its motley collection of jutting gun barrels coughed up black gobbets of smoke, and sent shells soaring over Renick's head.

The Korpsman to her right stiffened suddenly and toppled off his perch. As he fell, she saw that a bullet had shattered one lens of his gas mask. Another masked gunman stepped up to replace him in seconds. Renick didn't allow it to distract her. She was in her element now. She knew what she had to do.

She reloaded, found another target and squeezed off several more shots. An ork came thundering towards her. Its greasy hair was alight and the right side of its face was burnt black. It was already dead, it just didn't know it yet, but some sixth sense guided Renick's attention towards it. *It isn't going to stop…*

'Ten o'clock!' she yelled as she turned her weapon upon it. Both she and Creed landed good shots on it, but suddenly the burning ork pushed itself up from the ground and flew at her, spreadeagled, its fanged mouth leering, its liquefying right eye sliding out of its socket.

Renick ducked, at the same time twisting her lasgun around and jabbing upwards with its fixed bayonet. The ork overshot her, and her blade punctured its groin. It grunted, exhaling a blast of foetid air into her face, plunging head first into the trench. It almost took her gun with it; wrenching her neck, she yanked it free in a spatter of dark, viscous blood.

The ork's jarring impact would have snapped a human neck. It landed amid a throng of Korpsmen, awaiting their turns on the fire step. A duckboard broke in two beneath it. It writhed in the dirt, extinguishing its burning face. Rolling onto its back, it brought up a gun that looked like parts of many other guns welded together. Something clunked inside its rusted barrel. *If it starts spraying bullets in these close quarters…*

Renick snapped up her lasgun again, aiming into the trench this time, down at the prostrate xenos. Before she could fire, a Krieg Korpsman leapt towards her target. The makeshift gun made a terrible rattle, and bullets ripped through the Korpsman's body. He was dead before he landed, with a wet smack, atop his foe. The weight of his mutilated corpse pinned the ork's gun to its chest for vital seconds. Other Korpsmen moved in, with lasguns readied. They deferred to a cloaked quartermaster, who pressed a bolt pistol into the brute's half-melted eye. He fired once and then, because the ork was still twitching, again.

The Korpsmen rolled their dead comrade onto his back and began to strip his equipment from him. One handed his dog tags to the quartermaster, who read the numbers off them into a data-slate. None of them betrayed so much as a glimmer of emotion. Renick wondered if even they could tell each other apart without those numbers.

She returned her attention to the plain beyond the trench. She was just in time to see the ork tank blasted apart as a cannon shell struck it dead centre. Hot shrapnel glanced off her shoulder guards. A spluttering driver fought its way out of the wreckage. It wore a Cadian helmet jammed over its pointy green ears. Incensed, Renick fired at it before the Korpsmen around her could, and liked to think that hers had been the killing shot.

Reports flooded over the general vox-channel, from soldiers who no longer had eyes on the enemy. She added her voice to theirs and, a moment later, received the command to stand down, which she relayed to her squad.

The Krieg had other ideas. Instead of stepping back down

into the trenches, they were placing wooden ladders against the walls and swarming up them. Renick watched in astonishment as they disappeared over the parapet in their scores, in their hundreds; and their tanks, as if emboldened by a small but easy victory, were surging forwards too.

She half wondered if they meant to storm the captured hive right now.

'What happened?' asked Ferran.

'The ork attack had been repulsed,' said Inquisitor Ven Bruin. 'The Krieg decided to press their advantage. Two thousand went "over the top".'

The pair were in Ven Bruin's comfortable quarters, updating reports for their ordo. Ferran had slept through the previous night's events. Ven Bruin had closed his eyes for a couple of hours. He had found that the older he grew, the less sleep he required.

'They swept across no-man's-land,' he continued, 'killing any xenos stragglers they found, gaining roughly one point seven miles of ground.'

'And then?'

'And then they dug more trenches.'

'Hive Arathron's guns?'

'Had fallen silent. For a time, at least. Many, we think, were knocked out by the bombardment, though that can't be easily verified. Some started up again as the Korpsmen were digging.' Ven Bruin sighed, regretfully.

'How many casualties?' asked Ferran.

'The Krieg tanks advanced, drawing much of the fire,' Ven Bruin recounted, 'and of course the xenos' aim, at long range, was as slapdash as ever.'

'Naturally.'

'Two Demolishers were lost, though one was towed back into camp before dawn. Some parts may be salvaged, I believe. A couple of shells struck close to the working parties, and one right in their midst. The official death toll is almost seven hundred.'

Ferran scowled. 'Ten per cent of our forces.'

Ven Bruin nodded. 'But we are closer to our goal than we were yesterday.'

The Krieg were digging covered tunnels – saps, they called them – to link their new trenches to the old ones. They were wheeling their cannons through those tunnels, into fresh emplacements. Their shells now penetrated almost two miles further into the captured hive than they had before. It wasn't quite the breakthrough for which the inquisitor had prayed, but it was a start and he was duly thankful for it.

'Another commander,' he ventured, 'may have been more cautious.'

'Or less reckless,' Ferran countered.

Ven Bruin shook his head. 'The Krieg colonel made a calculation. He saw a gain to be made and weighed it against the likely cost.'

'And his soldiers accepted that cost.'

'With neither qualm nor hesitation. Earlier, Ferran, you suggested that the colonel had no fear of us because he felt no guilt. I believe it runs deeper than that. Any judgement we cared to pass upon him, I believe, he would accept as the Emperor's will for him.'

'As it would be.'

'My point is that the Krieg place little value upon their own lives. They see them as a resource, no different to an artillery shell, to be expended for the slightest advantage against a foe. That is more than simply confidence or courage.'

'Even on a mission in which they are expected to fail?'

'That makes them our best hope, in my opinion.'

Ferran's eyebrows beetled. 'Then attrition rates for Krieg regiments…?'

'Are far higher than average, yes. And yet, as you were about to note, new regiments continue to be raised, even as the old ones are replenished.'

'How is that possible?'

'I wish I could tell you,' Ven Bruin sighed.

'A world that, fifteen hundred years ago, burnt almost to a cinder. A world upon which civil war was waged for a further half-millennium.'

'Krieg may be a wasteland on the surface…'

'A death world, whose atmosphere is poison, upon which one would expect sickness and far worse to be widespread.'

'What goes on beneath that surface, I'm afraid I do not know. I suspect no living soul knows, outside of the Krieg themselves, and they certainly don't talk about it.'

'A world,' persisted Ferran, 'that, year upon year, reports increasing population growth.' Clearly, he had done some research.

'All I know for sure,' said Ven Bruin patiently, 'is that Larreth–'

'Inquisitor Larreth made her own inspection,' Ferran said, finishing the sentence for him.

'And reported her findings to the High Lords of Terra, who gave the Death Korps of Krieg their sanction.'

Ferran's eyes dropped to his data-slate. 'Yes, sir, they did,' he mumbled.

The siege of Hive Arathron ground on.

Sergeant Renick's squad pulled another Earthshaker shift. This time the routine came more easily to them, and they loaded and fired their great cannon as quickly as the Krieg crews did. Renick even obtained permission to alter the sights, to target a niche in a hive wall from which she had seen muzzle flashes.

By shift's end, those flashes had ceased and, later that night, the Korpsmen advanced a little further.

The Cadians spent most of their days in the encampment, maintaining a state of battle-readiness. Patience was a virtue rarely required of them, and the waiting wore on the less experienced of their number.

Only twice did Renick come close to real action again. The first was when an alarm was raised from the trenches. She was among the soldiers who descended into the network, bumping and jostling through its narrow tunnels. The forward trench was much farther than she remembered and before she even reached it, the fighting was over.

She heard the details from a fellow sergeant later. More orks had spilled out of the hive, straddling lopsided, smoke-belching bikes that, for all their ungainliness, had moved with rocket speed. Mounted guns had sprayed the air ahead of them with deadly clouds of bullets.

'They were zigzagging like crazy,' the sergeant lamented, 'and every time they fired those guns it sent them spinning, but they didn't care. Between their speed and the fumes they were pumping out, they were almost impossible to target.'

The Imperial forces had had three advantages, of course: numbers, cover from the trench walls and discipline. They had swiftly won the day. 'A few almost reached us, even so. One came close enough that I almost choked on its exhaust smoke.' The sergeant grimaced wryly. 'Made me wish I'd worn a gas mask like our friends.'

Renick's second taste of action came when squigs invaded the encampment.

She had come across these stunted aberrations before: little balls of pus and fury, barely more than heads on stumpy legs, scampering on clawed feet. Their features varied. Some had six eyes, others had none. Some bristled with spines or had vestigial horns or tails. All had great slavering mouths with fangs. No one quite knew what they were. A genetic resemblance to the orks could not be denied – though Renick had once seen a squig snatched up by an ork and thrust down its gullet.

They had appeared in the trenches two days earlier, seemingly from nowhere – until someone worked out that they were being *catapulted* from the hive. Some splattered upon landing, while Renick had heard tell of one impaled upon a Krieg helmet. Others rolled to their feet with astonishing resilience, and set about creating mayhem.

Renick was roused by urgent shouts, at exactly the moment that a squig tore its way through the side of her tent.

The creature's eyes were wide, lips pursed, its cheeks expanding. She threw up her blanket between them as it spat a jet of steaming liquid at her. Its bile ate through the thick fabric and stinging droplets splashed her arm. She hurled the blanket over the squig's head, blinding it as she went for her lasgun, always kept within arm's reach.

The blanket fell from the squig in tatters. It leapt at her, coiled legs propelling it three times its height into the air. The squig's jaws parted, and Renick stared down the cavern of its throat over a forked, black, slobbering tongue. She felt its sticky breath, its stench curling her nostril hairs. Never had she felt as exposed as she did in that moment, bereft of her armour – but at least she had her weapon.

She fired a full-auto burst at the dangling target of the creature's uvula. It screeched in agony as it cannoned into her shoulder. She was twisted around, stumbling into the tent's side, tearing through its canvas. She felt teeth grazing her skin, but then the squig fell limply away from her. It hit the ground and burst, spilling out putrid offal.

Voices were still raised outside and there was gunfire too, and somewhere a small explosion. Renick grabbed and quickly donned her breastplate. She jammed her helmet onto her head, but left her boots behind.

She emerged from her tent, as bright floodlumens glared from the roofs of the nearby huts. She blinked and, for a moment, could only discern silhouettes rushing about her. Then a squatter shape scampered across a small patch of open ground. She pursued it, and cornered the squig against the side of the latrines. It turned to leer at her, and she caught a glimpse of dark metal under its tongue.

'Grenade!' she cried. 'It has a grenade in its mouth!'

She had been aware of comrades rushing up behind her. Her warning stopped them in their tracks. They backed away, as did she, separating from each other, working their lasgun triggers for all they were worth. The squig tensed its legs to spring at them, but a beam flashed between its teeth before it could. Renick threw herself down and covered her head, as sizzling chunks of rancid flesh rained upon her.

By the medicae hut, she saw another squig impaled upon two troopers' bayonets. She spotted another squat body splayed beside the dwindling watchfire. A pair of feelers sprouting from its temples twitched, and she kicked the squig into the flames with a shudder of revulsion.

The Cadians spent the next ninety minutes searching every nook and cranny of the encampment. They ferreted another three squigs out of various holes, and blasted them to pieces. One managed to latch its filthy teeth on to a trooper's leg before it expired, leaving the limb mangled, bloody and probably, if Renick were any judge, infected.

They also found two more troopers dead in their beds, one's throat torn out, the other's skin blistered and black from head to toe.

They stoked the watchfire and doubled the guard for the remainder of the night, while the Cadian officers quietly closed the windows of their huts.

'Tomorrow…'

The war room was crowded with officers and their staff. Colonel Drakon felt forty pairs of eyes upon him, even those of the Krieg behind their masks, and one pair of eyes especially. The eyes of the witch hunter, Ven Bruin, a brooding presence in the corner. As if he wished to be inconspicuous, but he could not have stood out more.

'We make our move at thirteen hundred hours,' the Krieg colonel repeated, 'local time.'

For once in his life, Drakon didn't know what to say. He knew what he *wanted* to say. He wanted to ask his counterpart if he were insane, incorporating some well-chosen profanities for emphasis. If only the witch hunter had not been there, if it hadn't been for those eyes…

He frowned at the tactical hololith spread out before him, buying himself time. The display told him nothing he didn't already know. He mulled his options, finding them equally unpalatable. The best he could do was to proffer a bland query: 'Are you sure that's wise?'

'Our objective is–'

'I know what our objective is,' said Drakon, 'but I understood this to be a siege situation. Your cannons – our cannons – have barely begun to do their work.'

'With every day that passes, the xenos tighten their hold upon Hive Arathron. We know from experience that their numbers will increase exponentially.'

'I am well aware of that, but they started with a small enough force. Few survived the crash of their ship, and my shock troops fought them to a standstill before you arrived. Surely it makes sense to wait a few more days, a few more weeks, before we–'

'In the normal course of events,' the Krieg colonel said, speaking over him, 'that would indeed be our strategy. I have been instructed, however, that time is of the essence. The line–'

'The line must be held. Of course,' said Drakon with a grimace. He checked a flickering read-out on the display. 'So, you intend to send five thousand troopers across two and a half miles of exposed ground, mostly on foot, under heavy artillery fire.'

'The xenos are at their least active in the early afternoon. I will send the Baneblades forward, to take out their emplacements here and here.' The Krieg colonel indicated two points on the hololith with jabs of a swagger stick. 'Emperor willing, that will silence the enemy guns for several minutes, by which time–'

Drakon almost exploded. '"Emperor willing"?'

A pair of shrouded eyes were turned upon him. 'I have faith that He will be.'

Drakon bit back a rejoinder, aware again of Ven Bruin's presence. 'Just a few days' delay,' he implored again. 'We could expand the trenches further out across the plain, a little closer to our target. It could save hundreds, even thousands, of our troopers' lives.'

The Krieg colonel shook his head firmly. 'A gain outweighed by the xenos lives spawned in the meantime. Our ordinates have run the numbers, Colonel Drakon. Our odds of success in this mission are minimal.' Drakon grimaced again at that, because he knew it to be true. 'But this plan offers our best chance of a favourable outcome. We may retake part of the hive, at least – failing that, we can expect to focus the orks' attention upon us, draw more of them out into range of our cannons.'

'I'm sure we can get their attention,' he agreed dryly, 'but at what cost?'

'None greater than my Korpsmen are willing to pay, for the Emperor.'

And, with that, Drakon knew he had been checkmated. What more could he say, without giving Ven Bruin the impression that he was weak of faith? That his troopers, whom he knew to be the proudest, bravest soldiers in the Imperium, were actually less proud, less brave than those of the Krieg?

So, he nodded instead. 'Thirteen hundred hours,' he confirmed numbly. 'Tomorrow.'

They waited in the trenches.

Over five thousand soldiers stood shoulder to shoulder, elbow to elbow, packed so tightly that they couldn't have escaped if they had tried. The only spaces were left around the cannons, to allow their crews to continue to load and fire them. When their work ceased, the massed soldiers would know that their signal was imminent.

In fact, there were to be two signals. On the first, twelve hundred Korpsmen would go over the top. This first wave was expected to take the heaviest casualties, but artillery units would advance alongside them, as well as a phalanx of Death Riders on horseback. With the Emperor's favour, it was thought that a third of them might make the full distance to the hive. They would storm the orks' emplacements, if any remained, and engage the brutes in close combat – keeping them distracted from the second wave, sweeping up in turn.

The remaining members of the Cadian 432nd would be in that second wave. The Krieg colonel had made this decision himself, sparing Drakon from having to swallow his pride and ask him. He couldn't, he *wouldn't* expend his troopers' lives as cheaply as his counterpart did. *Especially now,* he thought, *when the number of Cadian lives across the galaxy is dwindling day upon day…*

Drakon too waited, in a tunnel leading to the forward trench. He checked his wrist chrono: *12:58*, it read. The display shimmered and changed to *12:59*. The cannons fell silent, leaving him with ringing in his ears. He strained to discern if the guns of Hive Arathron still thundered. He heard only the silence of the dead.

Then the signal crackled over the command channel.

Drakon raised a whistle to his lips and blew it hard. A score of other Krieg and Cadian officers did likewise, so no one could fail to get the message, and the pressure of bodies about him immediately eased.

He considered the courage of the Korpsmen now scaling the trench walls, beyond his range of vision. It shamed him to think that he had judged their lives less valuable than Cadian lives – but then, had their colonel not made that same judgement too?

Drakon looked at his chrono again. The second signal would be given exactly twenty minutes after the first. The signal for the Cadians and the rest of the Krieg to move out – and Colonel Drakon along with his regiment, because where else would he be?

The countdown had begun. He heard an ominous rumble from no-man's-land. *A Demolisher?* he wondered. *A Baneblade?* Or had that been the sound of ork guns, already firing from the hive?

434.M40

THE BETRAYAL

Hive Ferrograd's largest public square was packed out for the execution. Surrounding streets were clogged with people eager for the spectacle. Conspicuous among these were the blue-and-gold uniforms of the much-expanded 83rd Krieg Regiment. Today of all days, order had to be maintained – and had to be seen to be maintained.

Colonel Jurten was sending out a signal.

The condemned were brought out of the cathedral, having made their peace with the Emperor. They were led to the firing posts. Months in chains had left them sallow and emaciated. A priest walked beside them, waving his censer and bellowing hymns. His braying voice was drowned out by the crowd, jeering at the prisoners.

A hurled piece of overripe fruit sailed wide of its target and spattered on the holy man's robes. Guardsmen descended upon the thrower and whisked her away.

Ten autocrats were to die today. There had been twelve, but

the aged high autocrat had perished under interrogation, while one other had disappeared before she could be arrested. They shuffled to their fates in wretched silence, having learned the futility of protest. Nothing they could say would make a difference. They were part of a system that had enabled the ultimate treachery. They had turned a blind eye instead of acting, talked of compromise rather than conviction, wavered when they ought to have been strong.

Jurten had judged them guilty, every one of them.

So, the autocrats were chained to the posts and their faces hooded. Ten Guardsmen lined up before them, twenty-five feet distant. One for each of them. Jurten had given them bolt pistols, because the sound and explosive impact of the weapons would impress the spectators. He had chosen the most accomplished marksmen and given them two rounds each, because resources had to be conserved.

He waited for the priest to finish his reading. Then he brought the firing squad to attention, had them take aim. The crowd fell deathly silent, their bloodlust subsumed into a breathless trepidation. They would remember this moment for the rest of their lives.

Jurten barked out the order to fire.

The Chairman had the prisoner brought to his banqueting suite.

She was wrapped in an off-white shift, stained with blood and dirt. Her ankles, like her wrists, were manacled, hampering her walking. She was bundled through the door by two callow troopers of the Chairman's newly minted Krieg People's Army.

He dabbed gravy from his chin with a napkin. He pushed aside his plate with its picked-clean carcass. He sat back and regarded the prisoner along the considerable length of his dining table. 'Captain Sabella Jurten.'

Her eyes flicked to the goblet of wine at his elbow, and her tongue touched her cracked lips. 'Your magnificence,' she addressed him, hoarsely.

The Chairman's lips twitched in approval, though he preferred to be called 'your excellency' these days. It seemed less immodest.

'I assume you wish to talk about my father again,' said Captain Jurten boldly.

'Colonel Jurten continues to occupy Hive Ferrograd, in defiance of my just and lawful authority. He had its former... its *rightful* leaders shot this morning, before a baying crowd. One was a dear cousin of mine.'

'I see.' She didn't seem at all surprised.

'I warned him. Many times. I was crystal clear that any such actions would force me to retaliate... in kind.' Her face was cut, a purple bruise half hidden by the flame-red hair that had grown wild during her imprisonment. She was as spirited as he remembered her, however, holding his gaze defiantly. *She probably got that from him...*

'The colonel didn't earn his military honours by indulging in sentiment, sir.'

The Chairman's eyes narrowed with suspicion. 'You claimed to know little of him.'

'I may not have met him often,' she explained herself, 'but I've followed his career as best I could. I was curious about him. I know he was one of the youngest Imperial officers to receive the Macharian Cross. He led his regiment into the aeldari stronghold of the Shadow-Wind Forest. By rights, it should have been a massacre, but–'

'What point are you trying to make, captain?'

'That appealing to my father's feelings is like reasoning with the rushing river. You can threaten me, kill me if you must, and he might even mourn me. He might… But you won't deter him from his duty. You will not turn him from his course, because he believes that course was set for him by his God-Emperor.'

The Chairman pouted. 'Do you have a better suggestion?'

'He is only one soldier,' said Captain Jurten, 'and to win a war you need many.'

'Krieg isn't at war,' the Chairman snapped. 'Krieg has never been at war.' He pretended not to hear an ill-timed rattle of gunfire from outside his window.

'That is not how my father sees it, I assure you – and he commands an army, which I hear is growing by the day.' Now she sounded like General Krause. 'We cannot shake Colonel Jurten's faith in the Emperor, but we might shake his people's faith in him.'

The Chairman liked the sound of that. 'Go on.'

'Let me take a team into Ferrograd. Say, ten strong. I have a list of names in mind, people I trust implicitly. I know all the ways in and out, and I've had time to plan.'

'Ten soldiers? Is that all?'

'We'll find more inside. Many more. Good people, who support your reforms – supporters of *Krieg* – but who don't dare speak out at present for fear of reprisals. We can organise them, let them know they haven't been abandoned.'

'Yes. Yes.'

'A few symbolic strikes will make the cracks of doubt appear. Resistance to my father's occupation will grow – especially when it becomes known that I am the occupier's own daughter. *That* is how we use my name against him.'

The Chairman shifted his bulk in his chair. He rested his elbows on the table, his chin on his fists. 'I like it,' he purred, 'but fomenting an uprising takes time, and I need results now. So, what if I gave you your stealth team, Captain Jurten? What if you were to lead them into Ferrograd, get close to this upstart tyrant – and assassinate him? Ideally, fire the killing shot yourself.' He looked up at her sharply. 'Do you think you can do that for me?'

She didn't hesitate. 'Yes, sir, I think I can.'

The Chairman smiled and invited her to sit. He clicked his fingers and had wine poured for her. He had been right to give her this chance, he thought, despite his general's protestations. She had responded exactly as he had hoped she would.

He had always rather liked her, after all.

Marelle was woken by gunfire.

For a moment, in the darkness, she couldn't remember where she was. It was the smell that brought it back to her: the ever-present sewer stink of the underhive. Her stomach sank with the realisation of her plight, as it had done every day for months.

She scrambled out from under her blanket of rags. She crawled along the rusted pipe that jutted out of her tiny alcove. She couldn't make out much in the twilight world beyond. Then she saw lights along the service tunnel, bobbing towards her, and heard voices. Soldiers' voices, barking orders. They had come for her, at last.

Perhaps, she thought, if she crawled back into her alcove, they wouldn't see her. If they did, she would be cornered, so perhaps it was better to run. *Perhaps,* a small part of her thought, *it would be best to let them take me…*

For the thousandth time, she wondered how her life had come to this.

Marelle had been comfortable once. Her family name had gifted her political power. She had been a step away from becoming high autocrat of Ferrograd, once that aged fool Dremond succumbed to his creeping dementia. She had enough dirt on the rest of them to secure their votes.

She cursed the day she had allowed Colonel Jurten into her

orderly hive. Even more, she cursed the Chairman for his actions. On the day he had made his foolish and precipitate announcement – the day on which Jurten had marched into her committee chamber with his own demands – she had seen her future clearly, shackled to a firing post. The others, she felt sure, had seen it too, but only she had had the guile to fight it. *Perhaps I was the foolish one*, she thought.

Jurten had had all routes out of Ferrograd closed. Marelle had played the part of his staunchest, most strident supporter, while secretly calling in every favour she was owed or could extort. She had made her break hours before the inevitable coup. She had almost made it, until her last contact had betrayed her. On the hive's lower levels, her name and wealth meant nothing; and, without a bed to sleep in, nor a means to earn food tokens, the only way for her to go was down.

She had waited too long in indecision. The soldiers' lights had almost reached her. If she ran now, they couldn't miss her. If not, they would see her just as surely. There were at least twenty of them by her reckoning. She made out some of their shapes – and one shape unlike the others. A stooped figure shuffled between them, strange limbs peeking from the folds of its robes. *Too many strange limbs…*

She heard a clatter on the pipes behind her. Something brushed Marelle's skin and she yelped in disgust. A spindly, twisted, grey-faced figure sprang past her. Its skin was mottled with pustules; the thought that she had touched it sickened her.

The mutant landed in the tunnel in front of the soldiers, with a sharp crack of bone. It slobbered and jeered at them as if daring them to shoot it. Perhaps it too had tired of its tortured existence. Marelle had nothing in common with such a pestilential creature. *It* belonged here, she told herself, and it deserved to die here.

She had swung down from the pipes before she knew it. She was running.

Behind her, the tunnel was lit by lasgun flashes. The mutant's dying screech seemed to echo from its rounded walls forever. Sewer water slapped between her toes: she had been attacked, her shoes taken along with her jewellery, her first night here. She couldn't recall when last she had eaten, and she felt light-headed and weak from effort.

She had to keep going, she told herself, though to where she didn't know. *Just take the next turning and the next one after that, and you can lose them in the maze…*

She didn't hear the shot that killed her. She was falling before she knew why, before she felt the pain flaring in her back. She was lying on her face, six steps away from where her dash for freedom had begun. Her limbs and head were too heavy to lift.

She heard the soldiers tramping up to her, and wept frustrated tears. One prodded her between her ribs with his toecap. 'No need to waste another charge on this one,' he said gruffly. 'It's bleeding out badly.'

'Wonder where it got the fancy clothes,' another said.

'Picked them out of the garbage, by the state of them.'

'Its skin looks smooth. I don't see any obvious mutations.'

Another figure shuffled up to her, loomed over her. As Marelle's vision faded, she saw a blur of red. Multijointed arms splayed from it like the limbs of some huge, repulsive spider. *Mechanical arms*, she realised. The red robes hid the figure's face, but she caught the glint of a lens where its eye should have been, clicking and whirring.

She wondered what could bring an adept of the Cult Mechanicus down here.

The figure spoke in a voice like the creaking of dry parchment. 'The foulest mutations often cannot be detected by the eye.'

'Another one, sergeant,' someone shouted. 'Three o'clock.' There was a flurry of movement, the barking of guns again, and suddenly Marelle was left alone.

They didn't come for me, she thought. Her final thought. *They didn't even know me when they saw me. They couldn't tell me from the subhuman dross that infests this wretched underworld. My body will rot here, a feast for vermin, and no one will know my fate. It isn't fair. I had power. I used to be someone...*

The Chairman's speech had gone down well, so he had thought.

He had insisted on making a public appearance. He hadn't wanted anyone to think he was in hiding, though he had been. He had been surrounded by armed guards, of course, and the cheers and applause for his words may not have been entirely spontaneous.

He returned to his palace in the back of an armoured limousine. Its cushioned seats cradled him snugly, while aides fed and watered him and fanned his brow as he required. Still, never had he endured a less comfortable journey.

He couldn't see out of the claustrophobic compartment. He tried to imagine that his streets were quiet and orderly, but the constant buzzing of General Krause's earpiece shattered his illusions. Krause issued terse commands into his comm-bead, and more than once, the Chairman heard the muffled cracks of lasguns.

'No cause to worry, sir. Insurgents with banners, refusing to clear the roadway. My snipers took out one and the others appear to have reconsidered their options.'

'I don't like killing our own citizens,' the Chairman bleated.

'I know, sir. Only when we must. Some of these rabble arm themselves with metal bars or fashion crude promethium bombs, and we cannot risk your safety.'

'No, no, quite right,' agreed the Chairman hurriedly.

'This is not a matter for debate,' he had blustered to an exultant crowd, pounding his fleshy fist against his lectern. *'As your ruler, I know what is best for you.'*

He had the support of most of them, he had convinced himself of it. So, what was wrong with the malcontents among them, that they didn't wish to be free? *Brainwashed,* he decided, *in the churches that we allowed to be built here.* The council had argued for keeping those churches open. He resolved to have Krause find a priest who might have been preaching sedition and nail him to his altar.

The car braked and its engine hum subsided. The Chairman strained his ears for any hint of a threat from without, but the silence was almost eerie. Then he heard a ring of military boots. A side door was flung open and the vehicle was flooded with the harsh, unnatural light of his palace's courtyard.

Krause stepped out first and, once satisfied that all was well, nodded for others to follow. The Chairman hauled himself up off his cushion. He suppressed a grunt of effort, pretending that his knees weren't straining under his weight.

He looked for Krause and saw him, head down, growling more vox orders. Sensing the Chairman's enquiring eyes upon him, he broke off to explain: 'A riot in Auros' commercial sector, sir. A warehouse was torched, but the blaze has been brought under control. My major concern is that it seems as if members of the Home Guard–'

'People's Army.'

'The People's Army,' Krause corrected himself, 'stood back and allowed it to happen. Widespread looting has ensued on some of the lower levels.'

'Tell your officers to get a grip on it,' the Chairman demanded. 'I have authorised the use of choke grenades and shock mauls, and of course I will organise an immediate enquiry into the actions of–'

'What time is it? Surely past twenty hundred hours by now. I want it made known that any breach of curfew, tonight or any other night, will be punishable by… by…' The Chairman's voice trailed off. *I don't like killing our own citizens…*

'With all due respect, sir, I believe that the root of our problems–'

'We have discussed this, general,' he snapped, 'and you know my position. I cannot, will not, send troops to take back Ferrograd until the civil unrest here in Auros – and elsewhere, but especially in my capital hive – has been quashed.'

'For as long as Jurten defies your will in Ferrograd,' said Krause, visibly restraining his impatience, 'encouraging others to do likewise, we might never–'

'I have made my decision!' shrieked the Chairman with his customary petulance. He turned and marched away, clenching his fists until his fingernails bit into his palms.

Barely had he taken two steps when the bomb went off.

A blast of heat struck the Chairman's back and may have hurled him forward, or he may have stumbled in his terror. Either way, he flopped onto his stomach on the rockcrete, his stumpy limbs flailing. It seemed an age before a pair of troopers helped him to his feet and a jittery aide brushed his fine tunic down.

'What happened?' he panted, though the answer was already obvious.

His limo was ablaze. More soldiers were rushing from the buildings around the courtyard, paying out fire hoses. Krause reappeared in his eyeline. His uniform was singed, but unlike the Chairman he had managed to stay on his feet.

'I can only apologise, sir, for this lapse in security. I will find out who is responsible and I will have them shot.'

'The bomb… the bomb was in the car,' said the Chairman in a trembling voice. 'Had it gone off while I was in there… Had I stepped away a second later…'

He made his way indoors, feeling faint. He waved away the guards that attempted to fall in around him. 'Get away from me!' he bellowed at them. 'Leave me alone!'

Lieutenant Ionas scanned the data-slates covering his desk.

'Not much to report, sir,' he said. 'More looting in the textile district overnight. I've ordered an increased security presence there. Much calmer on the residential levels, just thirteen deaths recorded. Captain Kraemer is following up leads on the temple bombings – another two suspects were killed in a shoot-out this morning.'

Colonel Jurten grunted in approval. 'Be sure to make that information public.'

'We also recorded the usual quota of minor infractions, as would be expected in a settlement of this size. Nothing worthy of your attention.'

'Tell me about production yields.'

The question was expected, and Ionas' hand flashed to the appropriate slate. 'Averaging eighty-eight per cent of normal. Close to ninety-three in the food manufacturing division. Munitions stands at eighty-one per cent, but much of that shortfall can be attributed to the arson attack upon the Wulfram ordnance–'

Jurten waved away the explanation. 'I want production quotas in munitions increased by thirty-three per cent.'

'I'll inform the overseers, sir. It's, ah, likely that work shifts will have to be extended, which may cause further unrest, especially if it looks as if we're expecting an imminent attack.'

'An attack is precisely what we expect,' said Jurten, curtly.

'Yes, sir. Of course.'

'Hive Ferrograd's allegiance to the Emperor is an affront to the Chairman's authority. If he possessed a spine, or the humility to heed his military advisers, he'd have sent his army against us long before now. But even he cannot possibly prevaricate much longer. He must be aware that he has exhausted all the empty threats in his arsenal.'

An unpleasant memory flared bright in Ionas' head. A grainy holo-cast image of Captain Sabella Jurten on her knees, a pistol pressed to her temple. He wondered if the colonel still saw that image too, if it factored at all in his choices.

Restoring the Emperor's law to Ferrograd had been relatively simple. For most people, nothing much had changed. The Chairman had promised them increased wealth, but they had heard such promises before. He had sworn their children would no longer be taken from them, but had yet to explain what opportunities he offered them to surpass those of military service. So, upon being told an hour later that these promises were false, that they remained Imperial subjects after all, most had just shrugged and got on with their lives.

The remainder comprised a small fraction of the city's millions – outnumbering its security forces, true, but lacking organisation – and Jurten had cracked down hard on any hint of trouble-making. Public floggings and the recent execution had sent out a salutary message, which was slowly getting through. There were still a few frustrated secessionists out there, though, deluding themselves that something had been taken from them.

'The Chairman will see this as a provocation,' said Ionas.

'Giving him another reason to act,' said Jurten.

'Yes,' said the adjutant, 'quite.'

'If he doesn't move on us soon,' the colonel vowed, 'I shall be forced to move on him. Better it be the former than the latter, and sooner than later. His mistake was in fortifying his cities, not imagining that one might be seized from within. So, let him lay siege to our adamantium walls. Let our people see who their enemy truly is. Ferrograd can withstand an assault for months or even years.'

'Let the Chairman deplete his resources,' Ionas agreed, 'without recourse to Imperial forge worlds to replenish them.'

'While we build ours,' growled Jurten. *Without aid from the Imperium either…*

The Astra Militarum had taken weeks to respond to the colonel's report. They had acknowledged the situation on Krieg, but had made it clear that they had other battles to fight. Jurten's orders were to resist the Chairman's secessionist forces with all of his regiment's might. *A single regiment against a world,* Ionas thought, *but then look how much we have achieved already…*

Sometimes, when he closed his eyes, he found himself back in a cold, dark dungeon, bound by chains. He felt anew the horror that everything he had ever believed in, every thought in which he had ever taken solace, had betrayed him. Everything and everyone, apart from his steadfast commander. He had taken the brunt of Inquisitorial torture, and his faith had saved them all. His example made Ionas want to strive harder, serve better.

He had crunched the numbers many times, and each time with the same result. *This war we have chosen to fight is unwinnable,* he thought, *but if anyone can win it all the same, it is surely Colonel Jurten…*

'Looks like she's been dead a few days, ma'am.'

Captain Sabella Jurten looked down at the body with a frown. *Another mutant?* she wondered. It wore the tattered remnants of what must once have been fine clothes. Rats had gnawed its face, so it was unidentifiable.

The rats had scattered at the approach of Sabella's squad, but they hadn't gone far. She heard them skittering, squeaking, massing in the shadows around her. She held her lumen up over her head, but the shadows were stronger than its yellowish light.

She found the rusted pipe she had been following, and played her light along it. The pipe took a sharp upward turn and disappeared into the roof. Sabella clicked her tongue in frustration. 'We must have passed under the hive walls by now,' she murmured.

They left the faceless corpse behind them, plodding onwards. They checked every opening in the tunnel walls for steps or a ladder, or an upward-leading passageway. Sabella was aware of the skitters in the shadows growing louder. *Those rats are getting bigger...*

She tucked her squad against one wall and brought them to a halt. 'I know you're here,' she called into the gloom. 'We can hear you. Show yourselves.'

The sounds of movement ceased. Sabella listened to her heartbeat, and the creaking of flak armour plates as the troopers behind her adjusted their positions. Was that a ragged exhalation of air, or her own breaths echoing back to her?

A tangle of wire – one of many hanging from the roof like cobwebs – sparked bright blue and something bolted, only yards ahead of them. A misshapen figure with a limping, stumbling gait. Shadows enveloped it again, but its silhouette was flash-burnt into Sabella's retinas. Her squad opened fire and the figure squealed and fell, crawled a short way further on its stomach, then gave up with a heavy sigh.

This time, there was no doubting its nature. Its right arm was fused into a slimy mass of tentacles, which twitched as Sabella looked down at them. Sergeant Harkin pointed out a fresh bolt-wound to the mutant's calf, though no one had fired a bolt weapon. She wasn't surprised. 'So, there *was* a gunfight down here.'

That explained why they had encountered so few underhive denizens, at least live ones. The question was, who had shot them? Were soldiers cleaning out these tunnels? It was possible. They must have known, though, that this was a never-ending task; and surely they had more pressing problems above ground, in the hive proper?

She led her squad forward again, but they didn't get far. Firelight flared ahead of them, once, twice, three times, each time with a mechanical clunk. *A flamer,* thought Sabella. *Could've done with one of those ourselves…* Someone was burning out rats' nests or cremating corpses. They certainly weren't trying to hide their presence.

She directed her squad with silent gestures, then extinguished her light. She sidled into a rockcrete alcove, flattened herself against an iron door. She felt for its securing bolts and found them rusted, impossible to move without making a racket.

She saw Sergeant Harkin's boots disappearing as he hauled himself up onto a parallel pair of overhead pipes. Two troopers crouched behind a corroded copper steam boiler. Sabella couldn't see the rest of them. She braced her shoulder against the alcove's side and readied her lasgun. She didn't have to wait long.

Footsteps approached along the tunnel. A hushed order brought them to a halt. Sabella's troopers hadn't made a sound that she had heard, but a multi-scanner could have picked up their body heat. Probing lights swept past her alcove, as a stern male voice rang out: 'Who goes there?'

Not yet, she said to herself. *Let them think they're dealing with the usual underhive scum. Let them come a little closer…* The unseen commander was too cautious or too wily for that, though. He called out his challenge again. When again it went unanswered, he instructed a trooper to prime a frag grenade, in a voice deliberately loud enough to be overheard.

'Krieg Home Guard,' Sabella called out. She didn't give her name. She didn't know what reaction it would prompt. 'Identify yourselves.'

A pause. Then, in a mocking tone: 'Don't you mean the "Krieg People's Army"?'

'I said, identify yourselves,' she snapped.

'Sergeant Zabel. Of the Astra Militarum. The *Imperial* army.'

'I'm a Home Guard captain, Zabel. I outrank you. I order you to stand down your squad, so we can–'

The voice made a harsh noise, half snort, half laugh. 'You have no authority over anyone in Ferrograd, "captain". Only the Emperor and His representatives do.'

'Pardon me, Sergeant Zabel. I wondered why someone so loyal to the Emperor would be skulking about down here.'

'Our assignment is none of your business.'

'It might be.' She chose her next words carefully. 'If you're looking for a way out, then I know where to find one. You wouldn't be the first to desert from–'

'Throw down your weapons,' Sergeant Zabel bellowed, as if the word 'desert' had been a trigger for him, 'and step out where I can see you. No more warnings.'

Sabella had prepared for this moment. She hadn't expected it to come so soon, however. She had hoped to get a little further. She had hoped to be a little more sure. *He seems sincere enough*, she thought, *but what if I've misjudged him?* She didn't have a choice. All she could do was trust her instincts.

She put down her lasgun. She propped it against the iron door rather than laying it in sewer water. She stepped out with her hands raised. Lights blinded her, and she heard guns snapping round to cover her. She took a few steps along the tunnel, then stopped. She held her breath. No one shot her, which she took as a promising sign.

'How many more of you?' came Zabel's voice from behind the lights.

Sabella called over her shoulder: 'You heard the sergeant.'

She heard her squad emerging from their places of concealment behind her. 'Nine more,' she reported. 'Ten of us altogether.'

Zabel exchanged murmured words with one of his troopers, and a scanner bleeped. 'So, now you know I'm telling you the truth,' Sabella addressed him. 'There are just ten of us. Ten members – former members – of the Krieg Home Guard. Sent here by the Chairman, with the blessing of his Council of Autocrats.' She took a deep breath. This was the crucial moment. 'But loyal to the Emperor…

'We came to Hive Ferrograd because we wish to join you.' She waited for the echoes of that declaration to fade. When Zabel had still given no response, she continued: 'My name, by the way, is Captain Sabella Jurten – and I would appreciate it greatly, Sergeant Zabel, if you could take me to see my father.'

'How?' the Chairman of the Council of Autocrats wailed. 'How did this happen?'

He paced his well-appointed office, crimson-cheeked, quivering with anger. He snatched a data-slate from a startled scribe. He hurled it at the wall as if breaking it would make its news less true.

General Krause stood to attention, biting his tongue. *It happened because you ignored my warnings,* he wanted to say, *always thinking you knew better.* 'Captain Jurten was further in thrall to her father than… *we* imagined, sir.'

The Chairman stuck out his lower lip. 'This couldn't be… Could it be a trick? If her squad were captured, could she not have lied to…?'

'May I speak freely, sir? In private?'

The Chairman thought about it, then nodded in sullen assent. He turned to stare through his window, which wasn't a window. It showed the palace gardens as they had been centuries ago before dark, glowering buildings had come to overlook them. Krause cleared the room but for the pair of them. He waited for the Chairman to turn from his sepia-tinted illusion, and softened his tone as much as he was able. 'Well, sir? Is it not time? Time to face the fact that one of your cities has fallen to an occupying power.'

'Still, it remains home to tens of millions of my citizens.'

'Whom we would be fighting to free. Nor let us overlook the fact that many of those citizens are where they choose to be. How many have heard Jurten's incitements by now? How many flocked to Ferrograd to pledge their allegiance to his Emperor?'

The Chairman lowered himself into a chair, which squeaked in protest.

'Civilians die in war, sir,' said General Krause. 'That cannot be avoided.'

'I don't need your military experience to tell me that!'

'How many messages have you sent to Jurten? How many times have you offered to talk, to seek a compromise? He will not compromise. He will not surrender Ferrograd without a fight, nor rest until he has taken the rest of this world from us too.'

The Chairman nodded wretchedly. He was close to giving in. Why else had he agreed to send his staff away, but to keep them from seeing his weakness?

'Each day we delay only strengthens him,' said Krause, with the scent of victory in his nostrils. 'Each day, more people hear his message and believe his threats of holy retribution against any who dare to defy him. Each day, more ask themselves if we believe it too, if this is the reason we do not act against him.'

The Chairman swallowed. 'Do it.' His voice emerged as a squeak, so he cleared his throat and gave the order again.

'According to the plan I drew up, sir?' asked General Krause, eagerly.

'You have my authority to pursue any strategy you see fit. Requisition whatever resources you require. Um, that is, as long as I remain defended.'

'Of course…' The ghost of a smile crossed Krause's face, and he gave a little bow as he added, 'your excellency. I shall make the arrangements at once.'

'Send my aides back in as you leave,' the Chairman instructed. 'I will have them set up a public address for this evening. I will give Jurten one final chance to see reason.'

'Which he will decline.'

'I'll tell him that, if he cares about our people at all–'

'A sound strategy,' the general purred.

'–then he will respect our right to decide our own destiny. He'll leave Krieg forever, and… and take his followers into exile with him.'

'Else any blood spilt will be on his head alone.'

'I'll give him till midnight to respond. Then, on the stroke of twelve…'

'I shall order the bombardment of Hive Ferrograd's walls to commence – to cease only upon its return to the lawful control of Krieg's planetary government.' *Or else,* Krause didn't say, keeping the thought to himself, *after it has been razed to the ground.*

AFTER THE GREAT RIFT

THE PUSH

Sergeant Renick moved on the second whistle.

For the first few minutes, she didn't move far. Her stomach ached with anticipation as the trenches in front of her emptied. At last, it was her turn on one of the ladders. She scaled it and planted her knee in a sandbag, which deflated. Thousands of boots before her had trampled and burst it. She looked for the rest of her squad. She hauled Trooper Rask up behind her when the dry earth crumbled at his fingertips.

Then she was running.

She followed hundreds of pairs of Cadian boots and, ahead of them, two thousand masked Krieg Korpsmen. They fanned out across the plain, so she was no longer hemmed in as she had been. Still, with hundreds more shock troops surging up behind her, she was equally trapped. She couldn't have altered her direction if she'd tried to.

She kept running, hearing explosions around her. She kept running, even as she almost stumbled over Krieg corpses. They stared up at her blankly through their opaque lenses and she almost expected them to move, to jerk to life, to grab her ankle, to pull her down to join them in the dirt.

It was the most surreal, not to say horrific, experience of Renick's life. She was under enemy fire, but couldn't take cover because there was no cover to take. She couldn't fire back, because she saw no target. She had never felt so helpless before, so lacking in control of her own fate. She could only run, and pray that no shell landed close enough to wipe her out. *Trust in the Emperor…*

She saw Hive Arathron's walls ahead, through the throng. Her heart leapt with hope, but an age passed and they appeared to grow no closer. She stumbled over something else. Not a corpse this time but something warm, something that squealed and writhed and smelled. A puke-green head on stumpy little legs…

The squig snapped at her shin. She hammered it with her lasgun butt, fracturing its skull. The troopers behind her ran into her, driving her forwards. The squig's teeth caught in the thick weave of her trousers and it bounced alongside her like a punctured ball. A few more blows dislodged it, and severed an antenna.

Then the squig was behind her, out of sight, though she glimpsed others ahead. They weaved between the pounding feet of the Imperial soldiers, creating what mischief they could. She was almost glad to see them. She couldn't risk shooting in such close quarters, but she ran her bayonet through the eye of the next squig she passed, and felt less helpless.

Colonel Drakon's voice rasped over the vox-net. *'Pick up the pace. No slacking at the back there. These faceless latecomers think their world breeds tougher soldiers than Cadia does. I plan to make them eat those words.'* It gave Renick heart to know that he was out here with his regiment, taking the same risks as the rest of them.

It made her want to likewise inspire her squad. She turned

and yelled to them, 'Come on. We're almost there.' When she looked back, to her surprise, it turned out to be true.

The walls of the hive loomed over her. The troopers in front had slowed and were bunching up again. She found herself stepping on pulverised debris, which crunched underfoot. She heard the cracks of lasguns and the rattles of altogether more primitive weapons, from not too far ahead. She strained for a sight of the action.

She found it in the form of a muscular ork, horns of bone jutting from its helmet. It ploughed through the Imperial ranks, howling and slobbering, swinging meaty fists this way and that. Almost a dozen troopers, Krieg and Cadian alike, were clinging to it, straining to bring it down, hacking at its flesh with combat knives. It scraped two of them off against their fellows. It grabbed another Korpsman by his neck, dashed him to the ground and stamped on him. For a second, it was coming head-on towards Renick and no one seemed able to stop it. She drew her knife and braced herself to meet it.

The squirming weight upon it forced the ork to veer away from her, and at last it fell onto one knee, then the other. When Renick last saw it, before it disappeared beneath a heap of armoured bodies, its face was a mass of bloody bruises and both eyes were swollen shut, but the creature was still fighting.

It seemed another age before the crowd ahead of her dispersed. Renick clambered over a vast mound of rubble, which shifted treacherously, trying to drag her under. Half-ruined structures reared up around her, most already claimed by Cadian snipers. The familiar sounds of pitched battle roared in her ears. She paused at the apex of the mound to look down on city streets heaving with bodies.

'We made it,' Rask exulted, as a cold sweat of relief broke over Renick. 'Thank the Emperor, we made it through the walls!'

She took a half-second to consider her options. Then she plunged down the north-western face of the mound. A small Cadian force had captured a half-demolished building, possibly a gatehouse, but were struggling to hold it as orks battered at its straining doors. Renick's squad came howling up behind them, weapons blazing, throwing the greenskins into disarray, but only for a moment before they rounded on their attackers.

They had made it to Hive Arathron, but the real fight was only just beginning.

Colonel Drakon was still outside the hive, still jostling for access alongside the last of his shock troops, when he heard the noise above him: a violent clattering racket, punctuated by the crumps of a misfiring engine.

A mass of oil-spewing machinery was plummeting towards him, dropped from one of the hive's upper levels. Two sets of spinning rotor blades protruded from it, and nestled in its midst was a massive-headed ork, incongruously sporting a tiny pair of plastek goggles.

A pair of gun barrels peeked out from under its seat. As the ork yanked on a lever, double-handed, they spat out a torrent of bullets. The Cadians had nowhere to go, no shelter from the storm. Some were cut down, stumbling into their closely packed comrades. A bullet ricocheted off Drakon's helmet, next to his left ear.

'Stand your ground!' he bellowed as he levelled his bolt pistol.

He loosed off three, four shots into the heart of the contraption, but heard two pinging off its rotors. He had hoped to hit something vital, though he couldn't tell where its vital spots were. He'd have settled for wiping the grin off the pilot's face. Its tongue hung out between its fangs and it convulsed with raucous laughter.

Then something miraculous happened. The nose of the contraption jerked upwards as if pulled by a chain, and its descent was abruptly curtailed. Its belly sailed over Drakon's head, so close that with a leap he could have touched the xenos' foot, and a strong promethium smell assailed his nostrils. He turned to follow the machine's ungainly progress. Its rotors were actually holding it up, though the bulk of it hung like a dead weight underneath them.

It listed alarmingly to starboard, and a sergeant yelled, 'It's coming round again!'

Drakon had already voxed his Vulture pilots. They were trying to get a bead on the flyer, but its proximity to both hive and ground was a problem for the larger gunships. One came diving, screaming, out of a cloud formation. The heavy bolter in its nose flared angrily, but the Vulture had to bank away sharply before its kill was claimed.

Buffeted by its wake, the ork flyer struck sparks off the hive wall with its tail, but somehow remained aloft. It began a second strafing run, but this time its targets were prepared. A fusillade of las-beams sheared off its port-side rotor, and it spun into the wall once more and erupted into flame. A ragged Cadian cheer was choked off as burning debris rained down on their heads, and a blackened xenos carcass dropped into their midst.

'Keep moving,' Drakon commanded. 'Into the hive. Go! Go!'

They'd be safer inside, among tightly packed buildings, where flyers had less room to manoeuvre – for the orks would surely have built more of them.

He heard a telltale clatter above him, and another – and a third, this one behind him too – and knew it was already too late. Six more ork flyers had emerged from the hive behind the first. Six more clumsy contraptions, which swirled about the exposed troopers like fat, black, buzzing bees. The Vultures swooped in and picked one off, while a trooper's lucky shot sent a second reeling away, end over end.

The four remaining flyers opened fire.

Colonel Drakon's face was spattered with Cadian blood. He choked on the orders he had been about to give. He kept firing at the flyers, but almost blindly from the need to keep his head down. Two of them collided, and he hoped he'd had something to do with that. One of the remaining two had overshot him and was puttering away from him. He focused his fire on it, and saw its pilot jerk as bolts thudded into the back of its seat.

Pride froze into horror in an instant.

The flyer careened back around. Its nose dropped as the pilot slumped over its controls. Time seemed to stop for Drakon as the flyer came diving right at him. He was spared by an explosive engine misfire, knocking it off course. It ploughed through the troopers to his right with a screech of tortured metal that almost drowned out their dying cries.

The colonel himself was flung to his knees. He heard the guns of the last remaining flyer, a percussion track to the cacophony around him, and he considered staying down. His best hope might have been to use his dead comrades as cover, repulsive though the idea was to him. He couldn't bring himself to do it.

He lifted his head and saw hope.

The troopers between him and the hive had melted away, either fallen or escaped. A route through its fractured walls had suddenly cleared. Drakon could see right into the vast city, and to him at that moment it looked like the promised land. He shouted to his troopers, to any who could still hear, to follow him.

His heart pounded in his ears, and he didn't know where the surviving ork flyer was. He tried not to think about the fact that he was scrambling over dead comrades. He felt light-headed, and only now realised that some of the blood on his face was his own. A bullet must have clipped him, or some shrapnel. He would have to see to it, locate the wound and dress it. As soon as he could. As soon as he was safe.

He was almost there, had almost reached the portal. He reached out for it.

Renick was defending the gatehouse when the news came in.

Her squad had fought its way into the building through a mob of raging orks, granted with the aid of their fellows already inside. Between them, they had trapped their enemies in a deadly crossfire. She had lined her squad up behind a ruined wall; they worked their lasgun triggers for all they were worth as a second xenos wave came crashing towards them.

Things had been going well. The snatches of vox chatter she had picked up had mostly been positive. Though many had died in the dash across no-man's-land, that number had been smaller than expected. Renick had also heard – though she didn't know how to feel about this – that there had been far fewer Cadian losses than Krieg.

A Krieg squad had climbed up into a defensive emplacement and slaughtered a pair of squigs manning its cannon. They had sheared off the pin restricting its angle of fire and spun it to point into the hive instead of outwards. The sounds of battle had summoned eager orks from far and wide. A few strategically placed shells had impeded their progress, collapsing structures to block the approach roads.

They had been winning. Or so, from Renick's point of view, it had seemed.

And then they had lost their commander.

Another sergeant, a witness to the tragedy, voxed command headquarters over the regimental channel. He sounded as stunned as Renick felt. When Colonel Drakon died, it should have meant something. He had deserved a blaze of glory. He shouldn't, he *couldn't* have been shot in the back by some random festering xenos.

Another ork lumbered into her sights. Anger burnt in Renick's belly. She hadn't thought it possible to hate these stinking brutes more than she did. She aimed for its head and put a las-beam between its eyes. She shot it three more times before it had a chance to fall. 'For Drakon,' she bellowed, 'and for all the good soldiers who died with him!' *For all who have fallen inside this hive already, whose bodies lie unburied here. For our lost world…*

Another cry tore itself from Renick's throat and was taken up by others across the hectic battlefield, a communal roar of mourning but also of defiance: '*Cadia stands!*'

The xenos couldn't even let them have that moment.

They responded with a war cry of their own: a simple, bestial '*Waaagh!*' which swelled to drown out the Cadian voices. The Krieg's captured cannon boomed and another building fell, but still the orks found narrowing, twisting paths through the rubble. They dropped from the roadways of the levels above, with impacts that by rights should have shattered their bones.

Another mob swarmed towards the gatehouse, orks elbowing and kicking each other in a contest for pole position. Renick almost gave the order to fall back, but the memory of Drakon made her stubborn. 'Don't waste time taking aim,' she yelled. 'Fire! Fire! Fire!' A virtual tidal wave of green flesh bore down on them which their guns could hardly miss. She fired one-handed, though her lasgun bucked with each recoil, spraying out its bright beams haphazardly. Her left hand unclipped a frag grenade from her belt. Her fingers were coiled about the safety pin when she heard a tremendous rumbling behind her.

A squadron of Death Riders swept past her position. They

crashed into the wave and, incredibly, it broke over them. The riders clung to their masked horses with their knees, simultaneously shooting into the xenos mass and deterring attacks upon themselves with slashing sabre-blades. Their mounts lashed out as well with powerful hooves, battering their startled victims to the ground.

An entire platoon of Death Korpsmen advanced in the riders' wake. They charged the disoriented orks and actually managed to push them back. Their intervention robbed Renick of a clear target. A shot into the melee would more likely hit an ally than an enemy. Through gritted teeth, she told her squad to hold their fire.

She remembered what Colonel Drakon had said about the Krieg. *They think their world breeds tougher soldiers than Cadia does… Like hell*, she thought.

'Someone else can hold the gatehouse,' she decided. 'We need a target. I need something I can kill.' She could see no Cadian officers, so felt free to use her initiative. She led her squad over the wall and they followed her, trusting her implicitly.

They scurried beneath a groaning stone arch, upon which an Imperial eagle had broken its wing. They ducked into a shadowed alleyway, their armoured shoulders scraping the walls. Renick looked for a means of gaining height and found a rusted ladder. Its bolts were coming loose and it swayed alarmingly as she placed her foot on its first step.

Her plan was to come up on the orks' left flank, to find a vantage point from which to fire into the melee. To show the Krieg that Cadian soldiers avenged their own dead.

That plan was shredded in an instant by the roar of an engine.

Renick whirled around, in time to see a shape shooting past the end of the alley. An ork bike, like the ones that had attacked the trenches. *If its rider saw us…* She tugged at the ladder, and rockcrete dust sprinkled her shoulders. It would barely hold the weight of one person, let alone five, leaving only one escape route.

'We need to get out of here. Now!' Renick drove her squad ahead of her, and knew a second later that she'd made the right decision. The bike came scraping and screeching up the passageway behind them. She burst out of its far end and threw herself aside, even as guns chattered behind her.

She found herself in a cobbled courtyard, surrounded by creaking hab-buildings, their dark windows like dead eyes. Ahead of her, one block had fallen and, through its wreckage, she could see the ork mob straining to hold off their Krieg attackers. 'Can't go forwards, sergeant,' cried Rask. The bike shot out of the mouth of the alleyway beside her, and Renick didn't quite get her gun up in time to fire at it.

'Scatter!' she yelled. 'Find cover where you can.'

At least, she thought, the terrain gave them some advantage. As the ork rider wrestled its vehicle around, its worn tyres skidded on debris and nearly overturned it. The rider planted its right hand on the ground and actually *pushed* itself back upright. Baring stained, broken teeth, it gunned its throttle and bore down on Trooper Creed, who was caught out in the open. He feinted right, dived left, and bullets riddled the hab-block wall behind him.

The bike sheared away from the wall, an instant before collision. Two troopers disappeared through a door into one of the buildings. They appeared a moment later at a window, weapons blazing. Renick tried to do the same, but her closest door was boarded up from inside. She squeezed herself into the doorway instead, and added to the deadly las-beam gauntlet that criss-crossed the yard.

A tyre blew out and the ork bike skidded again; beams sliced through vehicle and rider alike. They spun into a mound of rubble, upon which the ork's neck broke with a sickening snap. Renick could have punched the air in triumph, but the feeling was short-lived.

The biker had not been alone – and another roared into the courtyard from the alleyway, with another and another close behind it.

Renick kicked at her door and heard the wood behind it splintering, but it refused to yield. An open window gaped across the yard, Rask yelling at her from behind it. She sprinted towards him. She made it almost halfway before she was surrounded. Five xenos bikes encircled her, their riders playing with their prey. One whirled a spiked chain above its head.

Her troopers hurled las-fire – three from windows, Trooper Creed from behind a decapitated statue in a corner – to little avail. The chain-wielding ork turned its handlebars inwards and hurtled towards Renick.

She sidestepped it, just, but the others were hemming her in. The ork's chain glanced off her helmet, making her head ring. She tried to turn, to fire after it, but couldn't keep her balance. She was sprawled on her back before she knew it, the ork bikes tightening their circle around her. She was going to die, like the colonel...

Salvation came in the form of the Krieg Death Riders.

Five of them – the same squadron that had passed her earlier? – thundered into the courtyard from the direction of the battle. Hoofbeats rang off the cobbles, and one iron shoe struck the ground an inch from Sergeant Renick's ear. The horsemen ploughed into the bikers, as they had into the orks without, breaking up their formation. Renick levered herself up onto one knee, still dizzy as combatants whirled about her.

An ork bike and a Krieg horse charged each other, exchanging streams of bullets. She expected one or both to veer away before they collided, but neither of them did. The impact left the bike a mangled wreck, the horse little better. Both riders were hurled from their mounts, making bone-breaking landings from which neither rose again.

Renick tried not to think about that, nor about how vulnerable she was in her present position. She raised her lasgun and focused on the view along its sights, sternly willing her blurred vision to clear, trying to ignore the bullets that ricocheted around her.

She fired whenever she saw green. One of her beams burst open an ork rider's throat. As it choked on its own blood, its bike hurtled full tilt into a hab-block, dashing it to pieces. Renick gave a grunt of satisfaction.

She looked for her next target, but found none. The ork bikes lay in ruins, their riders dead or dying. The last of them gamely hoisted itself to its feet and started towards her. A Death Rider galloped past it; its sabre-blade decapitated the brute with one swift motion.

One of the Krieg dismounted to examine his fallen comrade. He bowed his head and made the sign of the aquila, then climbed back up onto his horse. The remaining four riders cantered once about the courtyard, then back out the way they had come. Renick caught the eye of one – or thought she did – and, still too breathless to speak, expressed her gratitude for their help with a nod.

Her comrades rejoined her as she stood, a little shakily.

She heard a groan from nearby, putting her back on alert. She was startled to see that the fallen Death Rider still lived. She hurried over to him. He lay at an unnatural angle in the rubble, blood pooling about him. He was unconscious, but moaning in pain. His mask had torn, not enough for her to see his face, but allowing a lock of curly blond hair to peek through. She felt a sudden swell of sympathy towards him.

He was beyond saving, as his fellow Korpsman must have seen. Had he been Cadian, though, she wouldn't have left him to suffer like this. *Was he not worth a single bolt?* She hesitated only for a moment. She said a prayer over the Krieg man's body, then pressed her lasgun to his temple and released him from his misery.

'He saved my life,' she murmured, 'he and the others.'

Creed nodded in quiet approval. 'I saw what he did, the way he charged that bike, without flinching. It was… courageous of him.'

'Courageous, yes,' agreed Renick. It was a high compliment to pay to any non-Cadian, but even as she voiced it she felt doubtful. *Might a better word be 'reckless'?*

She had been reckless. She should have remained in the gatehouse, she knew that now. It had been an ideal defensive position. Her thirst for ork blood had led her squad into uncharted territory. That and her need to prove herself as *courageous* as the Krieg…

She had risked their lives for too small a chance of gain. For though she would gladly give her life in the Emperor's service – as would any other Cadian – she also knew that life was not to be squandered. Living to serve another day was a small victory too.

She breathed out heavily. 'Okay,' she said, 'I say we can hold this courtyard. Trooper Kell, see if you can find some wire in this wreckage and string it up across the alleyway behind us – neck high to a speeding ork biker. The rest of us will take up positions in the rubble and lend covering fire to our Death Korps friends out there. Jump to it.'

We can win this battle, she thought. *We have to win it, for Colonel Drakon's sake – and as long as the Emperor wills it, I intend to be alive to see it!*

* * *

In the war room, a sombre atmosphere prevailed, despite the hustle and bustle.

All eyes were upon the tabletop hololith that dominated the room. It displayed a schematic of Hive Arathron's lower eastern quadrant. Flickering icons denoted the last-known positions of Imperial and xenos units. The former were picked out in black and white, the latter in a putrid shade of green. The display stuttered as it refreshed every few seconds, in response to incoming information. Each time it did, the number of green icons grew.

Ven Bruin observed from the sidelines. He had considered joining the battle himself. His priority, however, was the mission that had brought him to this world. The one of which only he and Interrogator Ferran knew the details. For now, he had decided, he would wait and watch for a chance to act.

'We're losing ground in the northern sectors.'

'We can divert Kappa-Four Platoon to the north, with the colonel's permission.'

'Holding the south-western front.'

'Reports coming in of xenos artillery units approaching from bearing two-three-five.'

One voice cut through the others: that of the Krieg colonel, relayed over vox-speakers. He was ten miles away, in the thick of the fighting. His position was marked on the map by a large white skull, which pulsed in time with his words. *'Permission granted to divert Kappa-Four Platoon. Update me on the status of our own artillery.'*

'Still clearing a path into the hive, sir.'

'I'm getting five… six… seven tanks on bearing oh-two-zero. Most appear to be Imperial Rhinos, though none were lost in the previous engagement in Arathron. They must have been on the ork ship, so probably old, battle-damaged but heavily modified.'

'Contact lost with our squad on the captured Earthshaker.' A junior officer spoke calmly into his comm-bead. 'Does anyone have eyes on the captured Earthshaker? Report.'

The Krieg lieutenant left in charge here by the colonel leant over the hololith. 'Suggest laying krak grenades at grid reference oh-four-nine-seven-beta. Delta-Five Platoon can spare two squads for that duty. In the meantime…' His gloved fingers stroked the display, bringing up readings. 'Epsilons One through Four can intercept the ork tanks on a heading of–'

'*Do it,*' the colonel instructed.

Orders were issued, the display updated again. The ork tanks appeared as an ominous green stain at the table's edge. The black-and-white skull icons of the Epsilon platoons vectored towards them. *Foot-soldiers against heavy artillery…* The two clusters of icons met, and a fresh barrage of field reports blasted from Ven Bruin's earpiece.

The Krieg employed their sole advantage over the xenos: superior numbers. They rushed the looted Rhinos through a gauntlet of fire from their storm bolters. They were cut down in their scores, but some made it through. They swarmed over plasteel hulls, dragging ork gunners out of their turrets where they could or blasting them out with explosive charges. They poked grenades down gun barrels.

Three Rhinos burnt, and their crews came tumbling out with axes whirling. Almost twenty xenos had been crammed into each vehicle, so the Krieg's advantage was suddenly lost; the remaining tanks ground back and forth on their tracks, sponson guns chattering, their gunners not caring if they shot through their own kind to get to their foes.

One by one, skull icons blinked out on the display.

'*Epsilon captain to command HQ.*' The voice was breathless, but betrayed no panic. '*It is my duty to report near-total loss of Epsilon platoons One, Two, Three and Four. Enemy artillery has been impeded as directed. Two vehicles are disabled, with others sustaining varying degrees of damage. I pray to the Emperor that our efforts will be–'*

Contact with the speaker was lost in a ferocious burst of static.

The green stain resumed its inexorable spread. Four Krieg platoons – something close to one hundred and fifty Korpsmen – had surrendered their lives to delay it by approximately four minutes. Could it have been enough?

The members of Delta-Five Platoon had laid every krak grenade they had in the ork convoy's path. Now, at the instructions of the war room lieutenant, they scrambled clear of the roadway as the first looted Rhino rolled towards them.

Their sergeant's subsequent report was drowned out by thunderous explosions. Tense minutes passed before it was confirmed that another three tanks had been shattered. The smouldering shell of one lay on its side, blocking the road. Orks strained their backs to roll it away, hampered by Krieg Korpsmen sniping at them from the sidelines.

Amid this came news that an Imperial Baneblade had entered the city.

The sense of relief about the table was palpable, though the Krieg's masked faces were as unreadable as ever. It drained away quickly as more reports poured in.

'–Gamma-Two Platoon under heavy fire from–'

'–defensive wall in the north-eastern quadrant has broken, and the xenos–'

'–more ork tanks approaching on bearing oh-three-five–'

'–with copter blades, leaping from bridges and–'

'–rock shelf crumbled underneath them, and the captured Earthshaker was–'

'–ork tanks approaching on bearing–'

'–to report the near-total loss of Omicron-Seven Platoon–'

'–on bearing three-one-nine–'

Ven Bruin felt his heart growing heavy. A tendril of hope tugged him forward to inspect the tactical hololith more closely. It showed him that the situation was exactly as bad as it sounded. The number of black-and-white icons had diminished considerably, while green ones had remained steady or even increased. They surrounded the Imperial skulls and Cadian Gate symbols like a giant daemon claw, poised to crush its hapless victims.

It wasn't over yet, of course. A Baneblade roared into the fray, blasting two looted Rhinos to pieces and collapsing a hab-block on top of countless orks. It pulverised rubble beneath its three hundred-ton weight, but still its progress through the congested streets was achingly slow, and the display showed tanks moving in to flank it from the north and the south.

'*Lieutenant…*' The Krieg colonel's voice boomed over the vox-speakers again, and Ven Bruin tingled with foreboding. '*You have the best overview of our situation there.*'

'Yes, sir.'

'*Give me your tactical assessment.*'

'Unfortunately, sir, the xenos' strength and state of preparation exceeded our worst-case projections. Our casualty rate stands in the range of forty-one to forty-six per cent and we have failed to make the early breakthroughs upon which our strategy depended.'

'*Your conclusion?*'

'That advancing further into the occupied hive risks a serious collapse of the line. That our chances of holding what little ground we've gained are minimal. In short, sir, that this battle can't be won.'

A short, pregnant pause followed before the colonel responded, '*I concur.*'

By this time, Inquisitor Ven Bruin had already turned his back and, with a heavy sigh, marched out of the room. He needed air.

* * *

Sergeant Renick felt suffocated too when the order came in. She vented her despair, not with a sigh but with a full-throated scream of anguish.

She had felt the tide turning against her side, unable to stop it. Her squad had been compelled to cede the cobbled courtyard. Orks had dogged their heels back to the gatehouse, where they had regrouped. She could see the gap in the hive's outer wall through which they had gained access. How little progress they had made.

She clung to the thin strands of hope that each xenos slain provided. Her squad of five had claimed four times as many kills and played a part in many more. At some point, it had to make a difference. At some point, they had to stop coming.

Hadn't they been meant to win this time?

Instead, they were right back where they'd been before, the last time her regiment had fought inside Hive Arathron. *A fighting withdrawal...* A phrase designed to mask the bitter truth: that, despite all their strategies, despite their reinforcements, despite their prayers, for the second time they had been defeated. *We have failed the Emperor...*

Another bridge collapsed, dragging half a hab-block down with it from the level above. A mangled maglev carriage bounced out of the wreckage, smashing into the gatehouse wall. *We have failed our lost world of Cadia...*

A choking cloud enveloped Renick's squad. 'Hold... hold your positions!' she commanded. Through streaming eyes, she saw shadows looming through the dust. She took a shot at one and was rewarded by a guttural, indignant yelp. 'Another, there... at two o'clock,' she spluttered. *We have failed Colonel Drakon...*

'Two more at twelve,' Creed cautioned her.

'Trying to sneak up while we're blinded,' spat Rask, 'but we'll make them... make them regret...' He broke off, coughing.

Renick's lasgun was running dry. She slapped her last power pack into place, defiantly. *The colonel's sacrifice was all for nothing,* she thought.

There wasn't much she could do about that, nor about the many other good soldiers lost. Before she turned tail and ran away from their killers, however, she intended to slaughter as many of them as she possibly could.

ATTRITION

The sirens wailed out just minutes before the dawn alarm.

The day-shift workers of the south-west sector stumbled out of their cots, bleary-eyed and fearful. Having been under siege for eighteen months, they were used to waking, working, eating, sleeping to a soundtrack of booming cannons. They knew what they had to do.

Those that didn't were reminded by a calm but authoritative voice, broadcast by conical vox-speakers from every street corner. *'Extinguish all light sources... Take cover... Shelter underneath a staircase if you can, beneath a bed or table otherwise... Keep your gas mask to hand at all times...'* The voice, it was said, was that of Colonel Jurten himself, though no one knew for sure if this was true.

The sky of Krieg was visible to few hive-dwellers, but some fancied they heard droning overhead. Traitor bombs dropped between the pockmarked remnants of Ferrograd's once proud spires. They tumbled through several levels before becoming lodged. They brought whole blocks down, staircases and all, when they burst.

A half-ton bomb crashed through the roof of the Wulfram ordnance plant. It ripped out the walls and touched off a chain reaction of explosions that blew out neighbouring industrial and storage blocks.

Jurten joined the rescue teams as they combed the wreckage for survivors. For eighteen months he had been fighting a war at a distance, so he took every chance to flex his muscles and work up a sweat, to put the strength of his limbs to good use. His presence would also be an inspiration to others, or a threat; either one was fine with him.

'The traitors sent sixteen aircraft,' Lieutenant Ionas voxed him. 'Missile launchers took out six before they could reach us, and forced four more to turn back.'

'Then they let six slip through,' the colonel growled.

'An eleventh – the one that bombed Wulfram, we believe – took a hit from one of the mobile Hydras and may have crashed in District Fourteen-Alpha.'

'May have?'

'Still awaiting confirmation from fire crews at the scene, sir, but it's certain that something came down in that vicinity.'

Jurten frowned. Eleven bombers out of sixteen was not an unreasonable tally. Any enemy units destroyed could be counted as progress, as they weren't easily replaced. That was why the Chairman hadn't ordered an air raid in weeks, until today. *He must be growing frustrated, which could also benefit us…* The loss of Wulfram, on the other hand, was a serious blow to his own production capabilities. His gunners would have to conserve their ammunition, even more so than they already were.

'We need…' he grunted, straining to lift a heavy chunk of rockcrete by himself. 'We need a crane up here.'

'*I know, sir,*' said Ionas. '*I'm trying to get one to you, but the bridge at Fourteen-Gamma is out. Dozers are clearing a path through the residential sectors, but it'll take time. I could get more hands to you in the meantime. I could divert gunnery crews from–*'

Jurten interrupted him. 'No. No, the most important thing is to keep those cannons firing. We do not let our enemies see that we are weakened in the slightest.'

'*As you wish, Colonel Jurten.*'

The traitors bombarded the hive walls day and night, ironically with guns fashioned in Imperial forges. Some days, they took out an emplacement or broke through a wall. The loyalist defenders shelled their attackers in turn, with guns from those very same forges. So far, they had mostly succeeded in keeping them at bay.

Still, Ferrograd's walls, tough as they were, were not impregnable. Slowly, very slowly, they were being chipped away – just as slowly, very slowly, the traitors were depleting their resources. The loyalist guns had chipped away at their tanks' hides too – and some, whose crews had ventured too far forward, had been ruthlessly wiped out.

Jurten had sent small teams of infiltrators out into the enemy trenches. Many traitors had been slain by a silent knife in the back, their food stolen and equipment sabotaged. It was surprising how effective a simple rag could be, jammed into a Demolisher's exhaust pipe. The traitors had become wise to this tactic, however. Command headquarters had lost contact with three stealth teams in succession. No one had returned from any of them.

Jurten worked through the night, the next day and into the evening. He tore his gloves and scraped the hands beneath them bloody. Most of those he uncovered were already dead or badly wounded. The latter were of little use, not worth the treatment they would have required. He administered the Emperor's mercy to them. Still, the handful of lives saved justified his efforts. Every gun made a difference…

He lay in his bed that night, too tired to sleep. He listened to the booming cannons. Ionas had urged him to move his quarters deeper into the hive, where they would be safer. He liked to be able to hear the cannons, however. They kept him alert.

He could hear the stentorian voice from the vox-hailers too. *'The traitors launched a cowardly attack upon our homes, hoping to slay us in our beds. By the Emperor's grace, they failed. We shall mourn the loss of the brave workers whose lives they stole from us, but they shall be avenged. We shall rebuild our manufactoria, stronger and more productive than they ever were before. The Emperor shields us.*

'The traitors underestimated our military might. Our guns ripped their flimsy flyers apart. The traitor that bombed the Wulfram plant was recovered from the wreckage. He confessed his crimes and begged for the Emperor's forgiveness as he died from his wounds.'

The voice told Jurten's citizens what they needed to hear. It didn't always have to be true.

Krieg's war would be lost by the first side to exhaust its resources, and his side had had far fewer resources to begin with. Every soldier, every citizen of Ferrograd had to pull his or her weight, had to do the most they could with what they had. They had two major factors on their side. The first was their commitment. They were fighting for a cause that they believed in. The Chairman's forces fought for nothing.

Jurten's other big advantage was that he had Archmagos Greel.

Greel had attached himself to the 83rd Krieg Regiment some years ago. He had begun to appear at command meetings by virtue of his Adeptus Mechanicus rank. To begin with, Jurten had maintained a distance from him.

As a tech-priest, Greel was sworn to serve the Emperor, but saved his worship for his own Machine-God. *A false god…* He believed in the superiority of mechanisms over flesh, so had grafted augmetic limbs to himself. He may have replaced his own limbs; Jurten didn't know and didn't care to think about what Greel hid beneath his rust-red robes. He found it disconcerting enough looking into his whirring mechanical eye.

Since his return to Krieg, Jurten had found the archmagos indispensable.

Greel's coterie of acolytes performed the same tasks they always had, maintaining the regimental arsenal. He also had them cannibalising civilian vehicles and sifting through industrial junk heaps for usable components. They were patching up worn-out tanks, extending their lifespans. They bodged together new hybrid guns from the mangled remains of the old and somehow, through arcane means, coerced them into working.

Greel had drawn up plans to modify the loyalists' las-weapons. He had shown the prototype to Jurten. It was more powerful than the standard lasgun, but consumed more energy per shot. Jurten judged this an acceptable trade-off. Its users would simply have to pick their shots.

He had come to value Greel's utterly pragmatic nature. Never once, to his knowledge, had the tech-priest been swayed by emotion. Jurten wondered if he felt anything at all, or if the machines wired into his brain had shut off that part of him.

When the Chairman had threatened the life of Jurten's daughter, only Greel had told him what he had needed to hear: 'She is only one soldier.'

They met that morning for their regular debriefing. Jurten went to Greel, though it meant descending into the underhive. Greel was spending most of his time down here. Jurten had been aware that he had requisitioned work parties, but still he was surprised to see the extent of their activity. Lumoglobes were strung between the tunnel walls, casting a pale blue light. The sounds of picks and shovels rang off rockcrete, while the engines of oily construction vehicles idled.

'We cannot hold off the traitor army forever,' Greel opined, as the pair walked together. 'Already, they have driven us back from the outskirts of the city.'

'I am aware of that.'

'They surround us at all points of the compass, and also have air superiority.'

The colonel ground his back teeth.

'Which leaves us only one way to go,' said Greel, 'to remain a step ahead of them.'

'You're suggesting we cower underground like vermin?'

'No, colonel, not at all. But how many citizens were displaced in this latest bombing raid? I say we can make space for them, shelter them, right here. Retrenchment rather than retreat. These tunnels span the length and breadth of Ferrograd. They connect old storage cellars, bunkers, mining facilities and even slum hab-units from the days in which your ancestors lived and worked down here.'

'Many centuries ago,' the colonel muttered.

'Indeed. Before these levels were built over and almost forgotten – at best, considered a convenient repository for the hive's waste products.'

'This is a… noble endeavour,' conceded Jurten. 'It is also a long-term, labour-intensive project, for which I simply cannot spare the resources at present.'

They passed a squad of Guardsmen, who snapped to attention. The colonel returned their sergeant's salute. That made five squads he had seen, standing guard against the human and semi-human 'waste products' lurking in the underhive's shadows.

'Tomorrow is always too late, colonel, to plan for the long term.'

They were interrupted by a commotion up ahead of them. Jurten's instinct was to start forward, but Greel laid a gloved hand on his arm. He could only hope it was a flesh-and-blood hand.

A mob of panicked labourers came belting towards them. They were slowed, but not much, by the sight of the colonel's glowering countenance. He was affronted to see blue-and-gold uniforms among them. *If they dare flee from some weak-limbed mutant…* A sergeant stumbled to a halt before him, trying to speak, but he couldn't catch his breath. Jurten detected a sour mustard odour, felt it scratching at the corners of his eyes.

A handbell rang out somewhere, and warning voices were raised. 'We must have hit a gas pocket,' Greel said, matter-of-factly. The labourers about them downed tools, backing up along the tunnel. Jurten saw a yellow haze spreading slowly towards them and decided that withdrawal was indeed the wisest course.

They were passed by several figures in bulky fatigues, running towards the haze. They wore gas masks, connected by flexible hoses to rebreather units on their chests. 'They'll seal the breach if they can,' said Archmagos Greel. 'If not, we may have to abandon this whole area until the poison dissipates, which may take many months.'

'You're digging–' Jurten began, but found his throat constricted by the gas. He cleared it, irritably. 'You're digging through walls?'

'Reclaiming areas sealed up long ago. Unfortunately, at some point certain chemicals were stored in this area, in containers prone to corroding. You may wish to breathe through a handkerchief, colonel. A small dose of the gas should not cause lasting harm, but at higher concentrations it often triggers some rather unsightly mutations.'

Jurten did as the tech-priest suggested.

They turned into another tunnel, in which work continued as if nothing had happened. They had soon left the gas leak safely behind them, and Greel returned to his earlier point. 'You must be aware,' he said, 'that when citizens lose their homes or their workplaces, when they fall through the gaps in the system, when they don't know where their next meal is coming from, it is to here that they tend to gravitate.'

Jurten gave a grunt of reluctant acknowledgement.

'My workforce is made up of such refugees, who would otherwise be lost to us but are given a purpose by my project here, and somewhere to belong.'

They had circled back to the broad, stone steps at which their discussion had begun. Atop these, Jurten's Pegasus command vehicle was waiting to convey him to his next engagement. 'Let me speak to my adjutant,' he offered.

'There is one more, ah, factor of which I ought to make you aware.' Greel glanced around them, furtively. A mechanical feeler with something like a multi-scanner attached to its end peeked out of his robes, checking over his shoulder. Jurten pretended not to see it.

'Well?' he prompted.

'The Adeptus Mechanicus has certain records in its possession, relics of ages past. They point the ways to great vaults of ancient treasures, buried in the roots of certain hive cities across the worlds of mankind in order to preserve them during the Age of Strife.'

'I assume you mean technology,' said Jurten, disapproving. 'From the Dark Age.'

Greel didn't deny it. 'As some people like to call it.'

'You believe there is one of these… vaults here under Ferrograd?'

'I do, and surely it was by the will of…' – his human eye darted towards the colonel – 'our respective deities that we find ourselves confined here, of all cities, of all worlds.'

'What may this vault contain?'

'That is the question,' said Greel in his dry, cracked voice. 'Great wonders, perhaps. Machines whose functions have long since been forgotten–'

'Doubtless for good reason.'

'–but which may be of inestimable value in our current situation.'

'Weapons?' asked Jurten, shrewdly.

'Potentially powerful enough to hand us victory in this civil war,' said Greel, 'within weeks, or even sooner. Weapons with which we may reclaim Krieg for the Emperor.'

Jurten considered that prospect for a moment before he asked his next question. 'What manner of weapons?'

The colonel also met regularly with his daughter.

Captain Sabella Jurten was a fount of information. She had spent her life on Krieg, much of it close to power. She knew the autocrats. She knew their secrets, all the petty vendettas between them. Jurten had contacted most of them in their respective hives. He had threatened some, negotiated with others, fed misinformation to all. His aim was to keep them at each other's throats and undermining their weak leader.

Sabella couldn't tell him much about the Chairman that he didn't already know. The man's selfish motives were transparent enough. They often discussed him, even so, and today was no exception. 'My sources in the palace say he hasn't left his chambers in weeks,' said Captain Jurten. 'His latest public address was created from archive recordings. His personal apothecary calls upon him four times daily, but it's rumoured she can find no physical ailment and has diagnosed a sickness of the soul.'

'Perhaps he will do us all a favour and die,' growled Colonel Jurten.

'With your leave, sir, I believe I can make sure of it.'

He glared at her across the dinner plates. 'We have discussed this before.'

'He may pass away by himself or he may not. He may linger for years, with his toadies concealing his condition. He may even recover. Or we could put him out of his misery now, while he is vulnerable. Make an example of him in front of the world.'

'And if instead our soldiers are captured in the attempt?'

'I spoke with Archmagos Greel,' said Sabella. 'The tunnels he is digging underground could be our key to–'

'Those tunnels are not safe.'

'A single squad with rebreather units could make it through the gas pockets. I have looked at plans and taken measurements. I believe that, with minimal effort, we could break through into a network of natural caverns that runs beneath the earth in this region, and from there into a long-buried section of Auros' underhive.'

'The Chairman's palace is a long way from the underhive.'

'But I know all the routes between the two, including the blocked-off, secret passageways that nobody uses. I was in charge of palace security. It was my job to know. My squad could be under the Chairman's nose before he suspects a thing.'

The colonel pushed himself to his feet. He paced the room, being sure to keep his back to her. Few people would have noticed the stiffness in his left leg, had they not been look-ing for it. When he turned back to her, his face was studiedly impassive.

'Is this how you persuaded him?' he asked.

Words failed Sabella Jurten for a moment.

'Are these the words you used,' her father persisted, 'to talk the Chairman – your last commanding officer – into sending you here, to assassinate me?'

She had thought they were growing closer. These past months, she had spent more time with him than ever before. They discussed only strategy and administrative matters, nothing personal – neither had broached the subject of her mother – but still they were talking. She had believed she was earning her father's respect, not easily bestowed.

She was under no illusion about him, however. She knew exactly who he was. *A career soldier,* many had called him, but far more than that. The colonel was on a crusade, and that left no room in his life for anything else. So, she met his probing eyes, unblinking. 'My allegiance,' she said, 'is to the Emperor.'

She wasn't going to plead with him. He would think less of her if she did. Either he believed her – either he *knew* her – or he didn't.

The colonel was the first to lower his gaze.

'Who would replace him?' he asked gruffly.

'The Chairman? Difficult to say. Hive Argentus will push for High Autocrat Freudt, but he has enemies in Auros and may see the nomination as a poisoned chalice in the present circumstances. Marelle may yet reappear and stake a claim – though it's really more her style to find someone whose strings she can pull while remaining unaccountable.'

'Therefore the most likely outcome…?'

'Is that, while the autocrats squabble among themselves…'

'General Krause will take command of an interim military government.'

'Yes, sir, I would say that is probable.'

'And so, would have no one to hold him back.'

'As I understand it, the Chairman has not held Krause back in eighteen months.'

'That may be true.' Colonel Jurten retook his seat. He took a long draw from his glass and swilled water about his mouth, in thought. 'If I were to sanction this mission...' he rumbled at length.

'Yes, sir?' asked Captain Jurten, eagerly.

'If you were to infiltrate the Chairman's palace and kill that traitor in his bed...'

'I know I can do it, sir.'

'Then, once the deed is done, how do you plan on getting out of there alive?'

It isn't known exactly how the Chairman of Krieg's Council of Autocrats died.

Many versions of the story were told over the following years, from the one in which he gave his life to free his people, to the one in which the Emperor of Mankind vaporised him with a thunderbolt. Both sides in Krieg's civil war produced a raft of propaganda, beneath which the truth of the matter was inevitably smothered. The version accepted by the Ordo Hereticus, however, is the one now taught by the Krieg to their offspring, for history is written by the victors, after all.

The appeal of this story is that the Chairman died a broken shell of a man. Claiming sundry aches and pains, he made a permanent retreat to his bedchamber. There, he wallowed in his woes – not to mention in silk sheets, fine food and potent drink. He remained extremely comfortable, as long as he could blot out everything beyond his four walls. This was impossible to do, of course, and so his heart ached with resentful self-pity.

He gave in to lethargy, eventually struggling even to rise from his bed. He had been born to be a king. Instead, the Chairman clung to a title that meant little any more, presiding over a world irrevocably fractured.

All this he could blame on one man, whose name he frequently, vehemently cursed. He may have rued the day that he let Jurten's troop ship enter orbit. This would have meant admitting a fault in himself, though, so maybe he didn't.

The Chairman spent most of his days alone. He hated to be seen in his debilitated state, so had dismissed his aides but for a few that bathed him, changed his pyjamas and fed him. One evening, when he rang for an aide, nobody came. He huffed and puffed indignantly and swung the bell harder, until it flew out of his hand and cracked his dressing mirror.

A disturbance flared outside his door. Footsteps and raised voices.

The Chairman wailed, 'Is someone out–' His throat seized up as he heard gunshots, followed by a stifled cry. His overtaxed heart threatened to seize up too. Sweat ran cold down his back. He tried to roll himself out of bed, but got his legs caught up in his silk sheets.

He cowered as someone burst into the room. He recognised one of his own nursemaids, wild-eyed with panic. Tendrils of some noxious yellow gas followed him inside. 'They… they're…' the young man spluttered, slamming the door shut, bolting it and pushing a heavy chest up to it. 'They came out of nowhere. They set off some sort of… gas grenade. The guards… They shot the guards. Mr Chairman, we have to–'

'You will address me as "your highness",' he demanded, shrilly.

'Your highness…'

'Come, help me to my feet. It is your duty to protect your ruler, boy. Contrary to what our attackers may believe, we are neither trapped nor helpless in here. There is a catch in the back of the wardrobe, which opens a secret–' A hammering on the bedchamber door made his heart leap again. '*Help me up, damn your eyes!*'

He was poised on the edge of his mattress, reaching out a clammy hand to his aide, who was frozen for a second. Then the door was blasted into splinters, and the Chairman was sent crashing to the floor.

The yellow mist rolled into the room and collected about him. It burnt his lungs when he breathed in. He pushed himself up onto hands and knees, made dizzy by the effort. He reached out for assistance again and, for the first time in his life, a plea tumbled off his tongue. 'I'll give you anything you want...'

By the time he managed to raise his head, the aide was gone. The door of the Chairman's ornate wardrobe clicked shut.

Then he heard boots on broken wood behind him. It is said that, out of lifelong habit, he uttered a prayer to the Emperor, which went unanswered. He turned to be greeted by a sight even more horrifying than he had imagined. He saw monsters in the yellow fog, with leering skulls instead of faces, black staring eyes and distended snouts; and it is also said that, at this moment, the Chairman broke down in tears of bitter regret and repented of his heresies, though no one can know this for sure.

The last thing the Chairman's eyes saw was almost certainly the masked face of a loyalist soldier, looking down on him without pity, without malice, without any expression at all. By then the poison gas may have melted his skin and begun to dissolve his brain. It is likely that he would have experienced hallucinations.

It would have been an agonising death, and so it's likely that the soldier would have let it run its course rather than wasting ammunition on him.

The vox-hailers trumpeted the news throughout Hive Ferrograd. The Chairman – no mention was made of his cursed name – was dead. He had paid the price for his treachery, as would his misguided followers soon.

'*Our victory now is assured, for our enemies have lost their leader and lost heart. They see now, as clearly as we have always seen, that no sinner can long escape the Emperor's vengeance, and they have been shaken to their cores.*'

The announcement sparked celebrations in the city's churches, spilling out into the streets. There were hundreds of arrests for public order offences, driven by synthehol consumption – though Ionas asked the city enforcers not to punish offenders too harshly. He saw no need to consult with his commander about this.

Colonel Jurten's mood was black as he marched into the communications room. 'Let me see him,' he said gruffly. He stepped up onto a circular podium. Lights danced about him like giddy fireflies, scanning every inch of his body.

On an opposite podium, more lights traced out the very solid-looking image of General Krause. The two men had not faced each other this way before. Jurten had rebuffed Krause's previous attempts at dialogue, as he had those of the Chairman. No traitor had had anything to say that he wanted to hear. Until now.

They eyed each other with undisguised contempt. 'Your leader is dead,' said Jurten bluntly. 'I shall offer you the same choice he once offered me. Leave Krieg. Allow its people to return to the Emperor's embrace.'

'*Leave you to enslave them, you mean,*' sneered Krause, '*indoctrinate and abuse them, while your masters hunt me down like a dog.*'

'No, not like a dog. A dog deserves more dignity than a snivelling, stinking traitor. You betrayed your oath to the Emperor, Krause. You disgrace that uniform you wear.'

'*An oath made under sufferance,*' spat Krause, '*under threat of torture and death, and because I too was brainwashed, raised to believe that my life belonged to some ancient, half-dead husk propped up on a throne, light years away.*'

Jurten bristled at the blasphemy.

'I took up arms, fought in the Emperor's name, because I was told – we were all told – that honour would be our reward. As soon as I set foot on my first battlefield, as I was dropped into that carnage, I knew we had been lied to. Can't you see it?'

Aides and technicians stood stunned by Krause's words. Some covered their ears, while even Jurten was taken aback by such a brazen outburst. He motioned to Ionas, surreptitiously. The adjutant approached him, stopping short of the dancing lights. *Clear the room,* the colonel mouthed at him.

'I played the part expected of me,' continued Krause. *'The good soldier. I rose swiftly through the ranks. A commission released me from the unrelenting hell of the front lines.'*

'A good officer fights alongside his troops,' said Jurten, pointedly.

'So your Emperor tells you,' Krause snorted.

'It is the truth.'

'His truth, but there are others. There are truths that we have always known, but never dared acknowledge – and voices that will speak those truths, if only we are willing to listen to them. If only, Jurten, you would open your mind.'

'An open mind is an unsafe mind,' recited Jurten, automatically, 'and I see now that egotism has laid waste to yours. You are beyond redemption.'

Krause looked down at his boots and shrugged. *'I had to try to reason with you.'*

'Your leader is dead,' Jurten restated, 'and I swear to you in the Emperor's name–'

Krause's eyes blazed with sudden anger. *'You still don't get it, do you? Your Emperor has no power on Krieg. My army is superior to yours and it will crush you. It is only a matter of time. Or did you imagine that the loss of one man would break our spirit? Perhaps, Colonel Jurten, you might consider what you have lost today.'*

Jurten maintained his rigid stance, although his hip throbbed.

'*By now, you are aware that your five agents have not returned to you.*' The way he said the number, *five*, was deliberate. He wanted a reaction, which Jurten was determined not to give him. *So, all were discovered…*

'*It will not surprise you, I am sure, to hear that none of them survived.*'

'They understood the risk,' he growled, 'and accepted it.'

'*Did they? Or is that just what you expected them to say?*'

'True courage,' said Jurten, quoting another aphorism, 'lies in that distinction.'

Krause took a half-step towards the front edge of his podium. The end of his swagger stick, along with his right toecap, dissolved into a blur of pixels. '*For who among us really wants to die, when we could live instead? And, oh, your five assassins tried their very best to live. They knew their way around this palace. My sentries never saw them coming. From where could they have acquired such knowledge, I wonder?*'

'I have no patience for games. Say what you have to say.'

'*I came to know your daughter well, you know, when she was my prisoner.*'

'She told me about it. Every second.'

'*I knew she would betray us for a chance to earn your favour. The Chairman should have listened to me when I warned him. There is irony, I suppose, in the fact that his mistake returned to haunt him. But I knew… I knew that, once the alarm was raised, Sabella Jurten would flee along the secret passage from the Chairman's chambers. I knew the exact route she would take, and where to set my ambush for her…*'

Jurten had wanted an answer from Krause. Now he had it.

'*I made her remove the mask before I killed her. I wanted to see the fear on her face. She pleaded for her life. She told me she would do anything I demanded of her, if only–*'

'That is a damned lie!'

The image of his enemy leered at him. *'You'll never know for sure.'*

But Jurten did know. He and his daughter had discussed exactly this scenario. She had assured him that she would shoot herself before becoming a prisoner again, and certainly before she would give away his secrets; and he had believed her. He had only needed Krause to confirm that she had had the chance to do it.

He could have been lying about that too, but Jurten didn't think he was that wily.

Ionas had emptied the room of onlookers, as he had instructed. Only the colonel and a single engineer remained, and the latter's ears were covered with a headset. Jurten made a slashing gesture with his hand, a signal to cut off the transmission.

'My eyes were opened by the Chairman,' boasted Krause, in the seconds before his light image dissipated, *'but he outlived his use to me. His death neither moves me nor affects my plans in the slightest. Can you say the same about the death of your–'*

Jurten ground his teeth, glaring at the now empty podium before him.

He answered his enemy's final question aloud. He knew that no one but Ionas would hear him, but he couldn't cede the last word all the same.

'She is only one soldier...'

Krause stepped up his bombardment of the hive that night. The citizens of Ferrograd lay restlessly abed as the cannons thundered more relentlessly than ever. Many wondered if it was they who trembled, or the city's foundations far below them.

By dawn, the thunder had subsided to its customary level. The day-shift workers trudged to their manufactoria, the previous night's celebrations dampened by the morning's hangover. The voice that may have been Colonel Jurten's still lauded their recent success, but its promises were tempered by stern admonitions.

'Our victory will not be achieved in days or weeks. It requires hard work and sacrifice from every one of us. We cannot afford to falter. We cannot afford to tire. Each day, we must prove our faith in the Emperor anew – for it is our belief in Him that makes us strong.

'We cannot afford to doubt.

'Krieg harboured a viper in its midst. Complacency allowed its seductive poison to spread, and though the snake is dead now, that poison afflicts many of our countrymen still. That shame is for all of us to bear.

'We must be strong. We must have faith. We must not think of our own needs and wants at this time. We must do as the Emperor expects, and purge Krieg of the viper's poison. We must atone for our world's sins, show that we are still worthy of His favour.

'Praise be to the Emperor.'

AFTER THE GREAT RIFT

THE INEVITABLE

Ven Bruin was praying for guidance when Interrogator Ferran burst in on him.

'My apologies, inquisitor, but I felt you ought to hear this. The Krieg colonel–'

'Has withdrawn his forces from Hive Arathron.' Ven Bruin rose from his prostrate position. He had asked to be left alone. 'I was present when the decision was taken.'

'Then you…?'

'I trust his judgement.'

'I'm not so sure I do,' said Ferran. He obviously had something to say. Ven Bruin waved his subordinate into a seat. He poured out two drinks rather than calling for an aide.

'You told me of the Death Korps of Krieg's utmost commitment,' said Ferran. '"Entrust them with a mission," you said, "and they will pursue it relentlessly."'

'For as long as that mission is attainable. I'm sure I made that distinction.'

Ferran scowled, digging furrows in his brow. 'Any battle can be won if–'

'But a slim chance of victory may be outweighed by the cost of defeat.' Ven Bruin leaned back in his seat. 'The Krieg brought five thousand Korpsmen to this world. The last I heard, almost half that number had laid down their lives. It may be more by now.'

'I hadn't realised,' conceded Ferran.

'I understand this feels like a sudden reversal.'

'It does.'

'The colonel made a calculation.'

Ferran stared into his glass for several seconds before asking, in a more conciliatory tone, 'So, where does this leave us?'

'Awaiting further orders, but we know what they will likely be. We can pray for a miracle. We can pray that, somehow, more manpower may become available. The Adeptus Astartes might spare a force to aid us. We must, however, prepare for the worst.'

'Evacuation,' said Ferran, subdued.

Ven Bruin nodded. 'And then, perhaps, if it can be arranged, Exterminatus.'

'A world sacrificed for the sake of preserving the cordon.'

For the first time, he felt the full weight of his seventy years upon him. After a lifetime's service, he wondered, would this failure be his legacy? Ferran must have thought him old too, seeing him without his cloak and hat, his balding pate exposed. 'Though, begging your pardon, sir,' he said, 'what I meant was–'

'Where does this leave *our* mission?' Ven Bruin pre-empted him.

Ferran nodded. 'For the ordo.'

'I have asked the Emperor for guidance.'

'I… see, sir. Then I shall await your decision.' Ferran stood. 'But perhaps we should also speak with the colonel again. I should like to hear him justify his actions in his own words… and to look into his eyes as he does so.'

With a bow to his superior, he swept out of the room.

Ven Bruin watched him go with hooded eyes. He recalled a time when he had been so certain of himself. Once, he too would have sought someone to blame for such a setback as they had suffered. Someone had not been strong enough, not been devout enough. Someone had not done as the Emperor expected. *Perhaps Ferran ought to look closer to home.*

He had hidden the whip in the second that the door had been flung open. He recovered it from his boot now. He turned it over in his hands. He stroked its frayed, knotted cords. He felt a rush of warmth towards it, like it was an old friend. In his youth, it had often brought him clarity, and he had need of that now more than ever.

Was he being punished for his improper thoughts?

Or was the Emperor showing him the path to take…?

The journey to the hive, across no-man's-land, had seemed to take forever.

The long walk back seemed even longer. Some vehicles had ventured out from the encampment, but only to pick up the wounded and the dead.

With the orks' guns silenced, at least there was no immediate threat. A handful of greenskins had spilled out of the hive, but the fighting had not come close to Sergeant Renick. Her squad, unscathed but weary to their souls, trudged on across the dry, cracked mud. Never had her backpack felt so heavy.

She had fought for as long as she could. She had prayed, until the end, for some miracle to turn the tide back in the Emperor's favour, to sweep His enemies away.

She had witnessed the last stand of one of the massive Krieg Baneblades. It had planted itself in the middle of a roadway, a shield for the retreating foot-soldiers. The ramshackle ork tanks had come at it one, two, three at a time, wheezing as they clambered over debris heaps. Its battle cannon had roared with such explosive force that it seemed to shake the world, and one by one, the xenos vehicles had erupted into flame.

Their guns had battered the Baneblade in return, with little effect. Time and again, the smoke of a blast had cleared to reveal its target standing stoically. Renick had glimpsed the mask and helmet of a Krieg gunner perched up in his turret, and she could imagine no clearer symbol of human defiance.

It had been an illusion. The smoke had concealed cracks in the Baneblade's shell, and when next she had looked, there had been no gunner, no turret, just a smouldering crater. The great tank's other weapons – its heavy bolters and lascannons – had blazed on, but it was crippled now, and the xenos had scented its promethium blood and were circling it.

By then, she had backed up as far as the hive's outer wall. A commissar had screamed at her, 'Go! Go! Get out of here, now!' So, Renick had lowered her weapon, turned her back on that dismal scene and fled.

She passed an idling Centaur, decorated with Krieg skulls. Two Korpsmen knelt beside a dead comrade. They were stripping the body, as she had seen them doing in the trenches, and suddenly she realised that they only wanted its equipment. The Cadian dead, those that could be recovered, would be buried with honours. The Krieg would leave their own to rot.

The sun was poised on the horizon ahead of her. Its glare kept her from seeing how far she had to go. Eventually, however, she found trampled wire underfoot. A minute later, a trench yawned open before her and she descended into it.

The trenches already teemed with Korpsmen. The Earthshaker cannons were already manned and loaded, their crews awaiting orders. Off-duty Krieg were breaking out first aid kits in the dugouts. Renick felt grateful that her squad had been assigned no duties. Still, her tent seemed a long way away.

She followed other Cadians through a groaning tunnel. Some props had been dislodged and, inspecting them, she saw that they were chewed through. This put her on her guard and indeed, a moment later, she heard a familiar screech ahead of her.

Her fellows had unearthed an errant squig, but they were quick to deal with it. A dozen bayonets skewered the creature, continuing to pierce it long after it was dead. Rask and other Cadian troopers took out their frustrations upon the one target available. Sergeant Renick didn't blame them, but she did take offence at being sprayed with xenos bodily fluids. It was just as well, she admonished them, that the squig hadn't been of the acidic variety.

Her ears pricked up and, for a second, she wasn't sure why.

It was Trooper Creed who noticed it: 'The guns have started up again.' She had grown so accustomed to the sound that it had barely registered with her. The last soldier must have come in from the plain, she thought, and so the Earthshakers had been able to resume their work. They were bombarding the captured hive again.

For all the good it might do us.

A command vehicle wheeled into the camp, braking between its huts.

Its rear hatch opened and out stepped the Krieg colonel, his posture exuding grim determination. His command squad disembarked behind him. One wore a sling, but otherwise they showed little sign of their recent ordeal.

Interrogator Ferran barred the colonel's path. Majellus stood quietly at his shoulder, his hand resting lightly on his sheathed power sword. 'May we speak?' Ferran asked.

'Not right now,' came the gruff reply.

He was taken aback. Most people understood that when a witch hunter made a request, it was really a demand. He thought his tone had made that clear.

'I must report to high command,' said the colonel, 'and then convene a strategy meeting with my senior staff. Arrange that, would you?' This last was aimed at a junior officer who had emerged from a hut to greet him.

He tried to walk on, but Majellus blocked him again. 'I have a few questions to put to you,' said Ferran, 'which will not wait.'

'I can make time for you at oh seven hundred hours tomorrow,' said the colonel. 'In the meantime, my adjutant will assist you as much as he can. You understand, Interrogator Ferran' – the fact that he knew his name surprised Ferran – 'that I have plans to make upon which billions of lives depend.'

Ferran bridled. 'As an agent of the Ordo Hereticus, I must insist–'

'Do you have an accusation to make against me,' asked the colonel, 'or any soldier under my command?'

'At present, I do not, but–'

'Then it will be my duty and my honour to cooperate with your investigation. At oh seven hundred hours tomorrow.'

'That will be fine, colonel,' said a mild voice, approaching the group. 'Thank you.' Ferran didn't have to turn to identify the speaker.

The Krieg colonel shifted his gaze to Inquisitor Ven Bruin. He held it for a second, then afforded him a deferent nod. He swept past Ferran as if he weren't there, disappearing into his command hut. Ferran seethed at being undermined, but bit his tongue. Ven Bruin was still his master, if not for very much longer.

'I will take that meeting with the colonel tomorrow,' the

inquisitor said. 'I have reached a decision, which I must discuss with him. Your presence will not be required.'

Ferran glared after him as he too walked away. 'Sometimes…' he grumbled to himself. He felt Majellus' intense eyes upon him, and drew in a steadying breath. He reminded himself that Ven Bruin had earned his respect. *He has wisdom born of long experience; and, soon enough, his few remaining secrets will be mine too.*

Patience had never been one of his virtues.

More vehicles were returning from the plain. The medicae huts, both Krieg and Cadian, were swiftly filling up. A Chimera pressed into service as an ambulance pulled up, and a bloodied Korpsman was brought out on a stretcher. Another lay atop a gurney in the rear compartment. Ferran approached it, beckoning to the silent crusader to follow him. He leaned into the vehicle to examine its remaining occupant.

The Korpsman had received emergency treatment in transit. His greatcoat and armour had been peeled back, his shirt torn open. A crooked line of stitches stood out dark red against pale flesh. Still his mask remained in place, connected to the rebreather resting on his chest.

'What happened to you?' asked Ferran. He didn't know if the Korpsman would hear the question. He couldn't tell if his eyes were open or shut. He could hear laboured breathing, but it might have been produced by the machine.

'My squad was attempting to clear a stairwell,' said the Korpsman in a toneless, muffled voice. 'The battle was already lost by then.'

'Then why…?'

'My watchmaster thought we could climb up through a habblock to one of the upper levels. We could have stayed behind when the rest of our forces withdrew. That way, the Emperor would have a kill team stationed inside the hive, in case of need.'

'I see. Who sanctioned this plan?'

'I don't know, sir. A senior officer, perhaps the colonel himself.'

'I presume you were discovered.'

'There were xenos on the other side of the wreckage,' said the Korpsman. 'I regret to say I was not alert enough. A hand pushed through as I was digging. It seized me by the wrist. I was able to dislodge it with my shovel, but by then the xenos was on top of me. It... cut my stomach with a blade. I was not strong enough.'

Ferran stepped up into the vehicle beside him. 'Perhaps the blame was not entirely yours. Perhaps the orders you were given–'

'Orders are not to be questioned.'

'But you were on the ground inside the hive. You may speak freely to me. Would you agree with your colonel's assessment that–'

'Orders are not to be questioned.'

The Korpsman sounded agitated. It would do no good to push him further, Ferran judged. He hovered over him, uncertainly. His spiked helmet sat on a bench beside him, but the fabric of his gas mask covered the whole of his scalp.

Ferran found himself reaching towards it.

The Korpsman flinched as if struck. 'What are you doing, sir?'

'I thought I... could make you more comfortable.'

'Thank you, sir. The surgeon has already seen to that.'

'I'm sure you would breathe more easily with your face uncovered.'

'That isn't necessary, sir.' It wasn't the Korpsman who had spoken. The two stretcher-bearers had returned. They were Officio Medicae orderlies in dark blue scrubs. One of them had dried blood on his sleeve. 'His rebreather supplies him with the perfect oxygen mix for his height and build.'

'I'm sure it does,' said Ferran, smiling tightly.

He was clearly in the orderlies' way, though neither of them dared say so. He stepped out of the Chimera and left them to deal with their patient.

The colonel sat straight-backed behind his desk. He had neither moved nor spoken for almost a minute. Ven Bruin's gaze met its own reflection in the eyepieces of the colonel's mask. He understood why the presence of the Krieg unsettled Ferran so.

'This may,' said the colonel at length, 'change nothing. If this world is to be razed...'

'Then, Emperor willing, its secrets will die with it.'

'Though can we be completely certain of it?'

'This secret,' Ven Bruin pointed out, 'is hidden well. The xenos can know nothing of it, and they are unlikely to discover it by chance.'

'And yet,' said the colonel, 'they are known to be curious creatures.'

He rested his elbows on his desk and clasped his hands. It seemed a very human gesture. Ven Bruin wasn't sure why that surprised him. 'The risk is small but hardly negligible,' the colonel mused. 'The consequences, should the worst happen, would be catastrophic, not only for Octarius but for the Imperium itself.'

'Hence, I brought this information to you.'

The colonel nodded and sat back, his thinking evidently done. 'We must send a team into Arathron to locate this vault of secrets,' he decreed.

'I thought you might have one in place already?'

'No,' said the colonel darkly, 'not at present.'

'Then I wish to accompany that team,' Ven Bruin announced. 'You understand–'

'That this will likely be a suicide mission. Yes, colonel, I understand that fully.'

'Infiltration will be achieved by means of a Hades breaching drill, which carries no more than ten men. One squad of grenadiers. I can find a place for you, but only for you. Your retinue would have to stay behind.'

Ven Bruin nodded, unfazed. 'I alone know the vault's location – and, wishing no disrespect to you or your Korpsmen, colonel, I shall never speak that information aloud.'

'I assume,' said the colonel, 'you wish its contents destroyed?'

'If necessary,' Ven Bruin answered. 'If possible. First, I need to know exactly what we are dealing with. I need to be sure that the xenos have not breached the vault already–'

'Emperor forbid.'

'–and that it holds nothing worth… preserving. Unlikely as that seems.'

'May He guide your judgement,' said the colonel.

'When the time comes,' said Ven Bruin, 'I will require your Korpsmen to obey my instructions without question.'

'It need not be said, inquisitor.'

Another lengthy silence ensued. Ven Bruin toyed with his Inquisitorial seal, avoiding the Krieg colonel's blank-eyed gaze, and neither said what they were really thinking.

Troopers Rask and Creed hefted a shell into the Earthshaker's breech, grunting with the effort. Sergeant Renick checked her sights, took a step back and yanked the firing lanyard. The resulting thunderclap was muffled by the gauze stuffed into her ears.

Her back ached. She had lost track of time. She felt as if she had been carrying out her repetitive task forever. No longer could she even tell herself that she was doing any good. So what if her shells broke the hive's walls? What did it matter?

Her regiment had lost Hive Arathron once, then failed to retake it. There had been no official announcement, but everybody knew it: there would be no further attempt. Their goal now was merely to keep the orks contained for as long as they could.

It was rumoured that this world would be abandoned due to their failure. 'If that is so,' Renick had told her squad, 'then every shell we fire, every second we buy for the evacuation effort, will enable more lives to be saved.' *A scant few lives…*

Like them, she longed to be away from this place, for a ship to convey her to some other battle, one that could be won. She wanted to remember what victory felt like.

The orks themselves provided some respite from her miserable thoughts. As evening drew in, close to twenty emerged from the hive in their flying contraptions. Renick tried to get a bead on one, but it zipped in and out of her sights, and by the time her shell had crossed the distance between them, it was somewhere else entirely.

The koptas drew steadily closer, in a roundabout fashion. Their blades fought an ongoing battle with their unbalanced weight. They skipped and scraped across the ground, never able to gain much height. Meanwhile, the Krieg prepared for their imminent arrival. They poured out of their dugouts and retook their positions on the fire steps.

A Krieg lieutenant bade them hold fire until their targets were closer. He waited till the koptas were almost on top of the trenches, until Renick's lungs ached and she realised that she had bated her breath, before he gave the order.

Then the sky was filled with light and fury, such that she was half blinded and couldn't find a target to take aim at. She made out a shape, but it was already dropping like a stone. The kopta's pilot tried to bail out but caught its foot in tangled wiring and was dragged upside down to its demise. It might have been the very brute that had slain Colonel Drakon; Renick liked to think it was.

Some koptas, inevitably, made it through the lethal gauntlet. She ducked as one appeared above her head. Its guns chattered madly, but it couldn't find the angle to shoot down into the trenches, not while keeping its own nose up. It had also sustained heavy damage, trailing smoke. One of its rotors sheared off. It flew at Renick like an arrow and buried itself in the trench wall by her ear.

The kopta clipped the rear lip of the trench and careened away, in the process shedding hunks of bodywork, but another buzzed into view behind it. Directly overhead as it was, the Earthshaker couldn't target it. Renick and her squad drew lasguns instead, and joined a hundred other soldiers firing upwards.

The pilot clung to its controls one-handed. With the other, it brandished something horribly like a stick grenade. Renick wasn't the only one to shout a warning. Those that were able went scrambling into dugouts, while others flattened themselves against the trench floor. She squeezed herself into the gap between cannon and emplacement as the ork lobbed the bomb out of its cockpit and it spun, end over end, towards her.

It exploded while still in the air, driving shrapnel down into the trench but also ripping through the ork's own chassis. A hailstorm clattered against the Earthshaker's broad side. By the time Renick dared to raise her head, the kopta was nowhere to be seen.

Soldiers were picking themselves up around her, shouldering their guns again. Many had been bloodied, but none killed as far as she could see. They had been lucky. She checked herself for injuries. She had been lucky too. One member of her squad, Trooper Kell, had a twisted metal shard wedged in his forearm, but it could have been much worse.

Adrenaline still coursed through her veins, and she felt a grin tugging at her lips. 'Pretty sporting of the greenskins to come to us and let us kill them,' she remarked.

For the rest of her shift, which lasted ninety more minutes, she worked with renewed enthusiasm. She also kept a wary eye out for orks approaching the trenches on foot. It wouldn't have surprised her in the least to learn that some had crawled out of their vehicles' wreckage. She almost hoped they had, so she could gun them down again.

Renick slept in a dugout that night.

The Cadian shock troops had struck their tents and moved into the trenches, where there was now plenty of room to accommodate them. She had the impression that their own officers were none too happy about this. Her berth was a mere shelf, cut out of the earth, shored up with bits of timber. The rest of her squad had shelves below and to each side of her. Across the narrow trench from them were five Korpsmen. They slept in their masks, lying flat on their backs, their rebreather units ticking softly. Renick found herself pondering on the chances of a gas attack. Loud as the Krieg guns had sounded in the encampment, they were far louder here. She thought she would never get to sleep, until exhaustion overcame her. Even then, the sound of thunder permeated her fitful dreams.

The following morning, she ate with other sergeants and troopers alike, around a wooden table in a larger but still claustrophobic alcove. A portable generatorum buzzed in one corner, heating water to boil up rations and recaff. No Krieg were present and she wondered where they ate, or if they ate at all. 'None of us have seen it if they do,' Creed told her.

'I reckon they feed through those breathing tubes of theirs,' said Rask.

Renick shuddered at the thought. 'They're inhuman,' someone

muttered, and she nodded as if she agreed with the sentiment; but it was even worse than that, she feared.

What bothered her most about the Krieg was her suspicion, which had only grown in recent days, that they were very human after all. *For what must that be like?* she asked herself. *To spend a lifetime serving in these trenches? To see worlds only through dark lenses, and never feel their air upon your face?*

Raised voices and the howl of an engine disturbed her doleful reverie. Renick welcomed the distraction. She stood, stooping slightly so as not to scrape her helmet on the roof. She stepped out into one of the main arterial trenches.

The engine howl came from above her. An armoured vehicle was poised on the lip of the trench. It was more compact than the Demolisher tanks, but looked as heavy. Thirty or so Death Korpsmen thronged about it with digging tools. They eased its passage as it nosed its way forwards and downwards. Its tracks spun, struggling for purchase, kicking up soft earth in all directions. Duckboards were wedged underneath it, but immediately shattered.

For the final feet of its descent, it slid out of control, and Korpsmen scrambled to get out from underneath it before they were crushed. One wasn't fast enough. His legs were pinned beneath the behemoth. He groaned as he lay helpless in the dirt. Renick hadn't heard a sound like that from any of the Krieg before. A field chirurgeon hurried to him, as the vehicle rolled over him regardless.

It was some sort of mining or construction vehicle. A giant drilling head was mounted on the front of its chassis, making up at least a quarter of its length. The head comprised four interlocking power cutters, a gaping maw between them. The vehicle inched back and forth, orienting itself with the trench. Then it jerked forwards, scraping the walls on both sides, forcing Renick and others in its path to duck back into the dugouts.

Several figures descended into the trenches in its wake, among them the Krieg colonel. Renick also recognised the venerable, silver-bearded inquisitor, accompanied by his sizeable retinue. Something was definitely afoot, although she couldn't imagine what. *Could the rumours have been wrong?* she asked herself as the slow-motion procession passed her by, headed for the forward trench. *Could there be some hope, after all?*

The Korpsman crushed by the heavy drilling vehicle was dead. She hadn't seen it happen, didn't know if his injuries had taken him or if his own medic had helped him along.

Two Korpsmen hauled him away to a burial pit. His equipment, including his armour and helmet, had already been salvaged from him. His rebreather unit was gone too, but the gas mask remained. Even in death he was anonymous, even to those alongside whom he had fought. *Will anyone even say a prayer for him? How can they, if nobody knows his name?*

Who will remember him?

The Hades drill idled in the forward trench, pointed towards the distant hive.

A grenadier squad, Krieg veterans, formed up before their colonel. He reminded them briefly of their mission, and that the preservation of Inquisitor Ven Bruin's life was their highest priority. On their watchmaster's lead, they recited the Litany of Sacrifice: 'In life, war. In death, peace. In life, shame. In death, atonement.'

The colonel wished them Emperor-speed, and the watchmaster saluted. He loaded his troops into the waiting Hades, then turned to the inquisitor. 'We are ready for you, sir.'

Ferran looked the oily vehicle up and down, nose wrinkling in distaste. 'Once again, inquisitor, I wish to volunteer for this mission in your stead. At least take Majellus or one of the others with you.'

'Thank you, Interrogator Ferran,' said Ven Bruin curtly, 'but I must do this for myself. Should it happen that I fail to return–'

'God-Emperor forbid it.'

'–then you will be inquisitor in my stead. My mission will be yours to continue.' He waved away Ferran's effusive gratitude. 'Your first duty must be to report to the ordo. Tell them all we have seen on this world… everything we have learned.'

For a moment, it seemed like he had something else to say, but he decided against it. He turned away and climbed into the Hades' crew compartment. The Krieg watchmaster followed him. He had trouble squeezing himself into the confined space, but at last he slid the hatch shut behind him with a clunk.

Seconds later, the massive drilling head juddered into motion. It shrieked as the Hades edged forwards and its cutters bit into the trench wall. They gouged great holes out of the earth, shredding rock like tissue paper. The pulverised remains were sucked into the behemoth's great mouth and spewed out through its rear. Ferran and the rest of the onlookers stepped back to avoid its billowing discharge.

The drill receded from them, along a tunnel of its own creation. No sooner was it clear of the tunnel mouth than the latter caved in for lack of support. Where the Hades went, nobody could follow. Soon enough, it could not be seen at all, although the rumble of its engine was still heard and its cutters' piercing shriek was like a drill in Ferran's ears.

He was lost in his thoughts for a minute. Then he saw that the colonel had left. Ven Bruin's acolytes – *my acolytes now* – awaited his orders. He had none for them, other than to return to the encampment. For the present, they could only wait and pray; for what, most of them didn't know. They did as they were bade and asked no questions, but it was different for Ferran. Asking questions was his sacred duty.

He led the way back through the trenches. He passed Krieg soldiers mending uniforms, laundering bedclothes, maintaining weapons. He sent the acolytes ahead of him. He stooped his head and stepped into one of the larger dugouts. Four Korpsmen were seated about a table, stripping down their lasguns for cleaning and oiling. Ferran interposed himself between them. They continued to work without acknowledging his presence.

'"In life, shame,"' Ferran quoted.

'In death, atonement,' two of them responded, automatically.

'Is that truly what you believe, I wonder?'

None of them spoke, so Ferran pressed the issue. 'Atonement for what?'

'For Krieg's betrayal,' came the answer, 'fifteen hundred years ago.'

'And for no other reason?' That question also seemed to stump them. Ferran tried another tack. 'Tell me about your Colonel Jurten,' he said.

'Colonel Jurten saved our world.' He strained to hear a hint of reverence in the Korpsman's dispassionate tone.

He raised a bushy eyebrow in a studiedly cynical gesture. 'By laying waste to it?'

'He purged Krieg of its sins. He saved our people.'

'It could be argued that he committed a great sin himself. The weapons he deployed were remnants from the Dark Age of Technology. Their use was unsanctioned by any Imperial authority. The fallout from them taints your world to this day.'

'Colonel Jurten did his duty,' one of the Krieg intoned.

'To bring us back into the Emperor's light,' a second insisted.

'The Emperor gave him the tools to do so,' added a third.

Ferran had hoped to provoke them, but they spoke entirely without rancour. So confident were they in their beliefs that his accusations simply didn't trouble them.

He made another attempt. 'Krieg is… I believe the term for

it is "radioactive". Merely to step upon its surface unshielded is to sicken and, in short order, to suffer an agonising death. The skin sloughs from your bones. Your organs liquefy.'

'We do not walk the surface unshielded.'

'No. No, you have your suits and your masks, though even these, I hear, were not sufficient to protect Inquisitor Larreth.' He thought the Korpsmen recognised the name, though he had only their slightest head movements to go by. 'Still, you must remove the masks sometimes,' he ventured.

The Korpsmen neither confirmed nor denied the suggestion. 'Your children cannot be born masked,' Ferran persisted, 'and you must have mothers, fathers, families–'

'Our families,' said a Korpsman, 'are protected.'

'Sheltered by the bunkers,' said another, 'that Colonel Jurten dug for us.'

'At the behest of his most wise and loyal adviser, the arch-magos Greel.'

'I… see,' said Ferran, thoughtfully. 'And yet even Larreth, with the finest protective equipment and drugs available to her, sickened after her visit to your world. She reported stomach cramps and fever dreams, which bedevilled her until her dying day.'

'She was not Krieg,' said a Korpsman.

'It is natural, I suppose, that your people would have built up a level of tolerance.'

'Yes, Interrogator Ferran.'

'Through continued exposure to that poison,' Ferran stressed. 'But is that not a form of mutation in itself?'

'Sickness is not unknown among our people.'

'Even with your rebreather units? Even in your underground bunkers?'

'But mutations are abhorrent to us, as they are to the Emperor, as they were to Colonel Jurten. We suffer not the mutant to live.'

'And yet, your world's population continues to grow.'

'Those who bear the mutant's mark are identified and destroyed,' the Korpsman reiterated flatly.

'Are they?' Ferran's eyes flashed as he leaned in for the kill. 'How would I know, how would anybody know, if any of you were so afflicted? You claim the masks protect you – even here, even where the air is pure – but they conceal you too. They hide your faces and your eyes and the darkest of your secrets.'

'No one of Krieg would ever–'

'Might they hide the true reason for your shame?'

Ferran sat back, smiling like a predator that had trapped its prey. 'You'll understand,' he purred, 'if I must see it for myself. As an interrogator – an inquisitor-to-be – of the Ordo Hereticus, I require that you four remove your masks. Show me the true faces of the Krieg.'

For a moment, the Korpsmen just sat and stared at Ferran, but he didn't repeat his request. He met their blank eyes with his own obdurate glare and at last, as if some invisible cue had passed between them, they removed their helmets in unison and set them down on the table; and then they did as he had told them.

They tilted their heads forwards and peeled off their gas masks.

436.M40

THE ONLY OTHER OPTION

The traitors had broken through the northern perimeter again.

The pattern had become a familiar one. Another gun emplacement would fall to a well-targeted shell, or else a gun would simply fail. This would create a blind spot in Ferrograd's defences. The traitors would rise from their trenches – now encircling the hive at a distance of roughly two miles – and rush towards its walls. Colonel Jurten would lead his loyalist troops out to meet them.

Battle would normally be joined in the ruins of the outskirts. This time, the traitors had penetrated further into the hive, into a lower-level slum residential sector. It had been partially cleared, and the few remaining residents were fractious. Some resented being made to leave, others that they hadn't left yet.

Both attackers and defenders of the hive found roadblocks in their way, from barrels to barbed wire, to a burning sanitation truck propelled towards them. One loyalist squad fell foul of a makeshift nail bomb, set off by a tripwire. There would be a reckoning tomorrow, Jurten swore. First, he had to make it through tonight.

He plunged into the thick of the melee, as usual.

His weapons of choice were a chainsword wielded in his right hand, a laspistol in his left. The traitors recognised his badge of rank, if not his face, and they fought hard to get to him. Few made it close, and they soon regretted their bravado. The teeth of his sword shrieked as they bit through flak armour, into flesh and bone beneath. The traitors attacked from behind him and tried to outflank him, but they had reckoned without his command squad. Four hardened Krieg veterans had their colonel's back at all times.

And then there were Jurten's Death Riders. They thundered in from east and west at once. They crashed into the traitors' exposed flanks, trampling them under furious hooves. The horses had been Greel's idea. Though less durable than tanks, they were more easily replaced. Greel had already set up two breeding farms, and advanced a few ideas about how they could turn out stronger steeds.

Las-fire brought a horse down, but several traitors were pinned beneath its armour-plated hide. Another horse panicked, threw its rider and broke its legs attempting to flee, but the traitors' lines were broken too, and many ran for cover.

Jurten pursued a traitor squad into an alleyway. Too late, he saw that he was being led into an ambush. The traitors disappeared as muzzles flashed in the windows above him. He was struck in his right shoulder and his ribs, spun around and to the ground. He landed on his bad hip and a lance of pain stabbed through him, blurring his vision.

Gloved hands hauled him up and bundled him away. 'Don't need...' he rasped, but his throat was full of bile. He was dumped behind a stinking, overflowing trash compactor. Two veterans squeezed in beside him, and he realised that one had been shot in the arm. *My fault*, he thought, *for charging in without heed.*

The pain in his hip flared again as he shifted his position. He raised his head, which cued a fusillade of las-beams from above. He couldn't get an angle on the snipers with his pistol. He was well and truly pinned – and the traitors that had led him down this alley might still be nearby. Once again he cursed the obstacles he had faced in getting here. It should have been *his* men in the sniping positions.

'I'll call for backup, sir. If they can–'

'No,' Jurten interrupted the veteran trooper. 'They can't get to us without running the snipers' gauntlet.' He had one other option, though. He voxed command headquarters. 'Has Greel arrived there?'

'*Yes, sir, he's here.*'

'Have him stand by to implement the Hecatomb Protocol on my command.'

Lieutenant Ionas couldn't conceal his surprise. '*Yes, sir, but has it really come to that?*'

He wanted to answer, *Not yet. We can still beat them.* Instead he asked, 'Archmagos, can you hear me?'

'*I can hear you,*' came Greel's dry voice after a moment.

'I want a controlled demolition of one building only. I can't see a designation, but if you can get a fix on my position it's directly to my north. Can it be done?' Greel confirmed that it could. Jurten set his jaw grimly. 'Then detonate the charges in five...

'We're getting out of here,' he told his squad, raising his voice to reach them in their positions of cover. The two troopers with him helped him stand, even as a fierce explosion tore through the hab-block looming over them.

It began to fold in on itself, in inexorable slow motion. A

cyclone of pulverised rockcrete pursued the soldiers as they pelted back to the main street. Jurten found that he couldn't put weight on his left hip and, to his frustration, had to be half carried, arms about his troopers' shoulders. Almost as soon as they were clear of the alleyway, he fell and dragged them both down with him.

'I'll be able to stand in a moment,' he insisted, but somehow he was still prone when a field medic reached him. Fresh vox reports squawked in his ear. Traitor squads were popping up throughout the sector, employing hit-and-run tactics. Wherever they found themselves outnumbered, they dispersed, melting into nooks and crannies. There were many hiding places in these slums, and the traitors had clearly been enjoined to make full use of them.

'Could take all night to clear this place,' he heard one of his veterans opine.

'Like hunting rats in the sewers,' another agreed.

Jurten's watchmaster scowled as he hefted his lasgun. 'Wouldn't want to be a rat tonight.' The colonel approved of his attitude. *But at what cost?* he was forced to ask himself.

During previous skirmishes, he had maintained battlefield control. He had been able to keep the invaders contained. This time was different. He heard from a sergeant some way north of his position: '*Sir, the traitor tanks–*' was all he managed to get out before he was cut off, but it was enough.

A pair of Demolishers had been spotted approaching the hive. Evidently they had ploughed their ways through the outskirts, and even as Jurten mulled the dire implications of this, the ground beneath him shook with the thunder of their guns.

'*Standing by, Colonel Jurten.*' Archmagos Greel spoke without undue emotion, and yet somehow he always seemed to say far more than his words.

Jurten had to be dispassionate too. He had to make a rational decision, and his wounded pride could play no part in it. *We can still beat them… But the battle could rage across this level for hours, or even days, and some traitors might elude us still…*

In the end, it was a simple calculation. Krause could afford to lose more soldiers in this skirmish than Jurten could. He had plenty to spare to attack the hive from another direction, while the bulk of Jurten's men were bogged down here. It wasn't enough for the loyalist forces to fight harder, they had to fight smarter too. Sometimes they had to choose to lose a battle if they were to win the war.

He switched to the vox command channel. He informed his officers and sergeants of his decision, the words tasting bitter in his mouth. They were to withdraw from this sector, which would be collapsed behind them. The traitors would be buried in its rubble, as the snipers that had ambushed Jurten already had been. He spared a thought for the residents that would be buried too. *They should have left when they had the chance…* Still, even the weakest might have had some use to him alive.

A civilian ambulance had arrived for him. As he was lifted onto a stretcher, he voxed the archmagos again. 'Give us ten minutes to clear the sector,' he instructed, 'and not a second longer. Then bring it all down.'

'How is he?' asked Ionas.

'His wounds have been sutured,' said Archmagos Greel. 'He lost a lot of blood, but his organs escaped serious damage.'

'Then he will recover?'

Greel shook his head gravely. 'He shattered his left hip in the fall. The medicaes say he had an old break that never set properly. They say he will not walk again without support.'

Ionas took a moment to absorb the news. It could have been

worse, he decided. He had often asked Jurten to take a less active combat role, but the colonel had refused. He had always led his troops from the front, and that was not about to change. 'I am only one soldier,' he had said, and he would not hear otherwise.

'If he had died today…' Ionas breathed.

'We would have carried on as he'd have wished,' said Greel. 'We would have crushed the traitors in his name.'

'Of course. But still, the effect on morale…'

'The colonel is under sedation at present. He should address our people as soon as he is able, else rumours will proliferate.'

'I have already made those arrangements,' said Ionas.

'We need to make it known that Colonel Jurten is alive and healthy.' They had been walking as they talked. They halted at the entrance to the adjutant's office. 'And that he will fight on the front lines when the traitors' next attack comes.' Greel forestalled the predictable objection. 'It is what they need to hear. Morale, as you said, is important.'

'We can't hide the truth from them forever.'

Greel leaned closer to Ionas. His breath had an oily whiff about it. 'The colonel's hip cannot be healed, but it might be replaced. The blueprints for such an operation exist in the Adeptus Mechanicus archives. I have surgeons and enginseers fully capable of–'

'He would not hear of it,' protested Ionas.

'You think not?'

'To replace the flesh that fashions us in the Emperor's image with…' He checked himself as he remembered to whom he was speaking. He thought he heard something ticking softly beneath Greel's rust-red robes. 'The colonel would not agree to it,' he restated.

'I spoke to him as he was brought into the medicae facility. I explained that if he wishes to return to active service, then he has no option but to–'

'I don't believe it,' Ionas blurted out.

'Colonel Jurten,' Greel informed him with infinite patience, 'has given his consent to the procedure.'

Ionas was kept busy for the next few days.

There were lists of the dead from the collapsed sector to collate. Work rotas and hab allocations had to be adjusted. There were military casualties too, as some troopers had failed to disengage from the enemy in time. He had spared as many bodies as he could – not nearly enough – for rescue operations, and some survivors, a poor few, had been found.

They had also claimed a special prize. A traitor Demolisher had been unearthed, in salvageable condition. Its main gunner's neck was broken, but the rest of its crew were trapped in their compartment. After days without water and with little air, they had surrendered gladly. Their commander would be executed, the rest allowed to rethink their allegiances, as per Jurten's standing orders.

'They took up arms against the Emperor,' he had grumbled, the first time they had taken prisoners. 'For that, there can only be one punishment.'

'In ordinary times, I would agree with you,' Archmagos Greel had said, 'but these are not ordinary times, and these soldiers merely followed orders.'

'That is no excuse!' Jurten had barked, angrily.

'I seek not to excuse,' Greel had assured him, 'but to understand. These are men of weak conviction. They would follow you as readily as they did their traitor general – and, need I remind you, we need all the soldiers we can get.'

'I need *good, faithful* soldiers.'

Greel had shaken his head. 'We both know, colonel, that sometimes you only need warm bodies. Post these penitent traitors to the front lines of battle. Let them be the first to cross the minefields. They're pleading for forgiveness and a chance to prove their renewed faith. Why not give them that chance? Allow them to die in the Emperor's service.'

It had taken Jurten four days to give in. Ionas, who had overheard this conversation, sympathised with his dilemma. 'A necessary evil,' the colonel had once said, 'condemns us as would any other kind.' As Greel had pointed out, though, these weren't ordinary times.

Jurten chafed at being confined to a hospital bed. He refused to relinquish the burden of command, though Ionas knew his wishes in most matters by now. Ionas, therefore, had to update him hourly, obtaining his agreement to every trifling decision.

Data-slates stacked up on his desk, as an army of ordinates and scribes buzzed about him, awaiting his thumbprint on their orders. Ionas ignored messages from General Krause, surely wanting to crow about his pyrrhic victory. He composed instructions and updates to broadcast to the populace. He stressed that though a small part of the hive had been lost, its attackers had paid a steeper price.

He couldn't forget his conversation with Archmagos Greel. It weighed upon his mind, even while he was trying to sleep. He thought about the operation that Jurten had agreed to undergo. He had given in so much more quickly this time.

On the fateful morning, he watched the colonel being wheeled into a sterilised theatre. A fabric mask covered his nose and mouth, from which a hose snaked to a gas cylinder on the trolley beside him. Jurten twitched angrily in his sleep as if fighting the anaesthetic. He had never looked so vulnerable before.

Ionas sidled up to the watching Greel. 'How long will this take?' he asked him.

'For the artificial hip to be implanted,' said Greel, 'two or three hours. It may be several weeks before the colonel enjoys the full range of movement he once did, although that will depend to some extent on his own will to recover.'

'Do you need to be here?'

Greel's robes rustled as he turned to look at the lieutenant. Ionas wished he could see his face. 'I thought I might supervise the operation.'

'Which others could do just as well?' Ionas didn't wait for an answer. 'I wish to see something. I wish you to *show* me something.'

'May I ask for what reason, Lieutenant Ionas?'

'Because, as long as the colonel is unconscious, I speak with his full authority.'

'Perhaps this could wait until Colonel Jurten wakes and is able to–'

Ionas talked over Greel, determinedly. 'I want to see inside that vault, archmagos. I want to see it now. So, you can either take me there or you can tell me how to open it myself.'

Greel inclined his head, submitting with quiet equanimity.

They took a Pegasus into the bowels of the hive. Ionas hadn't been down here in a year, and he was astounded by how much it had changed in that time.

Huge spaces had been opened up and now teemed with industrious life. Small, basic hab-units had been hollowed out of rock at every level, linked by swaying plasteel gantries and rope ladders. Ionas saw churches, food distribution centres, apothecaries and trading posts. An ancient statue of an Imperial war hero, ten feet tall on a plinth of similar height, towered over him. It was doubtless salvaged from an abandoned sector, though the labour required to bring it here must have been intensive.

He would hardly have known he was underground at all. The light was unnatural, while the air was recycled and filtered, stale tasting – but how was that really so different from conditions on the hive's lower levels immediately above him?

Greel led him through a rock tunnel out onto a metal-mesh bridge, and suddenly they were looking down upon a factory floor. Immense machines cut, ground, drilled and stamped. They filled the air with dancing sparks, a burning odour and the shriek of tortured metal. Scurrying between them, labourers kept the hungry beasts fed, oiled and clean. Others manned factory lines. They assembled intricate components, filled bullets with fine powder, cut fuses, loaded heavy shell casings into carts.

Servitors oversaw the work. They lashed out with whips at anyone who slackened or just stumbled. Bred by the Adeptus Mechanicus, these part-living, part-mechanical drones were common throughout the Imperium. Rumour had it that some were once men who had transgressed against the Omnissiah. They lacked wills of their own and could only follow basic instructions. Ionas had never spared them much thought before, but now the mere sight of their metal limbs disturbed him.

'Much of the Wulfram plant's work has been transferred to this facility,' explained Greel. 'Within two months, we aim to match and then surpass the old plant's output.'

'Yes, yes,' said Ionas, who had thumb-printed the relevant reports. Being here, however, seeing this, was very different to studying numbers on a data-slate. Nor had those numbers told him everything, for surely Greel had begged and borrowed resources unaccounted for in his ordered records. The archmagos had created far more than just a shelter for potential future need. He was building a subterranean city.

A city over which, to all intents and purposes, he alone presided.

They left the busy manufactorum behind them and descended into a broad, well-lit thoroughfare. One side of the tunnel had been sundered, and the nose of an Imperial Termite drilling vehicle poked in through it. Ionas regarded it with a feeling of foreboding. 'Where did that come from?'

'An infiltration attempt about a month ago,' said Greel, almost dismissively. 'The traitors thought they could sneak in through empty underhive tunnels. Be assured, none of them survived to explain their mistake to their masters.'

'Why didn't I know of this?'

'I'm sure I had someone fill out a report,' said the archmagos vaguely.

They were waved through two security checkpoints and into a narrow, rough-hewn tunnel, which wended its way upwards. Their way was blocked by a sturdy metal hatch, bristling with bolts and latches. Ionas rapped on it and found it unyielding as expected. He suspected that it was adamantium.

A small generatorum squatted in the corner as if abandoned there. An augmetic arm emerged from Greel's robes to operate it without him having to stoop. 'The locking mechanisms are electrically powered,' he said, 'but the power supply has decayed over the millennia.' He ran a pair of wires from the generatorum to the door.

'I assume,' he said mildly as he worked, 'you know what this vault protects.'

'Colonel Jurten explained it to me.'

'But you wish to see for yourself. I wonder, what do you expect to learn?'

It was a good question, for which Ionas didn't have an answer. 'These weapons,' he ventured. 'How…?'

'How destructive are they?' Greel prompted him. 'Less so than some of the tools in the Emperor's arsenal. The cyclonic torpedoes of the Imperial Navy, for example.'

'But powerful enough to raze this world?'

'Most certainly, yes. If used en masse, they could easily crack Krieg in two. A single warhead exploded in the centre of a hive would melt its walls to slag and vaporise all human tissue within a radius of several miles. In addition–'

'Is that not enough?' Ionas breathed.

'–they poison the land they fall upon. It is said that for years, even generations after, no crops can grow there, and that the air itself burns the lungs and causes sickness and the most extreme mutations. Did Colonel Jurten not explain all this to you?'

Not quite so baldly, thought Ionas. 'He stated that these weapons must never be used.'

Greel had started up the generatorum. It hummed to itself for a minute. Then sixteen runes, arranged in a square pattern, lit up on the wall beside the hatch. 'Yes,' he said, 'the colonel has been perfectly clear about that.'

'Then why are they still here?' asked Ionas. 'Couldn't they be decommissioned?'

'Alas, we have only fragments of the weapons' schematics. Without knowing how they were assembled, we cannot know how to dismantle them safely. One mistake could cause an accidental detonation.'

'Even so, with traitors digging through the earth in this vicinity…'

'This vault has stood inviolable for thousands of years,' said Greel. 'There is no reason to believe that it won't do so for many thousands more.'

But that is not entirely true, Ionas almost said, *for you have found a way inside.*

The archmagos' hands, his human hands, played over the illuminated runes. Ionas tried to follow the sequence, but Greel positioned himself to block his view. A confirmatory beep came from the keypad, and a series of clicks and heavy clunks sounded from inside the door. Ionas took a step back, involuntarily.

Greel drew back a final bolt, which glistened with a recent application of oil. The heavy door cracked open and a whisper of cold air escaped from it. Spilling over the rim of the door was a deeper, blacker darkness than Ionas thought he had ever seen. Then lightning struck in that darkness, several times, before the light took hold and drove the dark away.

Ionas had never thought himself a nervous man. Still, he couldn't bring himself to step into that harsh, white light. He needed a moment to steel himself. He covered his hesitation with the question uppermost in his mind. 'Could these weapons win the war for us?'

'In a matter of moments,' said Greel.

He leant both hands against the vault door and pushed it decisively open. He stepped into the white light.

'What did you think of them?' asked Colonel Jurten.

Ionas looked up from his data-slates. 'Sir?'

Jurten sat across the desk from him, as he had been wont to do lately rather than standing. He gripped his walking cane between his knees. It was carved from dark wood, topped with a small silver skull whose grim expression matched its wielder's own.

Ionas knew exactly what Jurten was asking. He had been expecting the question for days. Jurten knew it too, and held his adjutant's gaze until he gave up the pretence.

'They were smaller than I had imagined them to be.'

The colonel nodded. 'I thought the same.'

'Which, in a way, only made them seem more terrible.'

'Thanks be to the Emperor,' said Jurten, 'that He placed the weapons here, beneath this hive, where we can keep them out of reach of our foes.'

'You believe even Krause would dare use them?'

'We are better off not knowing the answer to that question.'

'I… have been thinking, colonel, and if Krause only knew…'

'It would change nothing,' said Jurten with absolute certainty. 'He believes in his cause and no threat of force could ever induce him to betray it. Nor would I in his place. He would surely call my bluff and so then the decision would be mine. Having made that threat, would I back down and appear weak? Or else…?'

Ionas blanched at the very suggestion, but the colonel's eyes had grown distant. 'Krieg has been mired in civil war for years, and doubtless will remain so for many more. A single strike upon, say, Hive Auros–'

'And hundreds of millions would burn,' Ionas protested.

'Hundreds of thousands have already died.'

'But these would be civilians. Neither xenos nor mutants but ordinary citizens, who three years ago were loyal subjects of the Emperor and could be again. Many, I am positive, still are, only they are unable to proclaim it. We'd condemn them all for the actions of their leaders. Not only that, but we would taint our world itself.'

'Krieg is already tainted,' Jurten snarled. 'Any true and faithful subject of the Emperor must spit on its name.'

'And what… what if it didn't work? We could flatten Auros and the other hives could fight on, more hardened against us than ever. Colonel… I was under the impression that this decision had been made, that these profane weapons would be buried and forgotten.'

'An easy vow to make,' said Jurten darkly, 'but what about in days to come, when the enemy batters down our doors and we face the prospect of an ignominious defeat?'

As a rule, Colonel Jurten wasn't one to have questions, to voice doubts. He made pronouncements. It disturbed Ionas to hear him talking like this. 'Then that, sir, is when we must be strong.'

Jurten grunted. He pushed himself up from his seat, leaning on his skull-topped cane. It was clear that his artificial hip still bothered him, though Greel had said he was making excellent progress. He wore his uniform as proudly as ever he had, buttons and badges polished, but Ionas was startled to realise that the colonel looked old.

'What would it profit us to win this war, sir,' he entreated, 'were we to stray from the Emperor's path in the process? Perhaps those weapons… Perhaps the fact that they are here, beneath this hive of all the settlements on Krieg, is in itself a test.'

'That may be so,' agreed Jurten, 'but a test of what?' He turned towards the door and, as he limped away, he muttered something that Ionas barely caught, but which filled him with dread. 'I have already made so many compromises…'

The next push came from the east. More traitors than ever came pouring out of their trenches. This time, it was they who found a deadly ambush set for them.

Earthshaker cannons which they had thought destroyed had only been dormant. They waited until their targets had advanced too far to turn back. Then their shells pounded no-man's-land anew. Fire consumed traitors in their thousands, and stymied the advance of their artillery units.

The survivors, shaken, burnt and slashed by shrapnel, clambered through the hive's walls. They found no respite, for here too death awaited their arrival. Snipers lurked in every shadow of the ruined outskirts, behind every corner, in the blown-out windows of every half-standing structure. They turned the thoroughfares into shooting galleries, soon piling up traitor bodies in them. Then, when the traitors knew there was no hope, as they plumbed the depths of despair, the shooting stopped – and Colonel Jurten's ultimatum was issued.

Vox-hailers had been set up throughout the outskirts, ensuring that no traitor, wherever they cowered, was beyond the reach of his stentorian voice.

'You have one chance,' it said, *'one chance alone, to save your-selves. Reaffirm your allegiance to the Emperor, for He is the Master of Mankind and its protector. Swear that you will honour Him and serve Him, fight for Him, lay down your worthless lives for Him.*

'Drop your weapons. Step into the open. Get down on your knees with your hands behind your head and pray to Him. Wait for my troopers to collect you and obey their orders without question, for those orders come from me. You have my word that you will not be harmed. But first, I must see proof of your sincerity.

'Kill your treacherous officers. That is what the Emperor requires of you. That is how you can show your renewed faith in Him. That is your duty. Anyone above the rank of sergeant must be slain. You have five minutes to comply with this order, no more. Do so and He will welcome you back into His bosom. Death is your only other option.'

Silence fell for a minute, almost two. Then the first shots rang out across the ruins.

Vox reports confirmed that the traitors were fighting each other. Jurten told his sergeants to let the clashes play themselves out. The sounds died down as the five-minute deadline drew closer. Then came the first report of a traitor squad surrendering, swiftly followed by another and another, and then by many more.

Jurten waited at the end of a long, broad thoroughfare. He had picked this spot deliberately and had the approach to it cleared. Behind him stood the shell of an Imperial church, which had endured while the buildings around it were flattened.

He was flanked by half a dozen Demolisher tanks. One was the vehicle captured mere weeks earlier, repaired and redressed by Greel's enginseers. Behind him stood his command squad, weapons readied, while a standard bearer flew the Imperial flag. The wings of the double-headed eagle fluttered in an anaemic breeze.

Beneath this on the same pole was the quartered blue-and-gold flag of Krieg. This had once had a hammer at its centre, said to symbolise the planet's industry. To Jurten, it had symbolised Krieg's solemn promise to take up arms when called to by the Emperor. He had had a black skull replace the hammer. To him, it represented the death of his world's principles and mourning for what it had become.

The captured traitors were marched along the thoroughfare towards him. Stripped of their uniforms, they shuffled along with hands clasped over their bowed heads. One by one, they saw who they were shuffling towards, and Jurten enjoyed the looks of surprise and fear that dawned upon their faces. Was that conceited of him? he asked himself.

Their commanders had told them that he had been crippled, if not killed.

The traitors were bundled into waiting vehicles. Jurten watched another group approaching. A pair of stripped traitors were under the guard of a sergeant and three troopers. *Why only four,* he wondered, *when all squads were at full strength this morning?* Why were the escorts' heads down, avoiding his scrutiny as surely as their prisoners did?

He drew breath to yell a warning. At the same time, his eyes met the sergeant's eyes and there was no longer any doubt. The sergeant barked a cue and his five troopers sprang into action. Three snapped up their lasguns and fired. Their target was Jurten himself, but they didn't care who they struck; even their captured fellows were expendable. The traitors who had posed as captives drew knives from their shirtsleeves and charged.

Jurten stood his ground and drew his chainsword.

A part of him looked forward to flexing his muscles again. That part was disappointed. His command squad gunned down the traitors before they could reach him. Other loyalist squads were also regrouping, responding to the threat. They returned the traitor gunners' fire, driving them into cover. In the meantime, their prisoners had rediscovered their spirits. Some tried to break free, even wrestling their captors for their weapons.

Their sergeant bellowed at them, 'Kill their leader! Kill Jurten!'

He acted on old instincts. Almost before he knew it, he was charging the traitor sergeant's position behind a mound of rubble. He didn't have to look to know his squad was right behind him. Their las-beams sizzled past his ears, discouraging his target from raising his head. The traitor got off a few shots, even so, one glancing off a shoulder plate. As the incensed Jurten bore down on him, the traitor sergeant looked for somewhere to run, but he was cornered. He took his only other option.

With an insolent cry, the traitor leapt out of hiding. He met Jurten's charge with his bayonet levelled. Jurten sidestepped his thrust, pivoting on his left hip without even thinking about it. He set the teeth of his chainsword spinning. He swung it around in an arc, severing the traitor's head.

He spun around, teeth bared and nostrils flared, in search of another target. The rest of the impostor squad had been dealt with, however, preceding their leader into death. Order had also been restored among the prisoners, a few executions dampening the mood of the rest. He sent squads to root out any traitors still in hiding. Then he placed a captain in charge of the clean-up and took a groundcar back to headquarters.

Seated in its rear compartment, he ran his hand over the scar on his hip. He felt no pain. The truth was, he had not felt better in years – and not only physically. In the heat of the battle, he hadn't thought about the piece of metal inside him. Nor could he have performed as well without it. His loyalists had struck a great blow against the traitors, and Jurten had shown himself unbowed and still able to lead them.

Today, at least, victory was his. He had brought Krieg another small step closer towards serving the Emperor again. What else mattered, in the end?

AFTER THE GREAT RIFT

THE SACRIFICE

Ven Bruin felt smothered in the stuffy crew compartment.

His old bones rattled in sympathy with the Hades drill. His head rang with the screech of its diamantine-tipped cutters. He sweated under his heavy black cloak. He was wedged into his narrow seat, elbow to elbow, knee to knee with his kill team, nine Krieg grenadiers. None of them spoke, nor could he have heard them if they had.

From time to time, the drill would encounter an obstruction. Its shrill pitch would rise even further and an acrid burning smell would fill the compartment, masking the earthy scent of soldiers' sweat. The grenadier in the driver's seat would trigger the melta-cutter in the Hades' throat; it would buck like a startled horse before ploughing onwards again.

Ven Bruin barely registered when they had come to a stop. His head still rang, his bones still trembled, but the driver checked his instruments and announced that their fraught journey was finally over. The Krieg watchmaster slid the hatch open. He asked Ven Bruin to wait while he secured the area. Eight grenadiers clambered through the hatchway, closing it behind them. One stayed to watch over the inquisitor.

He looked at his silent guard. The grenadiers wore carapace armour including broad, flat breastplates. Like their colonel, in place of the standard rebreather, they carried overpressured respirator units on their backs. They wore masks like the rest of their kind, but screwed into these were metal faceplates in the shapes of skulls, with nasal cavities and teeth. Even these showed no expression, not the hint of a smile nor a scowl.

The grenadier, feeling Ven Bruin's eyes upon him, looked back at the inquisitor.

Ven Bruin felt the need to break the silence, so he asked, 'How long have you served?'

'Almost six years,' the grenadier replied, 'but I shall make my atonement soon.'

The hatch was thrown back again. The watchmaster had returned. 'It is safe for you to disembark, inquisitor,' he said. Ven Bruin thanked him.

It was a relief to heave himself out of the Hades, until the foetid stink of an underhive hit him. The drill rested in a low service tunnel. Dark water dribbled down rockcrete walls, pooling in the tunnel's centre. He took pains to balance on a crumbling walkway. They had cut through tangles of wire, likely plunging some sector of the hive into darkness.

A grenadier turned on the spot, finding his bearings, checking plans on a data-slate.

'Our goal is roughly four miles from here, watchmaster.'

'And a hundred feet up…' The watchmaster glanced up at the creaking roof. 'We'll get as close as we can on this sublevel, then look for a way to ascend. There are likely fewer orks down here, though the underhive will also have its predators.'

They set off along the tunnel, led by their map reader. While Ven Bruin stuck to the walkways, the Krieg didn't mind sloshing through sewer water. Two of them had lumens, creating a bubble of soft light about them. Two more hung back behind the light, lest anything snuck up on them.

They weren't alone down here, as the watchmaster had anticipated. Ven Bruin felt eyes on him from the shadows, saw movement in the corners of his vision, heard whispers of breath. Their lights seemed to draw all manner of vermin towards them, only for it to balk at the sight of them. He kept his pistol drawn and one hand on his sword hilt.

They passed an ancient water tank, which couldn't have seen rain in millennia. Ven Bruin heard a scrape behind it, saw a burst of flame, and something spun towards him. A grenadier leapt into the missile's path. It left a burning trail on Ven Bruin's retinas. *A bottle*, he realised, *with a lit cloth fuse, stinking of promethium…*

The bottle shattered as the grenadier batted it away. He reeled backwards, one arm of his greatcoat alight. Two comrades fell upon him and efficiently swiped out the flames. Another two rushed the water tank, firing, and Ven Bruin heard a squeal of terror, followed by a strangulated moan.

The grenadier who had deflected the promethium bomb was unhurt, protected by his armour and faceplate. The bomber, it appeared, was alone and definitely dead. It was – it had been – a mutant with a curved spine and a tumorous growth on its neck. It had a nest behind the tank, moulded from rotting refuse, in which it had collected scraps of metal as if they were gold coins. It had died in defence of this pitiful hoard.

'It must have been an Imperial citizen once,' intoned the Krieg watchmaster. 'It was offered the Emperor's protection. This was the life it chose and the death it deserved.'

And they moved on.

Their next encounter was more worrying.

They found an ork carcass lying face down in the sewage, a pickaxe between its shoulder blades. Ven Bruin gagged on its stench and had to breathe through his sleeve. He envied the Krieg their rebreathers.

More dead mutants were strewn about the tunnel. Swarms of black flies buzzed about them. So, the xenos had hunted down here, though not lately. The squad's field medic confirmed that the bodies were at least a week old. All the same, they extinguished their lights and proceeded with caution. They soon heard grunting and squealing ahead of them. It could have been rats, but it sounded like something bigger, and alien. A scan confirmed multiple heat sources, larger than rats, much smaller than orks or human beings.

'Squigs,' deduced the watchmaster, grimly. He muttered the word into his comm-bead, so as not to be overheard. Ven Bruin had been looped into the squad's vox-channel.

'We should back up and find another way around if we can,' he suggested, 'or else we–'

'Too late for that, inquisitor,' voxed the soldier with the scanner.

'Lights!' the watchmaster barked out loud.

The lumens flared, to reveal what they had already heard. Four squigs had caught their scent and came scampering towards them. Their tongues lolled out of their oversized heads, and they gibbered with childlike excitement. After days picking over old bones, they slobbered at the prospect of fresh kills.

'Leave none of them alive!' Ven Bruin commanded. 'If they live, they'll lead their ork masters here.' The Krieg had raised their heavy lasguns. They were Type XIVs, colloquially known as 'hellguns', for good reason. Their powerful blasts ripped through the stunted orkoids. Ven Bruin felt the heat emanating from the weapons as they fired. The unwieldy powercells required by them only added to the grenadiers' burdens.

More squigs sprang from the shadows, drawn by the noise and the light. Most were dealt with by the Krieg before they entered the shorter range of Ven Bruin's pistol. One, however, leapt at him from an overhead pipe with claws outstretched. The squig was squat and orange like a pumpkin. When Ven Bruin shot it between its four eyes, it burst like a frag grenade and showered him with chunks of rancid flesh.

The battle was short and one-sided. 'Did any escape?' asked Ven Bruin, after it was over. The grenadiers agreed that every squig they had spotted had been slaughtered. They couldn't guarantee, though, that none had slipped away unnoticed.

They took a sharp turn into a dank side passageway and double-timed along it, throwing caution to the wind. They continued to eschew the broader tunnels of the underhive for its darker, more treacherous routes, even when it meant a considerable diversion from their course. After some time, they stopped to rest and reorient themselves. They detected no sign of pursuit, but still Ven Bruin felt uneasy. *If the xenos search this sector for us, they might find more than they expected...*

He wondered if he ought to call off the mission, tell the watchmaster to turn back. He feared it might already be too late.

They broke into an abandoned sewage treatment and recycling plant. Its machines had been torn out but rusted tanks remained, half filled with congealed sludge. Dust coated every surface and the air was ripe with stale chlorine.

The watchmaster gripped the sides of a ladder and shook it. A network of overlooking gantries clattered. Somewhere, a screw was dislodged and bounced three times on its way to the floor. Pipework groaned and coughed up sewer gas.

'Should hold,' the watchmaster considered, 'if we're careful.'

Four grenadiers scaled the ladder and spread out across the gantries. They climbed more ladders where the light of their lumens revealed them. They soon found what they sought: an exit to a higher level, once used by the plant's workforce. It was blocked, which had also been expected. An explosive charge would have cleared the way, but the noise would invite attention. They set about the door with entrenching tools and discarded lengths of pipe tossed up to them. Old wood began to splinter.

Ven Bruin waited below, perched on the edge of a vat. He saw no point in concealing his tiredness. He couldn't match the Krieg for stoicism. The watchmaster stood beside him, alert. He had left two troopers behind to guard the entrance, while the last two checked for more potential access points. Ven Bruin heard a scrape of movement behind him, and thought one must have returned.

He stood and turned, in case, and so avoided the steaming jet of acid spit that would have struck him in the back. 'Squig!' he yelled as he drew his power sword and lit it up.

The squig tensed its legs as if to spring at his right shoulder. He saw through its feint, swung his blade to the left as it sprang, and carved it up neatly.

More shouts came from opposite directions at once. Orks were wrenching boards off windows at the back of the building, even as more charged the sundered entrance doors. The sentries, outnumbered, couldn't hold them. They fell back to where Ven Bruin and the watchmaster waited, ten green-skinned brutes hard on their heels. Two were felled by las-fire, but this failed to discourage the remainder.

Ven Bruin met them squarely with his sword. The orks' own

weapons were primitive as always, their hide armour no match for his energised blade. The Krieg, in contrast, fought with knives much smaller than the xenos' axes.

'Inquisitor,' came the watchmaster's strained voice through his earpiece, 'we'll hold them off while you get out of here. Go!' He hesitated, long enough for the soldier to add, 'This mission is over if we lose you.'

He was right. With a final volley of thrusts in the xenos' direction, Ven Bruin backed up to the ladder, jammed his sword back into its scabbard and climbed. He made it up only three rungs before something grabbed his ankle. He looked down into the bellowing maw of an ork with a single tuft of bristling black hair and a bone jammed through its flat nose. A livid, fresh scar sliced through its right eye, burn marks around its edges. Ven Bruin had cut it, but the pain had galvanised rather than deterred the creature.

He tried to shake it off him, but its grip was vice-like. Its fingers were crushing his bones. The ork was trying to drag him down. With one hand, he held on to a rung above him, the muscles along his arm screaming. He could feel his fingers slipping.

Ven Bruin drew his pistol. With no time to aim, he could only pray he didn't blow his own foot off. His first shot missed, but the second ignited the ork's hair. It howled again and let him go, trying frantically to beat out the flames, knocking itself half-insensate.

He resumed his climb, ignoring the pain in his ankle. As he attained the gantry, short of breath, it rocked violently and he flattened himself down on it. Beneath him, the dazed, half-bald ork had the ladder in both hands and was shaking it fiercely. A snap shot from a Krieg hellgun struck it in the neck and took it down at last.

The Krieg had spread across the lower level, keeping out of reach of their attackers where they could as this favoured their superior firepower. It occurred to Ven Bruin that his presence had only impeded them, forcing them to cluster around him. One ork had a gun but no clue how to aim it, spraying bullets in every direction. One pinged off the gantry's underside, right beneath his nose.

The two grenadiers from the back of the building had entered the battle. Two more fired down from above. The Krieg were gaining the upper hand, but more orks were squeezing in through windows, with no one there to stop them.

The gantries had almost stopped swaying, so Ven Bruin clambered to his feet. He fired a few shots of his own down into the melee. Then a Krieg voice in his ear reported that the exit door was open. 'As soon you can safely do so, disengage,' the watchmaster ordered his squad. Most had already managed to position themselves beside ladders, and some began climbing at once. He followed suit, hauling himself up onto the gantry above him. Smoke grenades were dropped below, but he outdistanced their rising clouds.

The walkways soon trembled again, this time with the beats of Krieg boots. The orks below let out bewildered howls as they groped blindly for their foes. Ven Bruin set his sights on a beckoning doorway. He couldn't remember when he had last exerted himself so hard – ten years before? Skull-masked grenadiers converged upon him. Two, finding themselves on a parallel gantry, climbed over its handrail and leapt across the intervening gap.

Ven Bruin reached the exit. Broken planks caught on his cloak as he pushed himself through. He emerged into a dimly lit, refuse-strewn, low-level hive street. He was greeted by two grenadiers, who immediately flanked him.

From behind him, inside the plant, there came a series of catastrophic crashes.

He didn't have to turn back to know what must have happened. The orks, instead of following the Krieg up onto the gantries, were tearing them down. Two more grenadiers came hurtling through the door in time; a third was framed in the doorway when the walkway under him collapsed. A comrade dived to catch his flailing hand. Another grabbed the rescuer's legs, to keep him from being pulled over the precipice too.

With a strenuous effort, both men were hauled to safety. They stood and dusted themselves down, exchanging no words of gratitude, nor even of relief. Perhaps they were thinking of the four comrades who hadn't made it out, their watchmaster among them.

'They could still be alive but trapped in there,' Ven Bruin noted.

'Then they will give their lives to delay our pursuers,' said a Krieg grenadier.

'As would we in their place,' another agreed. 'For the Emperor.'

'I have served the longest,' said a third. 'I shall act as watchmaster.'

Ven Bruin couldn't argue with their logic. 'Do we still have the map?' he asked.

They did, and it was brought to him. 'We have emerged into a manufacturing district,' said the grenadier who held it, 'which is good, because it seems to be deserted. A plate at the end of this thoroughfare reveals the sector designation, from which I can place us roughly… here.' He jabbed a finger at the faintly lit screen.

'You alone know our precise destination, inquisitor,' said the Krieg who had named himself watchmaster, 'so you will have to guide us from here on.'

They headed roughly west for thirteen blocks. Then Ven Bruin had the squad split up and search for a door, which he described to them. Two grenadiers insisted on sticking close to him.

Minutes ticked by until half an hour had passed, and still no door was found. He began to fear that his information was flawed. He had extracted it from the former planetary governor, whose terror had certainly been real. At the time, Ven Bruin would have sworn he was too afraid to lie.

They had encountered no other life so far, which was a mercy. He knew it wouldn't last. The orks they had left at the plant would not give up. They must have found another way up to this level by now. He thanked the Emperor when a grenadier voxed, *'Inquisitor, your attention is requested.'*

The narrow gap between two storehouse buildings was easily missed. It looked like an architectural flaw, but it opened into a covered alleyway, which ended in a rockcrete wall after just a few steps. Set into a recess near its end was a nondescript reinforced door without a handle. A faded sign read *Authorised Personnel Only.*

Ven Bruin reached into his cloak and produced a set of keys. He tried several in the door lock until one fitted. It turned easily enough and the door swung open. He stepped back and let two grenadiers walk through ahead of him. Their lumens picked out an ordinary storehouse floor, with shelving racks and discarded crates, all empty. Ven Bruin was about to follow the grenadiers inside when a multi-scanner pinged.

They snapped up their guns and one of them bellowed, 'Who goes there?'

Before the echoes of the challenge could die down, the grenadiers came under fire.

They separated, snapping off their lumens, merging into shadows. The acting watchmaster – Ven Bruin assumed it was him, though without a badge of rank he couldn't tell him apart from his fellows – held the rest of his squad back with a gesture.

Las-beams dispelled the darkness in staccato flashes.

Ven Bruin heard a human-sounding cry. A moment later, a vox report came in: *'All clear inside the building, watchmaster.'*

He was glad to get in from the alleyway, to lock the door behind him. He hoped the orks would overlook it, as his team almost had. Behind a stack of crates, two Krieg stood over a prone soldier. She wore the uniform of the local militia and was still alive, though she had been shot in the arm. She was shaking and sweating, and the sight of a witch hunter looming over her intensified those symptoms.

'Inquisitor, I... I beg the Emperor's forgiveness. I...'

'Who are you?' he snapped. 'What are you doing here?'

'Constable Hallam, sir,' she said, and she reeled off a service number. 'In the dark, I couldn't... I saw those skulls, those masks, and I thought...'

'What are you doing here?' Ven Bruin repeated.

Hallam pulled herself together, breathing through her pain. 'A special operation, assigned by the governor himself. We were to live here. Never leave this building. We have quarters upstairs and provisions to last us five years. I don't know... None of us knew what we were guarding, but it has to be something–'

'How many of you are there?' a grenadier barked.

'There were five, but our sergeant... We heard about the xenos through the emergency broadcast system. He took two constables out to assess the situation. I told him... I pleaded with him not to go. Even if the hive had been evacuated, our orders–'

'That accounts for four of you. The fifth?'

'He...' Hallam looked ashamed. 'We had been here, the two of us, for over a month. No word from the others. He began to... He said we should break into the vault. At first he said there might be weapons there, but then... then he talked about offering its treasures to the xenos, bargaining with them. I had no choice, inquisitor, I swear it. I had to...'

Ven Bruin turned to the nearest grenadier. 'Dress her wound,' he instructed, 'and find some water for her.'

He stepped away from the wounded soldier. He rounded another shelving unit. Just off-centre to the floor, a round metal plug bulged out of the rockcrete, roughly five feet wide. It gleamed in the pallid lumen-light. Three grenadiers gathered about it, along with the witch hunter. 'It looks new,' one of them remarked.

'Does that surprise you?' Ven Bruin muttered. He knelt to look at the protuberance more closely. The metal was smooth and bore no runes, but sprouting from it like toadstools were five spoked wheels of varying sizes.

'Watchmaster,' he said, 'take Hallam and your squad to those upstairs quarters.'

'Sir, could one of us not–'

'What I must do now, no one else must see,' said Ven Bruin firmly.

'I understand, inquisitor.'

He waited for the others to withdraw, and for some minutes after. As he was already on his knees, he used the time to pray. Then, with much trepidation, he reached for the largest locking wheel. He gripped it with both hands and turned it clockwise. Each time it passed through an arc of sixty degrees, he heard and felt a mechanical clunk. Upon the third of these, he shifted his grip to the next wheel and turned it anticlockwise.

He continued in this manner, through a sequence committed to his memory. He pushed all doubts, all other thoughts, out of his mind. He focused on the combination. He could not make a mistake. If he did, explosive charges would melt the locking mechanisms to slag and vaporise him.

The last wheel clunked into place.

The world seemed to freeze around Ven Bruin. He held his breath.

The metal plug shifted under his hands. A crack appeared in the floor around it, through which icy-cold steam escaped with a venomous hiss. When nothing else had happened after a minute, he teased his fingers under the edge of the plug and managed to lift it, just fractionally. He voxed the Krieg watchmaster.

Two minutes later, five Krieg grenadiers were spaced around the plug, in crouching positions. On Ven Bruin's cue, they lifted the heavy wedge of metal between them and slid it to one side. They revealed a large circular hole in the floor. Two ladders, placed across from each other, plunged into darkness.

'This vault,' explained Ven Bruin, 'was dug on the orders of the governor. I should say, the late former governor. Its contents are what brought me to this world.'

The grenadiers listened to him raptly. He felt unnerved by ten blank eyes upon him. He found it best to focus past them. They had come this far on faith. Now they had to know the truth – before they saw it for themselves.

'Somehow, he got his hands on certain… plans and, with the assistance of a rogue faction within the Adeptus Mechanicus, constructed certain… devices. Forbidden devices, which could have unleashed the fury of the warp upon us all.'

'Forbidden devices?' the Krieg watchmaster repeated. Ven Bruin thought he knew his voice by now. 'Weapons, inquisitor?'

'The governor confessed his sins to me,' he continued, 'on his deathbed.' The governor had, in fact, died under torture by Interrogator Ferran. 'To his last breath, he swore that his intentions had only been good, and I am minded to believe him. His true sin was his loss of faith. He feared a xenos attack and trusted not to the Emperor to protect him. He had these…' – he almost said *devices* again, obfuscating the issue by habit – 'weapons built to protect his people and himself. He lost his nerve when the true extent of their power became clear to him. He had the weapons hidden, where no one would think to look for them.'

He had said enough for now.

Ven Bruin stepped onto a ladder, tested his weight on it and began to descend. The watchmaster rounded the shaft and took the other ladder. He motioned to his squad to follow.

The further they descended, the colder Ven Bruin felt, even under his thick cloak.

The shaft was much deeper than he had expected and, after a few minutes, he felt he was underground again. He wondered how many workers it had taken to dig it, and to lower the forbidden weapons down it. Few, he imagined, would have known exactly what they were doing. All the same, suspicions would have formed, becoming rumours; and sooner or later, rumours always reached a witch hunter's ears.

At last, the light of the grenadiers' lumens fell on solid ground below. Ven Bruin stepped gratefully onto it and rubbed his cramped hands together. The watchmaster alighted from the ladder behind him. He drew his gun and signalled to the inquisitor to stay behind him. He stooped to walk through an arched opening. Ven Bruin followed.

The room beyond was hewn from dark rock, and smaller than he had imagined. A rack against the far wall was its only feature. Four strides would have taken him to it, but he faltered after two. The watchmaster stood beside him, as if similarly awestruck. The rest of the grenadiers crowded into the doorway behind them.

Secured to the rack by clamps with giant bolts were six grey cylinders. Each was almost twenty feet long and as broad as a man. Each had one rounded end and one flat, with short fins jutting from the latter in an 'X' pattern. A film of dust clung to them. Ven Bruin willed his feet to take him another step closer.

He reached to wipe the dust away, but thought again. He blew on a cylinder gently, uncovering a smooth, dull stretch of its surface. He saw no runes, no markings of any kind. The people who had put these devices together hadn't wished to boast of it. Anyone who knew of the cylinders' existence would surely already know their purpose.

'Pardon me, inquisitor.'

'What is it?' asked Ven Bruin, irritable at having his thoughts disturbed.

'The multi-scanner shows,' said a grenadier behind him, 'that the air in here is mildly toxic.' Ven Bruin sighed. He had known it was a possibility.

'Take my mask and rebreather, sir,' the grenadier offered.

Ven Bruin looked at him in surprise, but shook his head. 'I intend to spend no longer here than I must.'

'May I ask, sir, what you intend to do?' The watchmaster rephrased his question. 'What do you require from my squad?'

Ven Bruin's gaze lingered on the cylinders. 'If I could… were it not for the xenos and their badly timed arrival… I would bury these obscenities in rockcrete and drop them into the deepest part of the ocean, so they could never be recovered.'

'Indeed.'

'That is what the planetary governor ought to have done. The fact that he didn't suggests that a part of him, however small, still saw a use for these… these…'

'Weapons, sir. These weapons.'

Ven Bruin shot a glare at the Krieg watchmaster. It was, of course, met by his impassive mask. 'I have no way to dispose of these weapons,' he said carefully. 'Therefore, my only goal now is to ensure that the orks do not procure them.'

The watchmaster actually shuddered. 'Unthinkable.'

He took a step forward to join Ven Bruin by the rack. He

cocked his head as he examined the cylinders more closely. 'With five men, inquisitor, I doubt we could carry more than one of these cylinders at once. The return trip to the Hades–'

'No, no,' Ven Bruin agreed, 'that would be entirely impractical. Not to mention perilous. We cannot know if they are even... stable. I believe their functions are controlled by internal cogitators. Still, a large enough jolt might detonate them on the spot.'

Both inquisitor and watchmaster considered that point for a moment. Then they took a step away from the cylinders in unison.

'Then I see only one option remaining to us,' said the watchmaster.

Ven Bruin nodded. 'As do I.'

'We must guard these weapons with our lives.'

'Any one of them could reduce Hive Arathron to ruins.'

'Killing all the orks inside it,' said the watchmaster, a little too quickly.

'Should all six detonate together, in this underground chamber...'

'What would the consequences be, inquisitor?'

'I cannot know for certain. The devastation could spread to neighbouring hives. The air, the water of this world might be forever poisoned.'

'As on Krieg,' the watchmaster stated.

Ven Bruin was briefly lost for words. The parallel had occurred to him, of course it had, but to hear it drawn so baldly... 'There were many more weapons, ancient weapons, in the vault beneath Krieg,' he murmured. 'I hear they numbered in the hundreds.' *But what if the records are wrong?* he suddenly thought. *How can we know for sure? What if there* were *only six cylinders on Krieg? What if that was enough?*

'Of course, if it's true that this world has already been forsaken...'

The watchmaster spoke slowly, ponderously. Was he wary of how the witch hunter might receive his words? Or was it his own thoughts that disturbed him, the conclusions forming in a mind unused to thinking for itself?

'We should contact the colonel,' he suggested. 'Constable Hallam has a vox-caster with the requisite range, for use in the direst of emergencies.'

'Your colonel is aware of the situation,' Ven Bruin assured him, 'and agrees that I should handle it as I see fit.'

'Five soldiers is too few to hold this chamber,' the watchmaster pointed out.

'I fear there are too few soldiers on this planet to hold it forever.'

'The xenos must be kept from these weapons.'

'Indeed they must.'

'Whatever it takes? Inquisitor?'

Ven Bruin took a breath. He squared his shoulders and looked the Krieg watchmaster squarely in his eyepieces. 'Whatever it takes,' he confirmed.

'You should leave, sir,' said the watchmaster. 'My squad will escort you back to the encampment, if the Emperor allows it.'

'That isn't necessary, watchmaster. I knew when I undertook this mission–'

'Five soldiers is too few to hold this chamber. One can achieve the same result. The other four can better serve by escorting you to safety.'

Another grenadier stepped forward. 'If one must stay behind, watchmaster, I would like to volunteer for that assignment.'

'I would like to volunteer too,' said another, and the others followed suit.

'We have all lived too long,' said the watchmaster, 'but I have lived longer than any of you. I shall be the one to stay.'

The others accepted his decree without question. They took ration packs from their belt pouches and handed them to him, along with their canteens of water. They didn't have to be asked. In addition, each of them handed over a krak grenade.

No goodbyes were said, no final words. It finally fell to Ven Bruin to break the grim silence. 'We will reseal the vault as we leave, if we are able. No doubt the orks will find a way to break through it. Still, it may buy you – buy all of us – a little time.'

The watchmaster nodded in acknowledgement.

Ven Bruin glanced back at him once more, through the archway, as he placed his first foot on the ladder. The Krieg man stood stiffly in the centre of the weapons chamber, his thoughts as always concealed beneath his fatalistic mask.

They heard the orks as soon as they stepped out of the alleyway.

They heard their howls, and bursts of bullets shot into the air by ramshackle guns. The sounds came from every direction. Ven Bruin was torn. Did they turn back, hide behind the reinforced door and pray for the xenos to pass them by? Or did they make a run for it, perhaps try to lead them away?

He chose the latter. They had pored over the hive's layout and plotted a route back to the Hades drill that wouldn't take them over old ground. The kill team's new acting watchmaster led the way. They covered as much ground as they could before, inevitably, they were spotted. Whooping orks converged on them from opposite directions.

They set off a smoke grenade and, under its cover, ducked into another storehouse. The orks were left spluttering and gasping, and Ven Bruin's eyes teared up. He had to let the grenadiers guide him inside. Tinned goods had once been stored here, but looters, vandals and arsonists had visited since.

They made for a stairwell in one corner and clattered up flight after flight of stairs, seeking a higher-level exit. Smoke had got into the inquisitor's lungs, and they rattled and wheezed. They had brought Hallam with them, persuading her that her orders were now void, and she was struggling too.

They passed a narrow window, which gave an overview of their surroundings. Ven Bruin looked out at streets teeming with green flesh. He only had a moment, so couldn't locate the weapons store. Still, the scene crushed any hopes he may have harboured that it might not be discovered. It could only be a matter of time now, and precious little time at that.

He caught his breath and continued up the stairs, swept along by grenadiers above and below him. He heard the grunts and the pounding footsteps of xenos ascending behind him.

437.M40

JURTEN'S DAY

It was a day of celebration.

The Feast of the Emperor's Ascension had always been observed across Krieg. The Chairman had renamed it Independence Day but kept the date the same. That way, he could pretend to enjoy more popular support than he had.

In Ferrograd, the day had become one of remembrance and sober reflection. This year, however, Jurten had doubled rations and made synthehol available, albeit in watered-down form. A token reward for his citizens' hard work and patience. He ate with his senior staff, enjoying the same fare served at any table. This meant reconstituted protein steaks and fungus grown on the banks of an underground river uncovered by one of Greel's work crews. They ate by flickering candlelight, so as not to waste their fuel reserves.

The colonel had arrived late, having spent the morning in church. His was a brooding presence at the table's head, setting the tone for the gathering. Glasses and cutlery clinked, but little small talk was attempted. Jurten drank only water. He had put aside a bottle of amasec – the last in the hive – for this occasion, but when uncorked it turned out to have soured, which might have been for the best.

Today of all days he needed to keep a clear head.

He rose to his feet, and all activity ceased. The room throbbed to the familiar rhythm of exploding enemy shells. Jurten's keen eyes swept around the faces turned towards him. He noted which met his gaze and which could not. He lingered longest on the face of Lieutenant Ionas. Then he proposed the customary toast to the Emperor. 'May He bless our feast today and our endeavours in the days to come. May He grant us strength to smite the traitors in His name, and the wisdom to know how best to use it.'

It took his audience a moment to realise he was done. Perhaps they had expected an announcement. Archmagos Greel led them in the end. He raised his glass and proclaimed, 'To the Emperor!' to which the rest responded.

An old resentment flared in Jurten's chest. He thought Greel would rather have toasted his Machine-God. As valuable an adviser as he had become, he couldn't be trusted. Jurten couldn't trust anyone, not fully, only himself. His were the only motives that he knew beyond doubt to be pure. That was why he had to make this decision alone.

He refocused his attention on his meal. He forced himself to eat, though eating was the last thing he wanted to do.

Slowly, a new sound impinged itself upon his consciousness. He only heard it faintly; like the shells it came from the surface, some way above the rockcrete ceiling of his command bunker. The sound, even so, was unmistakable. It was an unremitting angry wail. The sound of air raid sirens.

* * *

General Krause was in a good mood as he entered his communications room.

His belly was full from the feast and he had drunk enough to feel relaxed. The war was going well, and he was especially pleased with the insult he had dealt to his enemies today. Jurten and his Imperial lackeys faced imminent defeat and now here was the proof of it. For the first time in over two years, they wanted to talk to him.

Krause stepped up onto a podium, lights whirling about him. An attendant servitor brushed lint from his jacket, took charge of his half-full wine glass and scuttled away. He waited for an image to form on the opposite podium, but it did not.

A hint of displeasure pricked at his contented bubble. 'Why can't I see him?'

'*Colonel Jurten is not here.*' The answer came over the vox-speakers spaced about the room, but in a voice he didn't know. '*I apologise for the deception.*'

'Who are you?' he demanded. 'Show yourself.'

'*I… can't do that, General Krause.*'

'Then I have nothing to say to you.'

'*General, please. What do you have to lose by hearing my proposal?*'

Something in the voice's tone – something urgent, something desperate – halted him with one foot on the floor. He eased it back onto the podium. 'Who are you?' he asked again.

'*A member of the colonel's staff. That is all I can tell you at present.*'

'Am I expected to believe he knows nothing of this?' He was almost disappointed. He had savoured the thought of Jurten crawling to him, pleading with him. At the same time, he had known it was too much to hope for.

'*I would like to negotiate the terms of our…*'

He seized on the voice's hesitation. 'Surrender? Say the word.'

'*Of our… surrender, yes.*'

'A surrender that you are in no position to offer.'

'At present, that is true.'

'And I have no reason to accept,' the general crowed. 'You've held out longer than I imagined possible, I will concede you that, but this war is almost over. Two-thirds of Ferrograd is rubble. Your leader cowers underground in sewer pipes, while your soldiers and civilians die for his lost cause in their thousands.'

'I wouldn't underestimate us, general. We're stronger than you think.'

'I doubt that. How did you enjoy the surprise gift I sent you for your false idol's coronation day? My bomber pilots tell me it provoked a storm.'

'Believe me, the last thing you want to do is provoke–'

'Why should I negotiate with you,' snapped Krause, 'when I am on the verge of crushing your dismal little insurgency forever?'

The unseen speaker bridled. *'You are the insurgents, not we. Krieg swore allegiance to the Golden Throne. And we… the colonel has weapons that you know nothing of yet.'*

'Still paying lip service to your withered Emperor?' Krause gave a spiteful laugh. 'Renounce Him and I might consider your proposal.'

'No, never!'

'Then I was right the first time. We have nothing to say to each other.'

'You misunderstand me, general. You think I fear what you might do to us? We are all of us ready and willing to die for a just cause.'

'Then more fool you.'

'I fear what Colonel Jurten may… what you may push him into doing to you.'

He almost laughed again; but again, something in the voice stopped him. 'If Jurten had weapons as you claim,' said Krause at length, 'if he believed they could turn the tide against us, then why would he hold back? For what possible reason?'

'The fact that he does should tell you all you need to know.'

'There are no weapons,' he snorted, but a small doubt gnawed at the back of his mind. Hadn't there been rumours, after all? He remembered the Chairman fretting about stories heard in childhood, of the Dark Age. Krause had been scornful at the time. He had told him he was worrying too much.

'What do you want from me?' he asked guardedly.

'Only what the Chairman offered us before, back in the beginning. Safe passage off-world, for my regiment and for any civilian who wishes to join us.'

'That is more than the Chairman offered.' *Still, a small enough price to pay for my enemy's utter humiliation…* 'I would want something in return.'

'Such as?'

'Such as Jurten. Hand him over to me as a prisoner of war.'

The owner of the voice took a moment to think about that. 'I doubt it will be possible. I know the colonel well enough to know that he would die before he–'

'That is my offer,' snapped Krause. 'Give me Jurten and we have a deal. The rest of you go free, as Krieg too will finally be free. If what you say is true, if you honestly wish to avert a disaster, then what is the life of one warmonger weighed against that?'

'I'll need some time,' said the voice.

'You know where I am,' said Krause, 'but I'd think fast if I were you – for I shall give you no quarter in the meantime. You may find this decision taken out of your hands.'

He signalled a technician to break off contact. He stepped down from the podium and looked for the servitor who had his wine. He took the glass and drained it in one gulp. He realised that he was grinning, and why not? It had been a very good day.

A day, he thought, *of celebration.*

* * *

Refugees were still arriving from the surface.

Some had been so defiant only hours ago, clinging to the remnants of their lives as bombs and shells fell about them. Some had imagined they could escape the city and seek sanctuary elsewhere. Their heads were downcast now, and they carried their few salvaged possessions on their backs.

The soldiers of the 83rd Krieg Regiment were well drilled in the process. Troopers took names and work histories and distributed bedrolls and food packs. They assigned the new arrivals to the spots in which they were to sleep. Certain tunnels had been set aside for this purpose and were lined with canvas tents and sheets pegged up to serve as curtains.

The refugees would be assigned to work parties by morning. It might be weeks or even months before hab-units became available for them – but the harder they toiled, the sooner that day would come. Few complained, and those that did and ignored the soldiers' warnings were marched back above ground at gunpoint.

'Our enemies believe they have won something today,' proclaimed the ever-present vox-hailers. 'They think us beaten but we shall rise again, far stronger than before. This craven attack, committed on this holy day of all days, only stiffens our resolve. It reminds us that there are no bounds to these traitors' depravity, nor to their conceit. For is this not the Emperor's day? And on this day of all days, no slight against His name – no assault upon His loyal servants – can remain unpunished.'

Such words were familiar by now, and they rarely meant much. The threats they voiced today, though – of all days – made Lieutenant Ionas very worried.

He led a procession of nine officers through the tent city. They pushed past civilians lugging buckets of water from standpipes. One batted aside a grimy labourer, who, worse the wear for drink, pleaded with her for more food for his children.

The contrast with the last feast day – the one called upon the Chairman's death – was stark. Back then, there had been cheers and even laughter. Now they were drowned out by tears and prayers. The churches were filled to overflowing. This morning's sermons had been broadcast through the hailers to reach the straining crowds outside their doors. Ionas looked around him and saw a people whose spirit had been broken.

He knew how they felt.

It had been months since he had eaten fresh food or breathed fresh air. He shared a tiny hab-unit with a junior officer. Its stone floor felt cold to his feet, even through the small rug he had procured. The ceiling hung low above his head and a mouldy-smelling fungus grew in one corner of it. He couldn't complain because the colonel endured the same conditions. He would say that sacrifices were for everyone to make.

Rank had no privileges in Jurten's world, just responsibilities.

Ionas led the way across the New Wulfram ordnance plant. The great machines below him were quieter than usual, but ticked and hummed to themselves restlessly. The thoroughfare beyond had been widened since his last visit, bright new tunnels branching from it. The stranded Termite was gone, presumably mounted on a transporter and pressed into service, though it was listed on no equipment inventory.

'Do we have much further to go?' asked Captain Voigt, impatiently.

'Almost there, sir,' said Ionas.

Voigt muttered something that Ionas didn't catch. He assumed it was another complaint about having to walk. Vehicle access to this part of the underhive was still tricky. Voigt's real problem, he suspected, was being this close to the unwashed masses. He twitched with suspicion and looked as if he had a permanent smell under his nose – which, to be fair, he did, but the rest of them were used to it by now.

Ionas had never warmed to Voigt, finding him fussy and unapproachable. He was vital to his plans, however. 'I promise you, sir, this will be worth the journey.' He had become well used to faking confidence.

The first security checkpoint was unmanned. The second had been abandoned too. With a growing unease, Ionas led the way up the rough-hewn tunnel to the adamantium hatch. He didn't know how to unlock it. He couldn't show his fellow officers what he had seen behind it. He had prayed that the hatch's mere existence would support his story well enough for them to ask more questions.

The hatch, however, stood ajar. White light streamed around its edges. Ionas approached it tentatively, drawing his pistol. 'Archmagos? Colonel Jurten?'

He pushed on the door and stepped through into the ancient vault.

He found it empty. Four metal racks still ran lengthways across the room, but he could see right through them. The cylinders that had filled them before – the shapes that had haunted his nightmares since – were gone. He felt a lump forming in his throat and thought his heart might have stopped beating. How many had there been? He hadn't had a chance to count them. In the nightmares, it always seemed like hundreds.

Ionas was dimly aware of voices behind him. The other officers had followed him into the vault and were exploring, wide-eyed. Even Voigt appeared impressed. They had questions for him about the indecipherable runes on the walls, about the hatch's antique but sophisticated locks, most of all about the empty racks. He couldn't answer them.

'We… we have to find the colonel,' was all he could manage to say.

* * *

Jurten watched as the last of the weapons was unloaded.

Secured to a trolley by stout iron chains, it was wheeled down the ramp of a truck. Two squads of soldiers steadied and guided its path. Its casing was jet black, but adorned with ancient warning runes in white, and with the image of a leering skull.

They wheeled their payload towards the silo doors. They didn't know, could hardly imagine, how deadly it truly was, but Jurten had impressed upon them that it was deadly enough, and to be handled with the utmost care. 'If that trolley gets away from you, pray that you don't by some freak chance survive to face my wrath.'

He had removed his vox-earpiece, wishing not to be distracted, but an aide informed him of an urgent message from his adjutant. He asked if it could wait. 'He says he is at "the vault",' the reply came, 'with Captain Voigt and the rest of your senior staff, and it cannot.'

Jurten gritted his teeth. He had been putting off this moment for months. No longer. It was time. 'Tell Ionas where we are,' he instructed, 'and tell him to come here.'

Six officers clambered into a pair of Tauroxes, while three more rode in the back of a canvas-covered truck. It was the best Ionas could summon at short notice.

He expected complaints from Captain Voigt, but he remained as sullen as the rest of them. Ionas wished he knew what they were thinking.

The coordinates that Jurten's aide had given him were close to the hive's geographical centre. The tunnel leading to them looked new and rarely used. They were forced to disembark at a roadblock. The colonel awaited them behind it. He stood with his hands clasped behind him, his expression grim.

Ionas saluted him. He opened his mouth to explain himself,

but the colonel motioned for the party to follow him, then turned on his heel and marched away.

A pair of iron doors set into a rock wall stood open. Assorted vehicles sat in front of these, one a truck with its loading ramp extended. Ionas glanced inside it as he passed, but it was empty. They stepped through the doors and traversed a short passageway, from the end of which he heard voices and heavy machinery. There were knots in Ionas' stomach and with every step he took, they tightened further.

'Is this what you wanted to see?' growled Colonel Jurten.

He led them into a vast round cavern. Soldiers and technicians clambered over scaffolding platforms and operated heavy-duty lifting equipment. A heavy black cylinder was being lowered onto a launch pad. A cylinder marked with warning skulls.

It appeared to be the last, as a score more like it were already in situ. They were propped up almost vertically, each leaning just a little towards the chamber's centre. Their lines converged at a circular metal blast door in the roof, several feet across and at least seventy above them. Ionas was aghast that all this had been built without his knowledge.

Of course, Archmagos Greel was at the centre of it all, supervising the installation of some manner of control shrine. He was facing away from the officers, but Ionas had the feeling that he could see them all the same.

'A silo,' he said numbly. 'You've built a missile silo.'

Colonel Jurten stared fixedly ahead of him. 'That is correct,' he rumbled.

'For the weapons.'

'Indeed.'

Ionas lowered his voice. 'The *forbidden* weapons.'

'Is this true, colonel?' Ionas was grateful when Captain Voigt stepped forward. 'Some of us had heard rumours, but...'

Jurten still didn't turn, didn't look any of them in the eye. 'We'll discuss this in private,' he decreed. He led them back along the passageway and turned off into a small, basic office. There were only three chairs and barely room for everyone to squeeze inside.

Jurten closed the door behind them and stood for a moment, lips pursed and head bowed in contemplation. Ionas thought he almost looked ashamed.

When he looked up again, however, his eyes were as steely as ever. 'Yes,' he confirmed, 'it is true.' And he told them what Ionas already knew, what the rest of them suspected. He told them what the weapons were and where they came from, and as he spoke, each of them grew paler, apart from Ionas, who felt the relief of a burden finally shared.

Voigt was the first to break the ensuing silence. 'Do you intend to use the weapons, sir?'

'I intend to prepare for that eventuality.'

Another officer spoke up. 'Then you foresee a circumstance in which–'

'How can you not?' snapped Jurten. 'We are losing this war.'

'But surely as long as the Emperor–'

'We are losing this war and we all know it. The traitors have driven us deeper and deeper underground, and soon we will have nowhere left to go. Soon, we will face a choice. Do we accept defeat? Do we accept failure and death? Or do we fight back with all our might? What would the Emperor have us do?'

'He would have us fight, of course,' said Captain Voigt, 'but even so…'

'If we do nothing with these weapons He has given us–'

The Emperor has nothing to do with those abominations, Ionas wanted to protest.

'–then Krieg will fall to Chaos and be damned. Employ the

weapons, and that…' Jurten hesitated, only for an instant. 'That choice will weigh upon our souls forever. For even the lesser of two evils, in His eyes, condemns us. That is why I kept this from you, all of you, for this is my burden to bear. A choice that I must make alone.'

'Those weapons,' said Ionas quietly, 'would ravage our world.'

Colonel Jurten clenched his fists. 'It wasn't so long ago that Krieg had never known war. That was its problem. Its people, *our* people, became soft. If we had known, if we could have seen the future, I would have dropped a ship full of orks on the capital hive city. I would have shown our bloated autocrats, I would have shown all of them, the truth.'

'At a cost of how many lives?' protested Voigt.

'A better world would have been forged in their funeral pyres.' Some of the other officers flinched visibly at Jurten's proclamation.

'You sound as if you have made up your mind.'

'The missiles will be ready to launch tonight. I have tried – I have prayed night and day for guidance – but I cannot think of a reason to hold back any longer.'

'Even on this holiest of days?' Voigt spluttered.

The colonel bared his teeth. 'When better for the fire of vengeance to rain down from the skies? A single missile would be despatched, to begin with. Hive Auros would be the target, as close to General Krause's command HQ as we can manage.'

'Sir, has this plan been examined by our strategists?' a young lieutenant asked.

'My guess would be,' Voigt answered her, shrewdly, 'only by Archmagos Greel. I see his cold metal hand in this. Can you deny it, sir?'

'Didn't we discuss this, Colonel Jurten?' Ionas pleaded. 'The risk of Krause calling our bluff, goading us into launching the rest of the missiles, is too great.'

Jurten glared at him. 'Who says I would be bluffing? Why should I even send those traitors a warning? Do they deserve a chance to save themselves?'

Another long, tense silence followed, during which all eyes turned to one man. Captain Voigt commanded the 83rd Regiment's Third Company and, since the loss of Captain Schmitz in battle a few months earlier, was its next highest-ranking officer. The others would follow his lead. He seemed to take an age to consider his options, until Ionas thought he couldn't bear the suspense any longer.

Jurten's patience ran out first. 'Anything to say, captain?'

Voigt nodded at length. 'Yes, sir. I think... I'm sure we all need time to reflect upon what we have just learned.' There was a general murmur of agreement. 'I would respectfully ask that you take no further action tonight.'

'Did I not make it clear,' Jurten growled, 'that this is my–'

'I'm sorry, sir,' Voigt interrupted, more forcefully, 'but now we know the truth, we cannot turn a blind eye to it. The Emperor also judges those who fail to act. Perhaps we may convene tomorrow to discuss the matter in depth?'

It seemed to Ionas, who knew the colonel best, that he was beginning to waver. Voigt had struck to the heart of his own doubts, and there was no Greel here to reassure him. Then the captain pushed the issue: 'In the meantime, we should seal up the silo and–'

'No,' the colonel thundered. 'There is nothing to discuss.'

'Sir, I must insist that–'

'I have set out our options and explained my thinking to you. I warn you, don't push me any further. Unless one of you has a better solution to offer? A miracle cure for all our problems?' Jurten glared at each of his officers in turn. Then he rounded on his adjutant. 'How about you, Lieutenant Ionas? You seem to think you have all the answers. No?'

'I only wish I did, sir.'

'Then I expect you, all of you, to keep the vows you made when you signed up to the Emperor's Imperial Guard. I am your commanding officer. I will decide our strategy, and you will implement my orders to the…'

He trailed off, unexpectedly. Ionas followed his narrowed eyes and saw that Voigt had drawn his pistol. His heart leapt into his throat. This was the moment he had known would come. The moment upon which the fate of his world hung.

'Don't do this, Voigt,' Jurten threatened in a throaty whisper.

'I'm sorry, colonel, but I have no choice either. I am relieving you of your command.'

'On what grounds?'

'On suspicion of treason against the Golden Throne, sir.'

The colonel's eyes bulged. His nostrils flared. His face turned red.

Then, just as Ionas thought he would explode, he seemed to get a grip on himself. 'That is within your rights,' Jurten conceded.

'Your weapons please, sir,' said Voigt, 'and I meant what I said. We will discuss this further. Tomorrow. Once we've had time to think.'

Jurten handed over his pistol and chainsword. Ionas took them, hardly able to look at him. He felt like the traitor that in Jurten's eyes he surely was. He expected the colonel to remonstrate with him, to shout him down with a few withering words, but he said nothing. Voigt lowered his gun. He decreed that Jurten would be confined to his quarters. Voigt himself and three more officers would escort him to them. The rest would stay behind to deal with the silo's closure.

Jurten complied with a meekness that Ionas had never seen in him before. He would have preferred it if the colonel *had* ranted and raved. He had never imagined that he would ever see him so defeated.

They emerged from the missile silo together. Jurten walked a short way ahead of the others. Voigt's pistol remained in its holster. No onlooker would have known anything was wrong, but for a certain stiffness in the officers' postures.

Voigt commandeered an armoured groundcar. He voxed ahead for the roadblock to be cleared for them. As he did so, Ionas caught a glint in Jurten's eye. He saw his lips moving as he muttered a command, a single word, into his comm-bead.

'Down!' Ionas yelled, as gunfire cracked around him.

Much of it was concentrated upon Voigt, who was caught in the open. Las-beams glanced off his armour, but one punched through his temple, and he crumpled. Another officer fell too; a third dropped to her knees, cast her weapon aside and raised her hands.

Ionas had dived behind the open truck and drawn his pistol, but there must have been at least six snipers, in niches in the rock walls looking down on him. He couldn't get a bead on any of them. He had only one viable target.

Jurten stood ramrod straight, unmoving, as beams sizzled past his ears. Ionas knew what he had to do.

Had he been more confident, had faster reflexes, more battle-field experience, he might have done it too. Before he could act, his weapon was shot from his hands, stinging his fingers. A rough voice behind him said, 'Come with us please, sir,' and troopers hauled him to his feet. Ionas assured them that he wouldn't try to resist them, but their grips upon his forearms didn't slacken.

The other surviving officer had been picked up too. She was bundled into the waiting groundcar. Ionas thought he was going to join her. Then Jurten gestured at the sergeant in charge of him, crooking his finger. He found himself dragged to where his commander waited, eyes glowering out of the shadow of his cap's brim.

Jurten's tone was deceptively mild. 'What deal did you make with Krause?'

Ionas saw no point in lying to him. 'He said he would let the rest of us, civilians and all, leave Krieg if I gave you to him.'

'And you agreed to this?'

'No.' He looked Jurten in the eye. He had never felt as brave as he did in that moment. It occurred to him that having no hope meant that neither was there anything to fear. 'But I should have done. I would have done. It would have been the lesser of two evils.'

A sergeant had retrieved Jurten's laspistol from Captain Voigt's body. The colonel clicked his fingers and the weapon was placed in his gloved hand.

'I wish it to be noted,' said Ionas, raising his voice so that all around could hear him, 'that what I did, I did for our world, and for the–'

Jurten shot him in the head.

'Disappointed?' asked General Krause.

His light image stood on the podium opposite Jurten. He tugged on his uniform jacket and straightened his cap.

Jurten didn't know what he meant, so waited for him to explain. *'You must have expected to be facing a monster by now,'* said Krause. *'Some misguided mutant, with a body as twisted as his soul. In fact, I am healthier than I have ever been.'*

'Not all mutations are visible,' Jurten growled.

'You need to believe that, I know. Either that or accept that your masters – our masters once – lied to us all those years. We can be free.'

'I wanted to tell you face to face,' said Colonel Jurten, 'that the deal you made with my adjutant is no longer valid. Lieutenant Ionas is dead.'

'Oh,' said Krause, unconcerned, *'was that his name?'*

'What happens next,' said Jurten, 'is on your head.'

And with that, he stepped down from his podium and marched out of the room.

He wasn't surprised to find Greel waiting for him outside. He always seemed to appear when Jurten's thoughts were troubled, always lurking in the corners of his new subterranean command centre. 'The traitor general refused to back down?' he said. It sounded more like a statement than a question.

'I saw it would be futile to ask him,' the colonel replied.

Greel nodded sagely. 'Then you've made your decision?' Seeing Jurten's grimace, he urged, 'I know how difficult this must be for you, but–'

The colonel flared. 'You don't know, Greel. Only flesh and blood can truly know.'

'–but prevarication will not change the facts of the matter. What have you learned today – in the past few months, for that matter – that has made any difference?'

'Krieg is my home.'

'What do you imagine a further delay might accomplish?'

'I was born here. Here is where I learned to love the Emperor. I prayed in the churches of this world, trained in its drill halls. I took a wife here. My daughter… Sabella… My daughter lived and died here.' Jurten closed his eyes and swallowed hard.

'Ionas was right,' he sighed, at length.

As always, he couldn't see Greel's expression. He knew from his silence, though, that he was surprised. A scribe emerged from a nearby room and two technicians scurried past them. They stepped into a pool of shadow beneath a faulty lumoglobe and waited until they had privacy again. Then, in a low murmur, the colonel continued.

'Ionas was right, that one missile cannot end this war.'

'The traitors could even track its launch trajectory, in which case…'

'Krieg is my home,' repeated Jurten, 'but it is diseased. Chaos has infected this world and corrupted its people. I hoped… I prayed that we might yet stem its inexorable spread. Cut out the Chaos tumour before the damage it wrought was irreversible. That false hope stayed my hand when perhaps… perhaps with a clearer head I might have acted.'

'No one has ever doubted your commitment to your cause.'

'But what do I do when that isn't enough?' demanded Jurten. 'I had to look into Krause's eyes today. I had to see what I have always known, that he is as committed to his beliefs as I am to mine. I had to know that there is no hope for redemption. If this world was ever to rise up against its leaders' heresy, it would have happened long ago. Instead, I find the Chaos taint has spread even into my own ranks, even to those closest to me.'

'The traitors will not cease the fight,' said Greel, 'as long as one of them yet lives.'

'Then, much as it pains me to say this,' said Jurten, 'Krieg is not my home any longer. My world, the world I knew, is lost. I cannot save it.'

Greel bowed his head. 'I concur.'

Jurten turned to him, eyes narrowed. 'How long have you known? Don't try to deny it, archmagos. You have been preparing for this moment since the day we came to Krieg. Since long before that, I shouldn't wonder. Since you first invited yourself to join my Imperial regiment. You have always been here to lend me counsel when I lost sight of the path to take. Has it always been so clear to you where that path would inevitably lead?'

'Rarely have I told you anything,' said Greel, 'that you didn't already know.'

Jurten took another moment to meditate on the truth of that statement.

'I have a vehicle waiting,' Greel prompted him at last, 'to return us to the silo. Are you ready to give the order, Colonel Jurten?'

He swallowed dryly. 'I am.'

They walked together. Jurten's feet felt heavier with every step he took, but he had no doubts any longer. He was resolved to do his duty. What other option did he have?

'The missiles will launch at one minute to midnight,' he declared, 'to mark the end of the holy day. No warning will be sent. There has been too much talk already. This world will be cleansed of its manifold sins by fire and fury.'

'And by the white heat of technology,' murmured Greel behind his hood.

'Today is the Feast of the Emperor's Ascension, after all,' growled Colonel Jurten. 'Today, tradition dictates that we should offer Him a sacrifice.'

THE FOG OF WAR

The word had come down to the troops that morning. A ship had arrived to collect them. It had already entered the system and would be in planetary orbit within hours. They wouldn't see another sunset on this world.

Sergeant Renick's squad had pulled their last laborious shift in the trenches. They were packing up their meagre possessions and striking their tents. The Imperial encampment was being dismantled around them. Technicians and servitors took the temporary buildings apart, stacking their walls on pallets for loading onto waiting trucks.

For a week now, the sky had been streaked with the contrails of drop-ships, converging upon the capital hive on the northern horizon. The partial evacuation of this world was under way. Renick couldn't keep her gaze from drifting upwards. Never had she been so eager to see the ships, although this time they would signify failure.

Heavy, dark clouds prevented her from seeing much. Cold

drops of rain spotted her cheeks. A Krieg Earthshaker was dragged past her on a trailer, hauled out of its emplacement with considerable effort. A formation of Demolishers and the last surviving Baneblade nudged out into no-man's-land to keep up the shelling of Hive Arathron. There had been little return fire from the orks in several days.

Nor had there been word of the kill team in their Hades, who had tunnelled their way towards the hive ten days ago. At least, no news had filtered down to Renick's level. Whatever their mission had been, she could only assume that – like everything else they had tried – it had been a failure.

It had been six days since Inquisitor Ven Bruin's last communication.

The Krieg colonel had briefed Interrogator Ferran in private. 'The kill team made it back to the Hades drill too late,' he had explained.

'The xenos had found it?'

'And pulled it apart. They are seeking another way out of the occupied hive. They were able to find a long-range vox-caster, intact, but they couldn't speak for long.'

'In case the xenos traced the source of their transmission,' Ferran had deduced. 'And did… did the inquisitor have anything else to say? About…?'

'They found the vault,' the colonel had confirmed without guile, 'and the weapons within, just as the inquisitor expected. They reached them before the xenos did.'

'Thanks be to the Emperor.'

'Ven Bruin believes, however, that the orks will not be very far behind them.'

Ferran's brow had furrowed. 'I see.'

'I have appraised Naval command of these events, and have

received an update from them. Exterminatus will take place approximately nine days from now. Evacuation efforts will be stepped up in the meantime.' The Krieg colonel had sounded like he was discussing some trivial point of administration, rather than the death of a planet.

Still, Ferran had sensed that he was holding something back. 'Unless?'

'Unless,' the colonel had replied in a tone heavy with unspoken meaning, 'something happens to alter our situation before then.'

Ferran felt he was getting better at reading the Krieg, after all.

Ven Bruin's time was almost up. A groundcar had arrived to take Ferran and the rest of the inquisitor's retinue north, to the capital hive, to its space port. He was to share transport with the Astra Militarum troops, at least until they had safely cleared the system.

'As soon as I am able,' he had confided in Majellus, 'I intend to return to the ordo. My first official act as an inquisitor will be to convene an enquiry. I shall be the first witch hunter since Larreth to visit Krieg.' He would know all the secrets that its Death Korps hid behind their masks. He was certain that, so far, he had barely scratched the surface.

He had taken out his earpiece, but a sudden flurry of activity around him told him that something was amiss. Sergeants and watchmasters yelled for their squads to form up on them. They dropped what they were doing, heading out towards the trenches. To their credit, neither Krieg nor Cadian showed the weariness they must have felt. Not in front of Ferran, anyhow.

He stopped a Cadian sergeant to ask her what was happening. 'The xenos, sir,' replied Renick. 'The orks. They've broken out of the hive in force. They're mounting a full-on attack on the trenches!'

* * *

It had begun with movements in the hive's ruined outskirts.

The spotters in the forward trench had alerted the gunners at once. Even through their magnoculars, however – and through a thin film of drizzle – they could see little. Damaged structures swayed, some falling, even where the shells of the Imperial cannons hadn't struck them. As if something massive, something powerful, were bulldozing through them.

Support structures crumpled. Whole levels crashed into each other. For a moment, it seemed as if the xenos in the hive, whatever they had been up to, had buried themselves.

Then a figure, some sixty-plus feet high, emerged from a cloud of dust.

It resembled a pot-bellied parody of an ork itself, with jagged metal fangs and piercing green lights for eyes. It was built up from layer upon layer of overlapping, mismatched metal plates, with all manner of weapons grafted to them.

It thrust a stumpy leg out in front of it and planted a metal foot in the softened earth. Its bulging torso teetered unsteadily forward as the leg bore the strain of its unbalanced mass. Its second foot crashed down in front of the first.

A select few Krieg grenadiers – along with their colonel, hearing a description via vox – were put in mind of the majestic Imperial Titans, which stalked across battlefields dispensing the Emperor's justice. This was a typical junk heap replica, of course. Titans were controlled from within by highly skilled crews. Orks rode the shoulders and hips of this one, and more could be seen inside its giant, gnashing mouth. They shook their fists, striking up a belligerent chant that could be heard across the plain: 'Stompa! Stompa! Stompa!'

The 'Stompa' lumbered forwards with ponderous strides, each twenty yards long. The Krieg gunners focused fire upon it, as did the tanks behind them. In exchange it spewed out bullets, shells and screaming rockets. It didn't seem to bother aiming, but it wreaked devastation all the same. A Demolisher tank was blown apart. An Earthshaker crew was lost in a terrible instant as a rocket streaked into their emplacement.

'Take out its legs!' came the cry from a Krieg captain, repeated and amplified by the watchmasters. Cannon sights were lowered accordingly, and when the leviathan's right foot next descended, flame trails converged upon the broad metal stanchion above it.

Armour plates were ripped away by blasts, exposing a skeletal framework of girders and wiring. Sparks erupted from the Stompa's right knee joint, and its huge head swayed this way and that as if in confusion.

It kept on coming, trailing black exhaust smoke from pipes in its rear. Its giant strides whittled down the distance to its sunken targets. Still the Korpsmen held their ground. The slain gunners were efficiently replaced; a new crew coaxed their spluttering cannon back into fitful service.

Almost before they knew it, the leviathan had reached them. Its giant head loomed above their heads. Its eyes' green beams swept over the huddled, masked figures like search-lumens. A hundred lasguns cracked, and a couple of orks plunged from the Stompa's shoulder, but mostly power packs were expended in vain.

A massive metal foot kicked an Earthshaker onto its back and stamped on it, shattering its barrel. Its crew recovered what ammunition they could and ran, but in place of a left arm the Stompa had a chainsword, so large it dwarfed the average human, spitting out gobbets of oil as it ground its gleaming teeth. With a lurch, the Stompa stooped and, with a mighty swipe, it cut a swathe through flak armour, flesh, muscle and bone.

A metal fist thrust forward, and a flamer attached to its right forearm swept along the trench. Two more Earthshaker crews were overtaken by a river of flame, and burnt to ashes. At the same time, hatches in the Stompa's torso flew open, and xenos streamed through them in their scores. They clambered and slid down the Stompa's uneven stepped sides.

Krieg and Cadian soldiers rushed into the trenches from the camp. They clashed with those attempting to get out. Their orders changed abruptly, officers now yelling at them to pull back for the Emperor's sake. At the same time, others yelled that they mustn't let any xenos past them. Grenadiers set up launchers to fling grenades at the looming leviathan, but they were no substitute for the cannons broken or abandoned.

Their best hope lay with their remaining artillery above ground. Four Demolishers roared towards the Stompa. They blasted it with everything they had, exhausting half their ammunition in a furious minute. It reeled and looked as if it might fall backwards, but it managed to right itself. Another huge stride brought its right foot down – upon a tunnel roof, which collapsed and crushed a Krieg squad underneath it.

The foot turned under the Stompa's unimaginable weight. It crumpled and the stress blew out the damaged joint above it. The Stompa crashed onto one knee in the trenches, its left foot still mired in the mud above. It almost tore itself in two right up the middle, plates sloughing from it in a veritable avalanche.

Its weapons were still active, though. Seeing soldiers teeming through the furrows around it like insects, it spat bullets and belched flames at them, while targeting its larger shells at the encroaching Imperial vehicles.

Orks also teemed through the trenches, not minding in the slightest that the Stompa killed many of them too. They howled with bloodthirsty glee as they ran down their fleeing enemies, some of whom turned to give them what they craved. The

Krieg fought with more savage abandon than usual, born of the knowledge that this would likely be their final battle. Even if they slew these xenos, they would only draw the leviathan's attention.

The Stompa's largest weapon protruded slightly off-centre from its chest: a colossal blast cannon, its report loud enough to split the heavens, its recoil throwing back the Stompa's head and sending its body into spasm. Its aim was appalling, but it could afford to be. Even a close miss was enough to blow a Demolisher off its tracks and onto its side. A direct hit blew the main turret off another tank and broiled the crew inside.

The leviathan was stuck in a half-reclining position. It thrashed its arms and pressed its one hand into the ground, seeking leverage to push itself back upright. The tank crews, with their colonel's voice booming in their ears, were determined to deny it.

One crew, their guns either mangled or run dry, bailed out but for their driver – who controlled the single weapon left to them, the Demolisher itself. He ran a gamut of exploding shells as he pointed his tank at the Stompa and stamped on the accelerator pedal.

The impact had force enough to crack the Stompa's wrist and cause it to slump again. It was well and truly stuck now, but still fighting for all it was worth. Inside, sweating ork grots desperately fed a greedy furnace. Meks rushed to patch hydraulic leaks, while pipes around them burst and showered them with boiling water.

A pair of Vulture gunships, scrambled in haste, flew overhead. The blast cannon roared and brought down one in a flaming wreck. The other dropped something round and black, which plummeted towards the Stompa's head. The orks in its mouth howled at the bomb as if to intimidate it into retreat. Met by a hail of bullets, it detonated prematurely, but still with a wave of concussive force and heat sufficient to melt its target's teeth.

A Goliath construction truck careened through the hive's outskirts.

Inquisitor Ven Bruin crouched in the compact vehicle's back, concealed by a creaking canvas awning. He clung to a ventilator grille to keep from being thrown against the sides. He was hungry, grimy and exhausted.

Beside him crouched a Krieg grenadier, the second of his kill team's surviving three members. The third was up front in the sealed-off driver's compartment. They had already sped past a small mob of orks, which had howled in excitement at the sound of squealing tyres and run alongside them for as long as they were able. Too late had they realised that the truck was in enemy hands, firing guns and hurling axes after it in vain.

The ork Stompa's egress from the hive had cleared a path of devastation they could follow. They didn't stop for squigs, splattering several against the truck's front grille, while others slipped beneath its wheels. They had resolved that, this time, nothing would turn them back. This wasn't their first escape attempt but it would be their last, succeed or fail.

Another mob appeared in front of them.

The driver put his foot down and bowled through the xenos like skittles. Some reacted fast enough to batter the Goliath as it passed them. A couple leapt onto it, finding handholds on its empty weapons turret. The driver threw his wheel around and scraped them off against a rockcrete base that had once supported a statue.

More guns rattled, and a bullet blew out the rear left tyre. Something heavy hit the roof above Ven Bruin's head, making it bow. A hefty green fist punched through the flimsy canvas, its knuckles almost scraping his left temple. The ork must have leapt from some vantage point above them. The driver swerved, trying to throw it off, one wheel rim striking sparks off asphalt.

The other grenadier strafed the roof, his hellgun shredding it but dislodging their unwanted stowaway. It slid off the back of the truck but somehow caught itself and, riding the axle, tore its way aboard. It was met by more blasts from the hellgun and from the inquisitor's equally aptly named inferno pistol. The next sharp turn flung a smouldering xenos corpse out of the truck, head first into a mound of rubble.

'Mission accomplished, inquisitor,' voxed the driver from his cab. 'We've made it through the hive walls out onto the plain. I see fighting ahead of us.'

Ven Bruin heard other vox-channels filling up with voices, as they entered the Imperial casters' range. 'Steer clear of it,' he ordered. He identified himself into his comm-bead and demanded to speak to the Krieg colonel.

He heard his terse voice only seconds later. 'Inquisitor?'

He relayed the message that he had himself received less than an hour ago. He boiled it down to five words, knowing it would be enough, fearing he might be overheard even over the secure command channel. 'Orks have found the vault,' he said.

'Acknowledged,' said the colonel after the briefest of pauses. 'What is your situation? Are you able to make it to safety?'

Ven Bruin confirmed that he could if the Emperor willed it so. He voxed his driver to head north and the Goliath veered left, the wheel with the shredded tyre scraping the ground again. They left behind the muffled sounds of cannon blasts and bombs. A single gun, behind Hive Arathron's intact northern wall, spat a few shells in their direction, one landing close enough to rock their suspension, but they soon outpaced this hazard too.

For the first time in ten days, Ven Bruin saw a future for

himself. He thought he might see his retirement, after all. He wasn't sure how to feel about that.

Six Krieg grenadiers had died to keep him alive, and had seemed grateful for the chance. Constable Hallam had given her life for him too. When feral underhive-dwellers with guns had pinned them down, she had nominated herself as the most expendable of them. She had run out and drawn the snipers' fire away before the inquisitor could stop her – before he could decide if he *wanted* to stop her.

He tried not to think about the fate of the seventh grenadier…

He wondered where his acolytes were, if they were even still alive. He wondered what they knew, what even Ferran had guessed, about his mission into Arathron. Did any of them have the slightest inkling of the horror about to be unleashed?

What would they think if they knew – *when they knew* – what he had done? Or rather, what he had allowed to be done, if that distinction even mattered. Would they think him deserving of the sacrifices made for him by so many noble souls?

Ferran was fighting in the trenches.

He was more used to facing human heretics than ravening xenos, but this was where the Emperor had placed him. His warriors accompanied him, the crusader Majellus chief among them. The rest of his acolytes, he had sent away.

So far, no ork had made it through the Death Korpsmen around him. He hadn't seen the Krieg in action close up before and he was impressed. They fought with skill and grim determination against foes larger and stronger than they were. This allowed him to stand back and choose his targets judiciously. He fired his bolt pistol only when he had a clear shot, and took satisfaction in blowing out the deviant brains of one xenos after another.

The massive Krieg Baneblade passed over his head on trench rails.

From snatches of vox chatter, he understood that the Stompa was damaged and had fallen, but was still a considerable threat. The hope was that the Baneblade could deliver the coup de grâce to it. In the meantime, with their leviathan distracted, the orks' attack was faltering. The Imperial forces had the breathing space they needed to regroup.

They were starting to beat the xenos back.

Then came an order from the Krieg colonel: *'All non-Krieg forces are to disengage from combat and pull back to the encampment.'* Ferran frowned. He had just begun to see a path to victory. Why would the colonel jeopardise that now?

A possible answer occurred to him, and it chilled him to the soul.

He almost didn't see the ork pounding towards him, snorting like a bull. His warriors closed ranks before it, protecting him. It slashed one with the edge of its axe, before reeling under a concentrated barrage of las-fire.

There were more orks behind it, though, and others coming up along a tunnel to Ferran's other side. He found himself suddenly surrounded. He couldn't understand how it had happened. The Krieg had seemingly melted away. One warrior, an Astra Militarum veteran, stumbled, and three orks fell upon him with claws and fangs. An axe swung too close to Ferran's throat for comfort. He drew his power sword and activated its energy blade.

Another of his warriors was a combat-servitor. It was capable of little more than trailing around after him, identifying threats and shooting them with an unwieldy gun arm. It planted heavy feet in the earth, head twitching as it gauged distances and bearings. Its arm snapped from side to side, loosing off shots that almost always struck their targets.

An ork rolled, with surprising agility, under every shot. Coming up beneath the servitor's chin, it thrust a stikkbomb into its gun barrel, then dived away from it. Though servitors felt no emotion, something like an expression of surprise crossed this one's face in the instant before its arm exploded. It didn't die immediately. Robbed of its single function, it stood still, blinking, bleeding, helpless.

By this time, Ferran was fully immersed in the fray. His sword parted a stone axe from its head. Its wielder tried to stab him with the splintered haft, which brought it close enough for him to plunge his blade into its stomach. His nostrils were twitching from the xenos' mossy odour; he almost retched at the stink of their blood.

Another acolyte had fallen, without him seeing it. More xenos squeezed into the narrow trench. He was backed up as far as its wall, his allies scattered. He wasn't too proud to vox for support. He gave his approximate coordinates. Hearing no reply, he voxed again: 'God-Emperor damn it, we're being overwhelmed back here!'

'*My squad is pinned down, Interrogator Ferran.*'

'*–too many orks between us and your–*'

'*–coming under heavy fire, but we shall endeavour to reach you as soon as we–*'

The excuses tumbled over each other. He had no reason to believe that they weren't entirely genuine. No reason whatsoever. '*I can't read these men at all,*' as he had told Inquisitor Ven Bruin, '*and not only because of the masks they wear.*'

Another ork yanked another stikkbomb out of a chain bandolier. It primed it, but was tackled by a warrior acolyte before it could throw it. They wrestled on the ground. The xenos swiftly got the better of its slighter foe, its hands around his throat. The grenade exploded between them, shrapnel ripping through both their bodies.

Ferran emptied his pistol's magazine, but couldn't get a moment to reload. He holstered the gun to grip his sword two-handed. Beset by three opponents at once, he could only hope to parry the crushing blows of their axes, clubs and fists. Leering faces filled his vision as ork stink filled his lungs. Inevitably, he took a glancing blow from a nail-studded club, and felt it might have cracked a rib.

An ork's head suddenly exploded. The brute's body toppled, to reveal a bloodied warrior behind it with a smoking pistol. And another ork behind her...

Ferran yelled out a warning, too late. The bit of an ork axe burst out of the warrior's chest. Blood welled from her mouth as her eyes froze over.

Majellus and Ferran fought their way to each other's side. There were no others left. The crusader carried a sword like the interrogator's own and a suppression shield, though the latter's charge was drained. Ferran counted half a dozen orks left standing, half of them wounded. It was just conceivable that they might hold them off long enough for help to arrive. *If indeed help is coming...*

He blocked another double-handed axe smash, which would have cleaved his head if it had struck him. An ork with a bleeding throat stood back, pumping bullets from a large black gun with a rotating barrel. Majellus blocked most with his shield, some ricocheting into the other xenos. He braced his back against the wall and struck between an ork's legs with his boot. It doubled up, groaning, and he brought his blade down on its neck.

Ferran slashed at an ork, tearing through its leather jerkin, drawing blood. A bullet had nicked his shoulder, and he felt it beginning to freeze. He whirled his sword in front of him, painting the air with light patterns, creating a defensive barrier into which he prayed the xenos wouldn't venture, just trying to buy himself a moment's respite. It wasn't enough. An axe blade swiped across his stomach, cutting through his armour, catching in his cloak and tearing through this too, tightening it around his throat.

It was in that moment that Interrogator Ferran lost hope.

Majellus had slain another of the orks, but it was not enough to save him. 'You can break one man,' he gasped as he was beaten to the ground, 'but you can never break the... the spirit of... mankind. As long as we have faith that... that the Emperor–'

Regrettably, he lost his tongue almost as soon as he had found it. An ork raised an axe above its head and slammed it into the crusader's chest. Another tried to snatch his power sword from him as he grunted his last. It gripped it by its coruscating blade and severed three of its own fingers. In other circumstances, that would have brought Ferran some pleasure.

A heavy, blunt instrument, he didn't see what, struck his right wrist and broke it. His own sword spun out of his hands. He reached across his body with his left hand, fumbling for his pistol and a fresh magazine for it. He sent a desperate prayer to his lips, but had no time to voice it. He was overrun and over-whelmed before he knew it.

An axe blade thunked into his shoulder and more bones splintered. Claws raked across his stomach. Blow upon shattering blow rained down upon him, until he couldn't feel them any longer through the fire that lit up his every nerve ending.

He heard laspistols, from somewhere a long way away.

He couldn't feel his legs. He slid down the trench wall, into a crumpled heap.

An ork, a single ork – he didn't know what had happened to the others – pinned him with one knee like a tree trunk. It took his head between a pair of meaty hands and tried to crush it. His left ear popped and went deaf. The ork threw its fanged mouth open and spattered him with drool. He thought it might try to bite his head off at the neck.

Then the ork was snatched away from him, he didn't know to where.

Ferran thanked the Emperor that his ordeal was over, that he could now know peace. His eyes closed and he drifted away.

An insistent shaking brought him back. He opened his eyes only with the utmost reluctance. They were met by the sight of a skull staring blank-eyed down at him. His heart froze in existential fear, until he recognised the faceplate of a Krieg grenadier; then he felt hope, but only for an instant.

He saw more blank Krieg masks above the first one. A whole squad had gathered around him. They had come, after all. Too late to save him, though. Someone was saying a prayer for him. He couldn't tell which of the Krieg it was, or if the words were only in his head.

He couldn't bear to die, he realised, while questions still burnt in his breast. He tried to voice them, but his tongue was swollen and blood clogged his throat. He managed to splutter out a single word before his eyes closed for the final time.

'*Why…?*' he pleaded.

It was a fitting last word for Interrogator Ferran.

Renick's squad had barely made it into the trenches when they received their new orders. She turned them round at once, thinking something must have happened back at camp, for why else would they have been pulled back there?

They saw orks only from a distance, fighting Korpsmen. 'I hate that we're turning our backs on them again,' Rask grumbled.

He cheered up a little as a pair of squigs bounded out of the melee and pursued them, snapping at the Cadians' ankles. 'Deal with them quickly,' snarled Renick. She had come to see them as merely a nuisance, but one she could have done without at that moment.

One squig was swiftly stabbed and bludgeoned to death. The other fled with a warbling shriek after Creed neatly sheared off its ear with a las-beam. Renick had to restrain the other troopers from running it down. 'We don't have time,' she reminded them.

She chivvied them up a trench ladder, one by one. The squig reappeared as she climbed up after them. Its mouth stretched almost as wide as its body. It flew at her and clamped its teeth on to her trailing foot. They bit through her boot, into her flesh. She tried to shake the clinging creature off her, slamming its head repeatedly into the wall.

The troopers above her pointed their lasguns down at it, but couldn't be sure that their beams wouldn't strike her instead. Renick let go of the ladder, fell the short distance to the trench floor. The squig's grip on her didn't slacken.

She rolled onto her back, snatched her own gun out of its sling. She drove its butt into her attacker's gnarled teeth until they broke. It tumbled away from her, affording the others clear shots at it, which they gladly took.

Her left foot was a mass of blood and protruding bone. Trooper Rask dropped back into the trench alongside her and booted the squig's scorched body away from them with a sneer. 'I'll vox for a stretcher,' Creed called down from above, but Renick shook her head.

'I can make it back to camp,' she insisted, 'if the rest of you help me.'

She popped a stimm tablet, which numbed her pain some-what as adrenaline flooded her system. With Creed pulling at her from above and Rask pushing from beneath, she made it up the short ladder, with much effort.

Little remained of the Imperial encampment by now. The

eastern horizon looked empty. Renick's injury slowed her squad down, allowing others to stream past them. Each squad was met by a junior officer with a data-slate. They were checked in and loaded into Chimera armoured transports, which then headed northwards in a convoy. 'I don't understand,' said Rask. 'Where are we being sent?'

The clamour of combat continued behind them, unabated. The trapped ork Stompa still fired its massive cannon, each blast making Renick wince. She tried to turn and look, but couldn't because of the troopers to each side of her, supporting her.

The junior officer took one look at Renick's foot and called for a chirurgeon, who guided her towards an old, beaten-up Samaritan-variant Chimera, made for ferrying wounded. 'I'll do what I can for you en route,' she promised.

'En route to where?' asked Renick, weakly.

'To the space port.'

She knew she should have expected that answer. Still, she couldn't quite believe it. 'We're leaving the Krieg to fight the xenos?'

The medic shrugged. 'Those are the colonel's orders.'

Creed and Rask helped her into the back of the Samaritan, then took their leave of her reluctantly. Renick heard engines screaming overhead and stole one last glimpse of the overcast sky. She saw the bright contrails of drop-ships streaking through the clouds.

In a rock-walled room, buried deep beneath the remnants of a once proud city, a lone Krieg soldier stood and waited.

He listened to the sound of the heavy drill above him. It had been whirring, grinding, shrieking, for eighty minutes now. It had paused only once, for a short time, during which he had heard a grenade going off.

When the drilling had begun, he had broadcast a warning over the general vox-channel. He had no way of knowing if it had been heard. His lumen had run out of power days ago, but the soldier didn't need it. He knew every inch of this vault by now. He knew where each of the six grey cylinders lay. He had clamped a magnetic krak grenade to each of them. Three more hung from his belt, while he cradled another in his arms.

He thought the drill was getting closer. Its vibrations travelled through the shelving racks around him and rattled his teeth. Occasionally, one of the cylinders would tick softly as if counting down the final seconds of the soldier's life.

At last the drill sputtered to a halt; but then came another sound, even more piercing and more dreadful. The sound of metal being wrenched and torn.

This continued for a few minutes longer, then a bestial cheer was raised. The soldier knew the hatch had been removed, because the xenos' voices howled around the shaft beneath it. The cheers died down, replaced by murmurs of wonder and anticipation. Then there came angry bellows and yelps of resentment, and a scuffle broke out.

The soldier waited in the darkness.

The xenos' fight was settled, and an iron rung creaked beneath a heavy brute's tread. He heard laboured, snorting breathing.

No one can know for sure what the Krieg soldier thought and felt in that moment. Was he proud to follow in the footsteps of his world's greatest hero? Or did he consider this one more sin to add to his people's ledger?

Light spilled into the room. It was a threatening red light, faint at first, becoming stronger as it felt its way across the floor to lick at the soldier's toes.

A figure stepped down from one of the ladders beyond the arched doorway: an ork with a looted spiked helmet and a glowing red augmetic eye. It turned to survey its new surroundings. It stiffened as it saw the soldier waiting in the shadows. Its lips curled away from its fangs. It hefted a gun the size of a small cannon.

And perhaps it saw what else lay in the shadows.

Perhaps it saw the trap that it had sprung and perhaps, just perhaps, in that fateful moment, for the first and last time in its life, that ork knew fear.

The Krieg soldier pulled the pin out of his grenade.

...

THE PURGING

A spotter, a young trooper, in the trenches saw them first.

Three sleek black rockets shot out from the ruins of Hive Ferrograd. Before he could activate his comm-bead, they were followed by three more. And then by three more. And three more. And three more.

The trooper's voice trembled as he raised the alert. 'At least a dozen… no, more like twenty… at least twenty of them.'

They had launched from somewhere deep in the hive's heart. As they crested its skeletal, dead spires, their paths diverged. Each missile arced away in a different direction, creating a fountain pattern of contrails behind them.

The trooper followed the closest through his magnoculars. Around him, his comrades scrambled for cover in their dugouts. Perched halfway up a trench ladder, he felt suddenly exposed. He willed his frozen legs to move.

Before they could, he realised that the missiles were still climbing. The trenches weren't their targets. For a second, he thought they might streak off into space, to threaten Krieg's defenders in their perpetual orbits, but no, they were levelling off.

'The hives,' he breathed over an open vox-channel. Was it possible that they could reach the other hives?

Hive Auros' augurs saw that very possibility, and alarms began to sound.

General Krause was halfway to bed when he was called back to his war room. 'On their current trajectory,' a breathless tech explained, 'one missile will strike in the south-eastern residential sector, third or fourth quadrant, while another–'

'Intercept them!' he demanded.

'We've scrambled the Lightnings, sir,' an officer reported. 'They'll try to shoot down the missiles before they hit.'

Krause was no longer listening. He elbowed a pair of aides aside and hunched over the augur array. He took in the blinking icons that represented each missile's position, numbers scrolling and updating beneath each of them. As they neared the edges of the main display, it zoomed out to keep them all in frame.

With a two-fingered swipe, he recentred the display upon Hive Auros. 'Send out an air raid warning across the at-risk area,' he instructed.

'Already done, sir.'

This is nothing to worry about, he told himself. *I imagine Jurten has been planning this for months, a gesture for his precious Emperor's day. But our walls remain strong. How much damage can a handful of missiles wreak?*

He tried not to think about the warning he'd been given, only hours before. *'You think I fear what you might do to us?'* He tried not to think about old rumours, dismissed long ago. Rumours of ancient, buried vaults and of their contents…

If Jurten really thought he had a chance, he'd have targeted military installations. Instead, he hopes to claim civilian lives. One final, futile gasp of defiance from an enemy who knows he has been beaten!

The trooper screamed in pain and fear.

He dropped his magnoculars and clutched his burning eyes. He tumbled down the ladder, landing in the trench on his back. He spluttered out a cry for help, but nobody came. He had been looking directly at a missile, magnified ten times, when it had exploded. The flash had been like nothing he had seen before.

It might have been the last thing he would ever see.

When hands clawed at him, the trooper fought them off by reflex. He heard voices, yelling and screaming, but dully as if through an armaglass barrier. His ears were deadened too. He put a hand to one and blood soaked into his glove. The high-pitched whine he could hear, he realised, was only inside his head.

The fire in his brain was subsiding, but he remained blind. All he could see was inky darkness, shot through with lightning patterns. He gave in to the hands and let them guide him, crawling painfully on elbows and knees. He tumbled into the shelter of a dugout, into the embrace of warm, sweaty bodies. 'I can't… can't see,' he repeated.

Someone mumbled a few words to him and must have seen his consternation, because he repeated them more loudly. 'I said, you and half the guys down here. It's just flash blindness, son. Should wear off in a minute or two, unless your optic nerve is scarred.'

But I was the only one looking through magnoculars, he thought. His face and neck smarted as if with a bad case of sunburn. 'What… what was that? What's happening?' he gasped.

'If you ask me, you're better off not seeing. It's like…' The voice was older, gravelly, belonging to a veteran sergeant. Most of the soldiers here were raw recruits, a skeleton crew sent out to man the trenches while the rest of their world partied.

'What is it?' the trooper demanded, feeling panic rising in his chest again.

'It looks like the end of the world.'

Inside the missile silo, there was absolute stillness and silence. Colonel Jurten raised his chin and stiffened his back. He would show no weakness, no failure of resolve, not even now. *Especially not now.*

Archmagos Greel stooped over the augurs, following the missiles' progress through Krieg's atmosphere. Shock waves had already rippled through the rock surrounding them, as through the precarious structures of Hive Ferrograd above them. The blast door in the roof had almost buckled as masonry had crashed down on top of it.

At last, Greel turned to face the colonel and reported, 'It is done.'

Jurten nodded. In a subdued tone, he thanked the few technicians who had remained with him. He had them shut off their machines. They had made the preparations, but it had been his finger on the trigger in the end. It could have been nobody else's.

He led a sombre procession out through the silo doors, which were closed and sealed behind him. The city was quiet too, far quieter than normal. Its residents slept off their day's libations, blissfully unaware, isolated in their subterranean bunkers. Jurten felt...

He tried not to feel anything at all.

He felt relieved. For how long had he borne the weight of an impossible choice upon his shoulders? That weight had lifted from him now. For good or ill, the decision had been taken, and there was no point in looking back.

This fragile silence would not last for long.

Centuries later and light years away, another world burnt in atomic fire.

'What in the name of the Throne hit us?' someone cried.

Sergeant Renick lay on a filthy Samaritan floor. Her head was bruised, but she felt no new broken bones. So sudden had the impact been that she hadn't had time to tense up, which had probably saved her.

She pushed herself up onto her elbows. Her plastered foot gave a shriek of protest. Her ears still rang from the explosion. The gurney upon which she had lain had fallen on top of her. Glass fragments showered her as she manhandled it aside. She recalled that the blacked-out windows in the ambulance's back doors had burst inwards.

She groaned as an elbow jabbed her ribs, winced as someone stumbled over her bad foot. The Samaritan's other occupants untangled themselves from each other. Aside from Renick's chirurgeon, there were two field medics and an unconscious Cadian trooper. One of the medics was bleeding profusely from his ear. The other reached the back doors, found them jammed and kicked them open.

A gust of hot, bitter, ashy wind stung Sergeant Renick's eyes.

She blinked until her vision cleared. She was propped up against the partition behind the driver's cab. She looked straight through the open doors, back the way they had just come. She blinked again in disbelief at what she saw.

She had thought they must have hit a mine, or been shelled by a cannon or bombed by a flyer. A conventional explosion. Instead, a great plume of thick, black smoke hung over the horizon to the south. It billowed outwards as it rose, so that more and more of the plain around it fell under its ominous shadow.

Renick heard a gasp of awe from someone behind her.

She couldn't quite take in the scale of it all. She didn't know how fast they had been travelling, how far they might have come. She couldn't see Hive Arathron at all. It had been engulfed. Did the fires reach as far as the trenches? As far as the camp? With no buildings left there, she couldn't tell, she had no point of reference.

'Is this... is this the start of it?' asked one of the medics.

She knew exactly what he meant. *Exterminatus.* Had they run out of time?

The Samaritan juddered and coughed as the driver failed to restart the engine. Renick forced herself to remember her training, to focus on practicalities. 'How far to the space port?'

'I don't know. A few miles, maybe,' responded the chirurgeon. 'Trouble is, we were one of the last vehicles out of camp. There's no one coming up behind us. I'm trying to raise someone, get a vehicle sent back for us, but–'

'But the vox-net is dead.' Renick could only hear static through her earpiece.

'I don't like the look of that cloud,' a medic murmured.

'And it's still spreading,' said Renick. 'If we can't get this Samaritan moving–'

'Proceed on foot, you mean? We have two casualties, sergeant, and only one gurney.'

'I saw a crutch back here.'

'And this patient is bleeding out again.' The chirurgeon knelt beside the unconscious shock trooper. 'He can't be moved. Frankly, even if I stay with him, without access to–'

Renick swallowed. 'Then we must leave him behind.'

'That is my decision to make, not yours,' the chirurgeon

admonished her. He cast his eyes downward. 'I am forced to concur, however.'

Renick tried to stand. She hated that a medic had to help her. The crutch was found and thrust into her hands. She tested her weight on it, gingerly, and was satisfied with the result. The driver turned the engine over once more, eliciting only a deep, metallic clunk and a deathly sounding rattle.

Renick faltered in the doorway of the Samaritan, her gaze drawn to the spreading cloud again. It seemed even larger than before, and already much closer.

'Shouldn't we stay with the ambulance?' one of the medics asked. 'At least we'd have some cover, rather than being caught out in the open.'

'I doubt it'd make much difference,' said Sergeant Renick firmly. 'If anyone wants to disagree with that assessment, feel free. But, right now, I don't want to know what happens when that cloud catches up with us, whether we have cover or not. I say we run. We run as fast as our good legs and this wooden prop will carry us – and we pray to the Emperor that He'll hold a drop-ship for us, and that we aren't already too late.'

Krieg's last feast day was over.

Even as midnight tolled, the first missile set light to the sky. For those unfortunate enough to bear witness to the spectacle, it seemed as if a score of new suns blazed fleetingly to life, only to consume themselves in that selfsame instant.

When their heat reached the surface, seconds later, it caused whole fields of wheat and corn to combust, while lakes directly underneath the missiles boiled dry.

Few people in the hive cities had a view of the sky. They heard the explosions all the same and felt them too, and some saw flashes of atomic light even in the lower-level gloom.

The brightest of days was swiftly followed by the darkest of all nights. Great clouds of smoke rolled in to steal the moon and stars away. Then the clouds were rent by jagged forks of lightning, thunder rumbled all the way around the globe, and rain began to fall.

In the trenches to the south of Hive Ferrograd's remains, a blind trooper couldn't see the rain, but he could hear it beating down. He cowered in his dugout, from the cries of his comrades caught outside.

Some had made a run for the armoured personnel carriers. Most of them hadn't made it. They returned with curses on their lips – some against the Emperor, of whom they had once sworn not to speak again – and with news that the rain was black and oily and it burnt.

Something stung the back of the blind trooper's hand. He yelped, causing everyone to start. 'You're sitting under a leak,' a voice muttered. He thought it was the sergeant again. 'It burnt through your glove. I'd draw your legs in too if I were you.'

He did as he was bade and hugged his knees. He gasped as he felt a drop of liquid creeping down his spine. It was cold, though. Sweat. It was just sweat.

He thought his vision might be returning. He was starting to make out vague shapes in the darkness. Then someone lit a match, and its light was like las-shots to both his eyes. He screwed them shut and listened to the urgent chatter around him.

'How long d'you think this is likely to–'

'–melted holes right through my armour–'

'–even the Gorgon's windscreen looked like it was bubbling and–'

'–told us this would happen, that if we defied the Emperor's will–'

'–must know what's happening out here. Surely they'll have to send us–'

The sergeant's voice, though quiet, somehow cut through all the others. 'I don't like the look of that roof much,' he said grimly, and a sudden hush fell upon the frightened young troopers around him as they raised their eyes upwards.

The blind trooper continued to stare at the patterns of light behind his eyelids. An ominous creak above his head, however, told him more than he wanted to know. He flinched as he felt another drip bouncing off his shoulder.

'We need to face facts,' said the sergeant. 'From what I saw out there, this unholy storm is not confined to just our trenches. Nobody is coming to rescue us, which leaves us with only two choices. Go out there, try to make it to the shelter of the hive–'

'And the rain will melt our flesh!' a young trooper protested.

'Then we stay put,' said the sergeant with admirable calm. 'We wait. Together. And we hope that, by some miracle, the storm lets up before…' Another creak, louder than the first and longer, made his point eloquently for him.

'Perhaps,' he ventured, 'a small prayer at this juncture might not go entirely amiss.'

The same black rain fell upon another world, another time.

Sergeant Renick's lungs burnt, her muscles ached, as she strove to outrace the oncoming storm. Another earth tremor stole her footing and, for the third time, she fell. This time, she landed on her crutch and it splintered.

For the third time, a medic picked her up. She had already tried to make him leave her and save himself. His reply every time had been, 'Just doing my duty.'

A spattering of rain bounced off her helmet. Wind whipped up dust around her boots. She saw a hole burnt in the sleeve of her fatigues, the skin beneath it reddening. She glanced back, regretting it at once. The storm's black mass was stealing up behind them like the shadow of the Grim Reaper himself.

Renick swallowed her pride and any claim of selflessness and accepted the proffered assistance. She focused on their goal, the hive ahead of them. It had already swallowed up her fellow travellers. It seemed so close and yet somehow it wasn't getting closer. She remembered the push towards Hive Arathron, how she had felt like she had been running forever. 'We made it last time,' she grunted. 'We'll make it again.'

Inside the hive, she knew she could find shelter. Inside the hive, she could commandeer a vehicle to the space port. Inside the hive was her escape route from this nightmare, from this God-Emperor-damned world. Inside the hive was an infinity away…

Thunder rippled through the sky above her head. The earth shook again in sympathy. The shadow of the storm crept slowly over her.

Constable Hallam was shaken awake.

She didn't know where she was at first. She didn't know why she was alive. Her head, her entire body, ached. She sloughed off a layer of debris as she tried to sit up.

The church. She had hidden out in a desecrated church. She had taken food at gunpoint from a ragged, tattooed street gang. Her arm had been itchy and painful. She had worried that her wound might have become infected. And then…

There had been light and heat and noise and pain, and then…

Her senses must have been overwhelmed. They had shut down to spare her. She might have been out cold for days or only seconds. She longed to return to that deep slumber.

She slumped there in the darkness, in the silence, in the cold, for either days or seconds longer. The roof had fallen in, she thought, but something – some fortuitously sited beam or statue – had protected her. A miracle. Like when, with a baying ork mob on her heels, she had stumbled upon a service shaft too narrow for them.

The Emperor Himself was watching over Hallam. He wanted her to live.

That thought galvanised her into action. She crawled in what she hoped was the direction of the doors. Her good hand sifted through pulverised rubble. Glass shards became embedded in her glove. She crawled for a long time and never found the doors, nor even the front wall of the church. She saw light ahead of her, however, and set a course towards it.

The light came from a guttering trash fire.

She had found her way out into a thoroughfare. Whole blocks around her, not only the church, had fallen. Walkways above her had collapsed and twisted into a metal tangle, which strained beneath a creaking mass of rockcrete. It was the whole hive, she realised with a gasp of horror. Hive Arathron had fallen. *The cursed xenos did this!* Hallam told herself. She preferred to believe that than to consider the alternative.

One wall of the church still stood defiantly. She recalled the ornamental stained-glass patterns of its windows, though some panes had been cracked. All were blown out now. There were shadows on the wall. Hallam couldn't see where they were cast from, nor did they flicker as the firelight did. The shadows remained still as she stared at them.

Stepping closer, she saw that the shadows were etched into the wall. The rockcrete around them had been bleached. She reached to trace a shadow with her hand, but pulled back in revulsion. The shapes, though indistinct, resembled orks. She saw no sign of ork bodies around her, however. Either they had been completely buried or…

Her stomach heaved and Hallam had to get away from there. She managed a few steps, fell, picked herself up and ran again.

A few steps more and she fell again. This time, she remained on her knees. Her chest hurt and she was panting. She felt the air was getting thinner. The roadway ahead of her was blocked. The roadway behind her too. She was trapped in an airtight pocket, and the fire was eating up her oxygen. Smoke from it filled her nostrils and tickled her throat.

That itch in her arm had spread across her body. She wanted to throw off her torn, soiled uniform and scratch herself until she had no skin left. What did the uniform mean now, anyway? What did her life mean? Why had the Emperor even bothered to spare her, if He could offer her no hope?

Not the Emperor, a small, unworthy part of her brain told her, *just a fluke of Hive Arathron's convoluted architecture. Blind, meaningless chance!*

Something behind her scraped and clattered. To her shame, Hallam let out a frightened yelp. A mound of debris was shifting as someone – *something* – clawed its way out from underneath it. Her eyes met the pale yellow eyes of an ork, which froze. It was smaller than most she had seen, with lighter skin. Its armour was basic, just strips of animal hide, and it carried no weapon.

In the ork's eyes, for a second, Hallam saw her own fear reflected. Then its snout twisted into a furious snarl. It bared its fangs. She reached for her lasgun. They might have been the only two survivors of this ravaged city, but what did it matter? All that mattered was the searing, visceral hatred they felt towards each other.

Three of the Imperial soldier's shots struck the xenos before it cannoned into her. The pair, locked in a furious embrace, reeled into the church's one surviving wall, another part of which crumbled to dust. The metal cradle overhead gave way with a screech.

So caught up in their eternal struggle were they that they hardly noticed a million tons of wreckage plummeting towards their heads.

Turbulence shook Ven Bruin's shuttle.

He gritted his teeth and gripped the sides of his cushioned command throne. Warning runes flared around him. *'Just caught the edge of the storm, inquisitor, sir,'* the pilot voxed him, the strain in his voice undercutting his reassuring words. *'The Aquila can withstand it.'*

In his mind, he still heard the screaming voices at the space port. He still felt resentful glares burning into his back. News of Arathron's destruction had only just begun to spread, but the protests had been building up for days. They had begun after the planetary governor, her staff and her closest friends had abandoned their world.

Ven Bruin was the shuttle's only passenger. Some of his acolytes, he gathered, had already made this journey, while others had not.

Another jolt rattled his teeth. He felt his throne had dropped out from beneath him for an instant. Had he not been strapped in, he might have been thrown from it. His instruments went wild, read-outs flickering and changing too quickly to be comprehended. He gathered that toxic chemicals had been detected in the local atmosphere, potentially corrosive enough to eat through ceramite and plasteel.

'How are we doing, pilot?' asked Ven Bruin, tersely.

'Can't give an ETA just yet, sir, I'm afraid. Half my instruments are in a spin, and visibility is down to near zero. Still, I've got to think that if we can just keep climbing…'

Why do they get to be saved, the protestors had been asking with their banners, their slogans, their glares, *when we do not?*

Perhaps the Emperor Himself had asked that question. Perhaps

He had willed that His inquisitor would not fly free of his sins, but would be forced back down to face their consequences. *Perhaps that would be for the best...*

The circumstances of General Krause's death, like those of the Chairman, are disputed.

It is known that a single bolt was fired, at point-blank range, into the right side of his head. It is less clear who pulled the trigger.

He was last seen – by anyone but, we must presume, his killer – in his war room. He stood with eyes lowered, fists clenched, unmoving in the eye of an ever-escalating hurricane.

'–detonated in the stratosphere, seeding it with tons of–'

'–same story from every other hive. Black rain is falling all across the globe.'

'–is razing forests in the southern–'

'–enough to turn fertile soil to ash, to kill birds and insects outright – and, sir, to melt human flesh and liquefy bones. We must issue a warning. All citizens must remain indoors, at least until this downpour ends, and even then–'

How much of this the general heard, we cannot know. He was like a granite block, unmoving as, one after another, the waves of catastrophe crashed over him.

'–from the flagship of our fleet. They say... Sir, they say it looks as if our world is... They say Krieg's atmosphere is burning. They're requesting orders.'

'–lost contact with our troops out in the–'

'–already seeping into the water supply. The augurs register toxicity levels of–'

'–wear down even rockcrete walls in time. Nowhere is safe.'

The voices rose in urgency and pitch, as shock and disbelief gave way to mounting panic. Still, Krause didn't stir, even when a new sound added to the clamour: the frantic whirrs of air filters and scrubbers cranked up to maximum power. 'Sir, the augurs say that even here, inside this room, the air–'

'–evacuate the hive, but there's nowhere left to evacuate to.'

'–move everybody downwards. Move the higher-level citizens down to the lower levels, where they'll have some measure of protection. The lower classes will have to make space for them, one way or another. Move down to the underhive or–'

'–cogitators are predicting the – is this right? – the total collapse of the planet's ecosystem within three days unless… unless something is done. What do we do, sir?'

'Sir? General Krause, sir. *What do we do?'*

One by one, the voices petered out, having nothing left to say.

Two by two, every eye in the room turned towards the mute form of General Krause, who raised his head at long last. His dark eyes glistened as they stared glassily between his aides and junior officers, at nothing. He drew a deep, shuddering breath, his nostrils flaring.

He turned and marched out of the room, without a word.

He left behind a stunned and hopeless silence.

His body was found four hours later, slumped across his desk. The door to his office had been locked from inside and had to be battered down to gain access. A broken, empty bottle lay beside Krause's left hand.

The obvious conclusion was that he had taken his own life, but no one wanted to admit to this. An Imperial assassin or a cowardly aide made for a more palatable story to tell Krieg's few survivors. In the long, hard years to come, they would need to believe that their leader hadn't simply given up.

The story found favour with Imperial loyalists too. Many disliked the thought of Krause evading the Emperor's justice by choosing the means of his own passing. They pointed out that he could have saved himself. He had bunkers in which he could have sheltered. He could have waited for the fires in the sky to die down and then fled in a shuttle.

It was harder to believe that he might have felt remorse, that he might have regretted some of the risks he'd taken and the warnings he had chosen to ignore. He might have blamed himself for his world's devastation, and the billions of deaths that would ensue. He might have chosen not to live with the guilt of his mistakes.

But that would mean the traitor general had a conscience.

Sergeant Renick had made it to the space port.

Her relief was short-lived, as her flight had not waited for her. The rest of her Cadian regiment had already shipped out. She had got a message to the troop ship, still in orbit, by patching into the port's vox-casters. 'Stand by,' she had been told, and that was all.

She sat against a fuel tank with her medic, her saviour. He had salved the burns on her arms and neck and was tending to his own. She didn't even know his name.

Outside, protestors had hammered on the roof of her truck and cracked its windows. The local militia had been unable or unwilling to contain them. In here, a subdued atmosphere prevailed. Well-dressed people craned their necks to stare up at the sky or they sat with heads in hands. Like her, they suspected that no one was coming to their rescue.

She felt queasy. She didn't know if it was nerves – the tension of the race for shelter, her ensuing disappointment – or if she had breathed in too much poisoned air.

The medic nudged her in the ribs. 'The sky. Look, sergeant. Look up at the sky.'

She did so, numb with apprehension.

The space port lay deep inside the hive. They had outdistanced the spreading mushroom cloud, but not forever. High above them, a circle of sky was outlined by the tips of looming dark spires. It had been ominously overcast, but now it had lightened somewhat. A shaft of sunlight played about the empty landing pads. 'Do you think…?' the medic ventured.

'I don't know.' Renick hardly dared to hope. Had the cloud reached the limits of its spread? Could they have been spared?

A squawk in her ear felt like blessed confirmation. *'Sergeant Renick, report to a Krieg quartermaster for allocation to a Devourer drop-ship.'*

'A Krieg…?' she repeated in confusion. 'But there are no…'

She heard a commotion from the main gates. With the medic's help, she pushed herself up into a standing position. The effort made her stomach lurch and blood rush to her head. She closed her eyes, breathed through it, praying that she only needed food and sleep.

The throaty roars of engines filled her ears.

A procession of vehicles swept onto the space port ramp. Huge, armoured vehicles: Gorgons, Trojans, Leman Russ Demolishers. Renick gaped at them in disbelief, at their trench rails and dozer blades, at the helmeted-skull decals that adorned them. They were fewer than before, but no less impressive than they had been when she had first seen them.

The mobile platforms that had once borne cannons were mostly empty now. A single Baneblade had lost its main gun and was coughing up smoke. The vehicles of the Krieg 43rd Siege Regiment were battered but defiant, as were the Krieg soldiers that poured from them, as silent and inscrutable as ever in their greatcoats and rebreather masks.

Then came the Death Riders on their masked and armoured horses, sitting just as straight-backed as they had all those weeks ago. Renick wished she could have seen the protestors outside as they had approached. She imagined that few had dared try to block their paths. She imagined that little ever could.

The Death Korps of Krieg had walked through nuclear fire and had emerged from it unbowed. She felt proud of them, proud to share a cause with them, proud that they too served the Emperor. They were glorious. Indomitable.

Some thought the storm would never end.

After days, at last, it burnt itself out and the silence of the necropolis prevailed.

More days and nights, impossible to tell apart, passed by. Then a lone figure stepped from the ruins of a once proud hive. His feet became the first to tread upon the blasted surface. His were the first prints in the layer of ash that blanketed the planet.

Colonel Jurten took a long, deep breath.

The air was thin and clogged with particles of soot. Hence he had brought his own supply, piped from a unit on his chest through a flexible hose into a full face mask. It tasted stale and left a slight tang of rubber on his tongue.

He had been warned that the air would burn his skin, so was wrapped from head to toe in durable materials. A coal-black, armour-weave greatcoat was fastened tight about him, a shield against the cold. A black haze blotted out the stars and showed no signs of parting yet. The sun had not shone upon this world in days and might never again. Without his layers of insulation, his blood would have frozen.

Scanning the horizon, he could just make out the smog-wreathed outline of another hive. From this far away, he could almost imagine that life inside continued as it always had. He knew better. Half-melted spires formed unnatural shapes. No lights streamed from the hive's windows, no flyers weaved between its structures, no smoke poured from its industrial stacks.

'You don't have to go out there,' Archmagos Greel had advised him.

He had been wrong. Jurten had had to see this for himself, regardless of the risks to him. So, Greel had ensured that he was as protected as he could be. He could face the consequences of his actions, of the choices he had made. He didn't have to feel a thing.

'I won't ask for your forgiveness,' he murmured to his Emperor, 'only that you bless your loyal servants in our future endeavours. The time of purging is over. Of the world I once loved, only this wasteland remains. My duty now is clear. I shall build a new world, a better and more devout world, upon the ashes of the old one.

'One day, Krieg will rise again.'

442–444.M40

THE FUTURE

The mutant had had a name once. He could almost remember it too.

Raim? Rahm? Hadn't there been a rank to go with it? He might have been a captain. It seemed so long ago, but he felt it had meant something then.

Now all he had was the pounding of his own feet on ash and clinker. The pounding of a straining heartbeat in his ears. And pounding hoofbeats, sweeping up behind him.

The sounds grew louder, echoing between the looming slag heaps. He tried to run from them, but found himself hurtling towards them. He altered his direction, but somehow the pounding came from ahead of him still.

He ought to have stayed in the bunker. There had been a bunker once, hadn't there? Hadn't there been candles, tinned food and water from a tapped pipe, clean enough to keep down in small doses? But didn't he also remember being beaten, cast out by huddled refugees with frightened eyes? After all he had done for them. Hadn't he protected them?

Ash and dust, kicked up by his flight, caught in his throat. He stumbled and fell, barking his hands and knees. He struggled to stand with his weak arm and curved spine as the pounding built to a thunderous peak and he found himself suddenly encircled.

The mutant let out a frightened whine. He had heard tell of Death Riders: gaunt, mounted figures who stalked the chem-wastes, hunting down their prey. It had been said that they were Colonel Jurten's soldiers, returned from beyond death itself.

He ought to have stayed in his cave. He had only broken cover because his stomach had been empty and because his itching was unbearable. He had hoped to find a fresh carcass to sustain him. He had wanted to bathe his skin in river sludge.

The riders were empty-eyed, faceless, as the rumours had described them. They were armoured like warriors, but they wore no regimental colours. They were clad in mourning black. Even their horses wore metal shields over their heads, as if their faces were too horrific to be seen. 'Who...?' The mutant's voice, long unused, rasped in his raw throat and tripped over his swollen tongue. '*What* are you?'

The riders regarded him with blank indifference. One jerked the reins of his mount, which trotted forward. He might have been the leader, as his shoulders bore strange rank insignia. He drew a thin, curved blade.

Raim – Rahm? – had once worn insignia too. The tatters of a blue-and-gold uniform still clung to his arm. He remembered that he had had a weapon, and he snatched it from his belt. He aimed it at the rider's eyes and squeezed the trigger.

The pistol had long since lost its charge. It whined pitifully, as did its wielder. The blade was now poised above his head.

'Why… why do this?' he whispered. 'You destroyed our world. You won the war. What more could you possibly want from us?'

The Death Rider spoke in a flat, hollow voice. 'Swear allegiance to the Emperor,' he commanded.

'I… I swear it,' said the mutant. The adrenaline that had been rushing through him drained away. He felt weak and deeply weary. He felt tears flowing from his eyes as if a dam had burst. 'I swear it. I do. Praise be to the Emperor.'

The Death Rider nodded as if satisfied.

The thin blade flashed through the air and sliced off the mutant's head.

Colonel Jurten's eyes opened. As always, his first act was to thank the Emperor for another day of life. He took no day for granted.

His artificial hip had locked again. He levered himself stiffly off his bunk and tested his weight on it until, with a resentful creak, it acceded to his will. His uniform hung behind his door, looking threadbare, reserved now for formal occasions. He pulled on his usual dark fatigues and greatcoat. It had been a long time since he had had a valet to dress him.

He inspected himself in a cracked mirror. He looked old. *I am old*, he reminded himself, but he looked older. His every compromise, his every sacrifice, was etched into his drawn, sallow face. He had always cropped his hair close, but now he had only grizzled stubble. He had shaved his head since the morning he had found hair on his pillow.

The lens of his augmetic right eye whirred and clicked, adjusting its focal length. It never quite got it right, but it was an improvement on the natural eye that had withered in its socket. He donned his synth-leather gloves, covering his flaking skin. *'You must have expected to be facing a monster by now,'* General Krause had once sneered at him.

He pulled his cap down over the tips of his ears and reached for the door.

The underground city never slept. The sounds of industry resonated through it as Jurten climbed down from his hab-unit. Hammers rang off anvils in the forges. Drills rattled and screeched. A bell chimed to signal the change of shift, and weary labourers spilled out of the manufactoria and headed for their beds.

Those that noticed Jurten at all made sure to steer clear of him. Where once they had regarded him with awe, now they averted their eyes from him, shunning him as if the stench of death clung to him. They spoke few words, because they had little to say. Even the announcements from the public vox-hailers were less frequent than they had been. They offered bland sermons on the topics of duty and necessity, which hadn't changed in months.

Jurten strode into his command headquarters. A young adjutant leapt up from behind a desk, saluting. He reeled off the usual litany of figures. Jurten stayed him with a raised hand and a pained expression. 'Anything I need to know, lieutenant?'

The adjutant thumbed at his data-slate, lips pursed. He couldn't have been older than sixteen and the colonel had no memory of seeing him before. He had so many young adjutants, these days. 'You, ah, might be pleased to hear, sir, that our water purification targets–'

'Anything else?'

'New Wulfram reports minor setbacks in development of the new Ragnarok battle tank.'

'How minor?'

'Potentially a week or two's delay. I've requested a further report by shift's end. On the plus side, production of high-explosive shells has been stepped up ahead of schedule and is now at its highest level since the end of the war.'

'The war is not over yet,' Jurten growled.

'No, sir. One more thing, sir. The archmagos is waiting in your office.'

'I will not live to see our world reborn,' said Colonel Jurten.

'Indeed not. Nor will I.' He could always rely on Greel to be honest with him, where others might have held out false hope or hidden behind platitudes.

Jurten could be honest with Greel too. He didn't have to hide how tired he felt after so short a walk from his hab. He leaned back in his chair and closed his eyes. He needed a drink, but he made himself wait. He didn't want to use up his water ration.

'I analysed the latest batch of samples last night,' said Greel.

'There has been no improvement, I assume?'

The tech-priest shook his head. 'It has only been a few years, Colonel Jurten. We knew it would likely be far longer before–'

'But there has been no improvement in those years. None at all.'

'Our air remains as toxic as it ever was.'

'Is it possible, archmagos, that Krieg–'

'That its ecosystem might have been damaged beyond saving? That Krieg might remain a dead planet forever? Yes, colonel, it is possible. Does that change your opinion of what you – of what we – did? If you could make that choice again, would it be any different?'

Jurten didn't have to think about his answer. He had pondered the question over many sleepless nights. 'No. It would not.'

'This world does not matter, colonel.'

'Krieg is–' he began to protest.

'This world is just a lump of rock. Krieg is the people who gained mastery over this world. It is the sum of their achievements.

Those people have suffered a great setback, but they can recover. They can rebuild. They can still be saved.'

'Billions of Krieg's people died,' said Jurten pointedly.

'So that many times more – a limitless number of future generations – may live good, faithful lives,' Greel countered.

'There are still some who would stand in the way of that goal.'

Greel nodded. 'Some. Far fewer than there were.'

'We've no way of knowing how many traitors survived.'

'They were less prepared for the Purging than we were.'

The Purging… Jurten noted Greel's casual usage of the term. 'Still, they were far more numerous than us to begin with. By now, they will have dug down as deeply as we have.'

'And they will be building, as are we.'

'Soon,' vowed Jurten. 'Soon, our tanks shall roll across Krieg's blasted wastelands. Soon, our shells shall batter the remnants of their cities. Soon, we shall root our enemies out of their boltholes and force them to answer for their heresies. Soon…'

Not soon enough, he feared.

'The traitors will fight to their last breaths,' said Greel, quietly.

'I've no doubt of it.' For all of Jurten's efforts, all his sacrifices, what had he truly achieved? He had won no resounding victory, only evened up the odds against him a little. His real fight had only just begun, and, just as before, he fought alone.

He doubted that any of the Chairman's cruisers, his vaunted ring of steel, remained in orbit, and those that did would be airless husks by now. Their captains would have faced a stark choice between braving the storms still raging through Krieg's stratosphere and attempting to flee. In the latter case, without a Navigator to enable a warp jump, they would likely have run out of air and fuel long before they could reach a safe port.

It made no difference. Even if he'd had an astropath, a means of contacting the Departmento Munitorum, why would they aid him now? What could they hope to gain by it, when Krieg itself had become a man-made death world, a prize no longer worth the taking?

One day… thought Jurten.

He imagined, one day, an Imperial delegation arriving upon a grand cruiser. He imagined himself taking a shuttle to greet it. *Only it will not be me…* One of his descendants, perhaps, would announce that Krieg's long civil war was over. Its loyalists had triumphed over the secessionist traitors and were ready to serve the Emperor once more. He would offer the Emperor a world. *No, not a world, its people!* An army more loyal, more resilient, than any even He had seen before.

Jurten's eyes had closed again. His mind had wandered, as it often did lately, to other days. Greel's voice brought him back to the present. 'One day,' he said, 'Krieg's surface may be safe to walk again, but that day may not come for generations yet, and while we do nothing but await it–'

'We give the traitors time to recover from their losses,' agreed Jurten.

'We need to build an army that can fight in these conditions. We need to create a people that can *thrive* in these conditions, and we must do it before our enemies can, for we must assume that they too–'

Jurten frowned. 'We have had this conversation before, arch-magos.'

'Indeed we have.'

'Have I not compromised enough?' the colonel roared, his old fire flaring in his heart again, if only for an instant.

'On the contrary,' Greel replied implacably, 'I'd say we have sacrificed too much. Too much to sit back and see it count for nothing. Having started along this path, Colonel Jurten, we cannot – we must not – turn back now.'

'The military academy is working to full capacity,' said Jurten.

'It isn't enough,' insisted Greel.

'Every man, every woman in the city has been drafted into our armed forces.'

'It isn't enough.'

'God-Emperor damn it, we aren't talking about warhorses here!'

'The principle remains the same.'

'Some would say those words are heretical, Greel.'

'No doubt some would, but I accepted the truth of them long ago. I believe that, in your head, you can accept it too. It is only your heart that disagrees.'

Only your heart… As if that ought to mean nothing. *Perhaps because Greel's heart is only cold machinery,* thought Jurten. Perhaps, this time, *he* was the one who could not see. 'I won't do it,' he said stubbornly, 'There are still lines I will not cross.'

Greel didn't press the point. He seemed to accept the colonel's decision, but Jurten suspected he was really just biding his time. He *would* have that water, he decided: a mouthful, at least, to wash down his anti-sickness tablets.

Another passing-out parade at the academy. How many had Jurten attended now?

The graduating platoon formed up for their commander's inspection. They were fully kitted out with bulging backpacks and belt pouches. Each of their sloped lasguns was of the new, more powerful type, distinctive heat sinks screwed to their barrels.

Each Guardsman wore a rebreather, mask and spiked helmet, so he couldn't see their faces. Nor did their builds vary much. Months of gruelling training had made them hard and lean. They were of similar heights too, being of similar young ages.

He marched along each of their ranks, seeing little to distinguish each Guardsman from the next. Eighty-six of them in all. He asked questions of a handful of them. Their answers were abrupt and to the point. 'Why are you here?' he asked them.

'To fight and to die, sir, for the Emperor.'

'My world is dead, sir, and my life is His to command.'

'There is no peace in life, sir, but in death we atone for our world's sins.'

Jurten thought about what Greel had said, about Krieg being made up of its people. These were the people, this was the Krieg, he had created. He felt proud of them, and yet somehow saddened by them too. He told himself that neither was appropriate.

They were what they had to be, no more. They were the soldiers his world needed.

At last, the day came when Jurten led his soldiers into battle once more.

It didn't happen quite as he had pictured it. He had been forced to accept the advice of his medicaes. He was too weak to take his rightful place at the head of his infantry. Instead, he sat up in the turret of his trusty old Pegasus.

He ensured his troops could see him, even if they could only recognise him by his badges of rank. His face was masked as theirs were, and he couldn't help but think this for the best. When he felt able, when he had breath enough, he motivated them over the vox-net.

The wheels of their vehicles churned up thick layers of ash. Their engine roars shattered the silence of years. Anyone watching from the hive ahead of them could scarcely have missed their approach. He almost hoped there *was* somebody watching – for the sight of his regiment, his army, on the march, would have struck holy terror into them.

The battered form of Hive Argentus rose before them. At Jurten's command, his Demolisher tanks surged forward, cannons thundering. They targeted known gun emplacements in the outer walls. Their bombardment lasted several minutes before he called a halt to it. He sent his infantry into the smoke before it cleared.

Death Rider scouts had reported that the eastern gates were sundered. Hundreds of masked soldiers poured through them, separating into squads of ten and fanning out. Some found their way along the hive's dark thoroughfares impeded by collapsed buildings, some by man-made barricades. They blasted through the latter with grenades, sending sandbags, coils of wire and shards of planking up into the air. Within minutes, they were teeming through the outermost sectors of the hive.

They were joined by the newly constructed Ragnaroks: great slab-sided tanks with square turrets and huge caterpillar tracks. Only six had rolled off the assembly lines thus far, and this was their first field test. They were unsophisticated, slow, unwieldy, designed for easy assembly, and yet they packed a punch. Their battle cannons blasted obstructions to debris, which was then pulverised beneath their tracks. They cleared a path in which the Demolishers and Jurten's command vehicle followed.

'Does anyone have eyes on the enemy yet?' voxed Jurten, grinding his back teeth.

'No trace yet, sir.'

'All clear here, colonel.'

More replies came in, all negative. Some, from the squads farthest from him, he could barely hear through static. That had been expected. What was the term Greel had used? *Electro-something interference* in the air, limiting vox range.

He remembered the flare gun in his belt, brought as an emergency backup communications system. He took it out and fired it. The flare streaked through gantries above him, exploding prematurely as it struck one, raining bright light down around him.

The light revealed Hive Argentus in all its dusty, cobwebbed decrepitude. Perhaps the city truly was dead, but for those webs' denizens: squat, hardy arachnids with blood-red shells, only glimpsed as they scuttled into shadows. Could Jurten's augurs too have been rendered unreliable by the tainted atmosphere?

Then came the vox report he had been waiting for. 'They're here, sir.'

The traitors appeared as if from nowhere. As if the racket made by Jurten's invaders had been enough, at last, to raise the city's ghosts. They stumbled out of rockcrete shelters, blinking. They bubbled up from underhive tunnels like disturbed cockroaches. Four, five, six squads at once, and then more, found themselves under attack.

Jurten heard gunfire – the anaemic cracks of lasguns and the heavier barks of the new loyalist variant – and eagerly urged his driver towards the familiar sounds.

The Pegasus' headlights found and paralysed a figure in the road ahead of him. It was hunched and scrawny and might have been a mutant, though Jurten saw no definite sign of it. The figure was swaddled in layers of filthy rags. It wore a respirator over its nose and mouth, and a pair of thick flying goggles. It displayed no military markings but carried a lasgun, which it threw down at the sight of Jurten's vehicle bearing down upon it.

The traitor raised his or her hands.

Jurten shot it in the head and had his Pegasus ride over its twitching body. The vehicle's lumens now picked out other fleeting figures as they ran for cover. He holstered his pistol and took the grips of the Pegasus' inbuilt heavy bolter. He switched it to full-auto and strafed the ground ahead of him in a ninety-degree arc. His rounds punched through walls, barrels and abandoned vehicles, finding their targets wherever they cowered.

His ammunition belt was being swallowed at a rate of knots, however. Reluctantly, he eased up on the trigger. He felt he had made his point. He had revealed the skulking traitors and set them to flight. His troopers could pick off the rest of them.

'Remember,' he instructed them, 'these people are our enemies. They are the Emperor's enemies. Soldiers or civilians, each is as guilty as the rest. Each has had chances to atone and has declined them. For what they have done to this once peaceful world, they can never be forgiven. We offer them no mercy. Only death.'

The sounds of battle across the outskirts intensified. Vox chatter told him that the traitors were starting to regroup. They were fighting back, but their weapons were feeble compared to the loyalists' weapons. Their armour was flimsy compared to the loyalists' armour. Their will was weak compared to the loyalists' will.

One nest of traitors took the dishonourable way out. They detonated explosives pre-planted about their hidey-hole, hoping to burn their attackers with them. Jurten waited tensely for an update. *'They took out our sergeant,'* came the tremulous voice of a young man trying to be brave, *'and two of our troopers need medical assistance. But the traitors… We counted eight bodies. I don't know how many more were buried.'*

'Well done, soldier,' the colonel responded. 'You have command of your squad now.'

'I… Yes, sir. Thank you, sir.'

'I know you won't let me down.'

He heard the rattle of an automatic weapon to his right. Bolts whistled past his exposed upper body and pinged off the Pegasus' hull. His driver shouted up to him: 'Heat sensors place the sniper on a bearing of oh-two-zero, sir.' Rotating his turret, he found himself facing the lower windows of a towering hab-block.

He yanked on the lanyard of an auto-launcher, which spat out three grenades at once. Two hit the block's side, but the third sailed through an empty window frame behind which he had glimpsed movement. He saw the flash of its explosion, thought he might have heard a scream. Whether he was right or not, no more bolts came his way.

His lips curled back from his teeth in triumph. He yelled down to his driver, 'Find me another target!' Colonel Jurten was back in his element. For the first time in a long time, he felt blood pumping through his veins again.

'Did we do it? Did we take Argentus?'

He felt sure he had asked before, but he couldn't remember the answer.

'We control eighty-three per cent of its eastern sector,' Greel told him patiently. 'The traitors have dug in across the rest of the city. It will take us time to root them out, as we discussed, especially given our need to avoid extensive casualties.'

'I was there...' He smiled fondly at the memory.

'Yes, Colonel Jurten, you were there. You led the initial charge into the traitor-held city. Almost half the ground we now hold was taken by you in those first few hours.'

'How long...?'

'That was eight months ago.'

Eight months... It felt like longer. At the same time, it felt like no time at all. How long had he spent in this hated medicae bed? How many mornings had he opened his eyes to stare up at the same bland patch of ceiling? Each time he did so, it felt like a gesture of defiance.

Jurten hated feeling helpless. At first, he had hated the machines that surrounded his bed, their needles sunk into his veins, clicking smugly to themselves, but now he hardly noticed them at all. He insisted on receiving daily briefings, but struggled to retain much useful information from them.

'The other hives?' he asked.

'Remain silent,' said Greel, 'but they may not for much longer. The latest readings from Auros suggest an increased level of industrial emissions. Captain Henkel has pulled three platoons back from the front to bolster our defences in case of–'

'No,' croaked Jurten. 'We must... take Argentus first, must press the attack.'

'We must also protect what we have built here,' argued Greel, 'as we continue to build on it. With more resources, of course, we might have been able to–'

'Have I not made it clear that we will work with what we have?'

'Every one of your Korpsmen is aware of your directives.'

'Every one of my...?' Jurten's brow wrinkled.

'My pardon, colonel. That is what the people have been calling our reborn army. A "Death Korps". The Death Korps of Krieg. I hear the name is taking hold within their own ranks too.'

'Hmm.' Jurten wasn't sure how to take that news.

'Henkel has created a new rank of quartermaster, to manage our–'

'Can Henkel win this war?' Jurten interrupted, bluntly.

'I'm sure you know, he is a most efficient officer,' said Greel.

'But can he win this war?'

Greel sighed. 'I fear that he cannot.'

'Tell me why not.'

Greel's mechanical eye whirred, refocusing on Jurten. Not for the first time, the colonel wondered how old the tech-priest was. *He* never seemed to tire nor sicken. Perhaps there was too little left of his flesh-and-blood body to suffer such weakness. 'Because, by the time he sees what must be done, it will be far too late.'

Jurten sighed and closed his eyes.

'We agreed long ago that this war will outlast us both,' said Greel, 'but that doesn't matter. The outcome will depend upon decisions taken now. It depends on *your* decisions.'

'I am old,' complained Jurten. 'I am ill. Can't someone else shoulder that burden?'

'They could,' said Greel. 'That too depends on you. Are you ready to relinquish your command? Let someone else decide?'

In any debate, he always seemed to cut straight to Jurten's weakness.

'Some years ago, I urged you to consider the long term, to make provisions for the dark days we knew must come. You listened to me then, and so we have the advantage over our enemies now. I urge you, colonel, to think of the future again.'

'I think of little but.'

'From the start, you and I understood what few others did, or perhaps what they lacked the courage to face. We understood that Krieg's war would become one of attrition. To the side that can more effectively replenish its resources–'

'–will go the ultimate victory. I know that, Greel.'

'And what more precious resource do we have than our–'

'No!' cried Jurten, drowning out the words he couldn't bear to hear again.

This time, however, Greel did not give in. 'You might not see the war's end, colonel, but you and only you can win it for us. One word from you will tip the balance. My genetors and I will attend to the practicalities.'

'Yes,' Jurten growled, 'I'm sure you will.'

The tech-priest's voice hardened suddenly. 'Your body is failing you, Jurten. It's time to make your choice. Will you die with your work unfinished – hoping and praying that you have done enough, while feeling you ought to have done more? Or will you rest content in the knowledge that you have secured a future for your people? That you have done as much as – even more than – your Emperor could ever have asked of you?'

Colonel Jurten passed away that night.

He spent his final hours drifting in and out of sleep, contemplating the decisions he had taken. He wondered how history would remember him. As a hero? It was just as likely he would be considered a villain. The man who had destroyed a world. His own world. *For even the lesser of two evils, in His eyes, condemns us…*

He knew he shouldn't care. It was hubris to imagine that his reputation mattered. For what was he, after all? Hardly a man, as everything that had made him such he had been compelled to surrender. He had been just a tool in the Emperor's hands, for which he felt honoured.

One day, they'll see, he thought. *They'll look at what I did and what it led to, and they will understand. Not all of them, perhaps, but some… One day…*

There were no ceremonies held. No days of mourning were declared.

Heartfelt prayers were voiced in the packed churches, but otherwise life – and work, always work – went on as normal. This was at Jurten's own insistence. Often he had said that he was only one soldier, no more important than any other.

'And, though he may be gone,' said the voice that sounded like his voice, echoing through caves and tunnels, 'never will he be forgotten. For he cleansed our world of its sins and set us on the long, hard path towards atonement.'

Nor was there much talk of a replacement. Though the matter wasn't formally discussed, no officer felt it right to claim the vacant rank of colonel. It was far too soon.

Perhaps, deep down, they also felt it easier to proceed as if Jurten hadn't left them. Just to follow the path he had set out for them. That way, the weight of his choices could rest upon his memory alone. None of them would be culpable. As far as history was concerned, they could remain nameless. And faceless.

'Our duty is clear now, for each and every one of us.

'We must redouble our commitment to our labours. We must strive to build the future that our saviour envisaged for us. Through our efforts, Krieg will rise again, stronger and more faithful than before. And we shall do this in Colonel Jurten's name.

'And in the name of the Emperor.'

Greel attended his first command meeting in several months.

He was here only because he had been summoned. Otherwise, he saw no need. He had plenty to occupy his time, and Henkel was a decent, solid officer. He lacked his predecessor's fortitude, but then who could say any different? Greel trusted him to keep the war on course, while overseeing the minutiae of city administration.

Henkel could never have brought the Krieg this far, but he was the right leader to take them forwards from here. For the next few years, at least. For as long as he was able.

Greel looked around the war room table. Every officer present was wearing his rebreather mask, even here, even this far underground. Even had he seen their faces, he doubted he would have known most of them. No one addressed him directly. They discussed glitches in the supply of first aid kits to their troopers, and an adjutant read out a positive report from the newly established hydroponics dome.

They considered reports from the front. That morning, a vehicle had sped out of Argentus and headed for the capital hive. It had screeched along congealed tarmac until it hit a roadblock, tried to plough on across rough terrain and had floundered in a rut. Death Riders had run its fleeing occupants down.

'The next one,' a young lieutenant warned, 'could make it through, or the hives might somehow re-establish contact with each other. If Auros sends out reinforcements...'

'We cannot take that chance,' agreed the captain.

They decided to pull half their forces out of Argentus, and retask their artillery units. Hive Auros would be surrounded. The goal, for the present, would simply be containment. The loyalist soldiers would be issued with tools for digging trenches. They were to prepare for what would likely be a prolonged siege.

Henkel turned towards his tech-priest, at last. He requested a full report into his current projects. This was no less than Greel had expected, and for which he had prepared. He produced a data-slate from inside his robes and cleared his throat. He spoke in quiet, measured tones for several minutes. He omitted no detail, suspecting that Henkel knew most of them already.

Greel told the assembled officers more than they needed to know, more than they could understand, and his frankness stunned them into silence. 'None of you were aware of this?' he asked with feigned surprise. 'Colonel Jurten never briefed you?'

'He did not,' said Henkel stiffly. 'Then the colonel...?'

'We spoke only hours before his passing. He was concerned, as was I, about the future. The Purging has taken its toll on us too – our population has remained almost static ever since. New births have barely kept pace with the growing number of mutations and deaths. At this rate, I project that within–'

'We are all aware of the problem,' the captain grumbled.

'Then you understand why the colonel approved this procedure.'

The officers exchanged uneasy glances. They had planned to hold an inquisition. Instead, they were the ones being put on the spot by their suspect.

'With due respect, archmagos,' another captain ventured, 'how can we be sure of that? Or even that the colonel's mind was…?' He trailed off, uncomfortably.

'We all knew and respected him. We know that he took no decision lightly. He was also determined that our suffering, our toils, must count for something. What is the point, he asked me, in rebuilding shattered industries, manufacturing arms and equipment, if there might come a time when no one remains to wield them? Our children, he always said, are our most precious resource…'

That statement elicited murmurs of cautious agreement.

'The vitae womb,' said Greel, 'will make our children stronger. Strong enough to reclaim our world for the Emperor and, in time, to return to the stars.'

He swept the table with his cold, augmetic glare. 'And Colonel Jurten gave it his approval, with almost his final breath. He chose to take that upon his conscience, so that no one else would have to. And the last thing he said to me – before his eyes closed and I left his bedside for the final time – was that this would be his final compromise.'

AFTER THE GREAT RIFT

A BLIND EYE

'Are we certain the danger has passed?'

The planetary governor looked immaculate in her dress uniform with her rows of medals, but her tired eyes betrayed the stress of recent weeks.

'The fallout from the atomic explosion,' explained a rust-cloaked genetor of the Adeptus Mechanicus, 'was mostly confined to the area of Hive Arathron, though a small amount will certainly have drifted on the breeze to other population centres.'

'Including my capital hive.'

'The effects of which appear to be negligible thus far.'

The *Memento Mori* was a Galaxy troop ship assigned to the Death Korps of Krieg, decorated inside and out with their customary morbid imagery. The governor was present aboard it in hololithic form only. Her exodus ship was in wide orbit near the system's edge. Still, there were solid bodies enough to pack out the communications deck.

Among these were the Krieg colonel commanding the 43rd

Siege Regiment, a commissar who did most of his talking for him, and the pensive Inquisitor Ven Bruin.

Hovering above another podium was the light image of a glowering lord general, whose flagship had recently dropped out of warp space. *'But there will be long-term effects?'* he growled through his white beard.

'There is much we are yet to relearn about–'

'Are my people safe, tech-priest?' the governor snapped.

'The bomb site must be quarantined, of course,' said the genetor, 'to a radius of six miles at least and for no less than fifteen years. No one must enter the contaminated zone without protection. Beyond its perimeter, we'd expect to see a marked increase in minor mutations – tumours, cataracts, skin rashes – along with diseases of the blood.'

'That hardly sounds "negligible".'

'Such conditions would remain relatively rare, and should lessen in frequency within a few generations. I would recommend that medicaes–'

'Generations?' the governor spluttered.

'The death toll could have been far worse,' said the Krieg colonel, gruffly. 'Perhaps you should be grateful for that mercy.'

His commissar broke the ensuing uncomfortable silence. 'What the colonel means is–'

'He's right,' the lord general barked. *'Ten hours ago, we were looking at Exterminatus. To say nothing of the consequences, had the xenos worked out how to use those weapons instead of having them blow up in their faces.'*

'Unthinkable,' the commissar agreed.

Ven Bruin stared down at his own feet. Only he and the colonel knew the true cause of Arathron's destruction, and neither volunteered that information. Their reports had said no more than they needed to say.

He was used to keeping secrets. His work with the ordo demanded it. Often a lie was permissible, expedient even, in the service of a greater truth. Never had he kept a secret from the ordo itself, however, and the guilt of it festered in his heart.

'*If the Emperor has indeed chosen to spare my people,*' said the governor, '*then of course I am grateful for His mercy. Still, sir*' – she addressed the lord general directly – '*I wonder at the wisdom of risking more lives to a hazard so barely understood?*'

So, now she reveals her true motives, thought Ven Bruin.

He cleared his throat politely, demanding attention. 'Madam governor,' he said, 'your people are afraid. They are confused. They feel abandoned at a time of global crisis. The greatest peril your world faces is that those feelings will turn them away from the Emperor. Leadership is needed now. Your people need to see that you are not afraid to live among them. They need to feel protected.'

The Cadian shock troops held a service in the ship's chapel. A Ministorum priest asked the Emperor to bless their fallen comrades' souls. Their acting colonel read out every one of their names, though it took him almost an hour to do so.

The Krieg attended normal daily services. No names were read at these. Their priest – the same priest – spoke in non-specific terms about those who had trodden their path before them. He asked the Emperor to bless the soldiers present, to give them strength to follow in the footsteps of their honoured dead. 'We will remember them,' he had declared at the Cadian service, though there had been so many names that no one could remember more than a fraction of them. He made no such promise to the Krieg.

The *Memento Mori* docked at an Imperial void station. Four hundred and sixty-three Cadians marched down the loading ramps. The short warp jump had given them time to clean and repair their uniforms, and they held their heads high as always. Still, there was a palpable air of despondency about them.

The Krieg remained aboard and were joined by fresh troops from their home world's training centres. They were already waiting in a loading bay. They tramped along the troop ship's passageways, pouring into its great assembly hall.

Ven Bruin watched them from an overlooking gallery. Their drill was flawless, every Korpsman in perfect accord with every other. Their footsteps rang in perfect unison, sympathetic vibrations rippling outwards from them through the deck plates. He tried to imagine what they looked like under their masks. They could only have been boys. Once they had been absorbed into the regiment's depleted squads, however, he would have no way of telling them apart from the older, seasoned veterans.

The colonel addressed the new arrivals. He welcomed them into the ranks of the Krieg 43rd. He congratulated them on proving themselves worthy and told them how they would be rewarded. 'You will die in the Emperor's service, for the sins of our ancestors and in the hope of our world's eventual redemption. Your life, each of our lives, will count.'

Ven Bruin was also meant to disembark at the station.

He was to have hopped another flight and worked his way back to the ordo. He had had a change of mind. The memory of Interrogator Ferran had much to do with it. He sat on the edge of his bunk in his sparse quarters, as shutters closed over the windows behind him. The *Memento Mori* was about to leap back into the warp.

He cradled his whip in his lap. Its knots were stiff and dark with crusted blood.

He had questioned several Korpsmen who had witnessed his apprentice's demise. Their stories had all been the same.

'The xenos broke through our defences and overpowered him. We fought as hard as we could to get to him. Alas, we were seconds too late.' None of them had sounded especially regretful, but why would they?

Three Korpsmen reported to Ven Bruin's quarters. He was surprised to see them until they explained that their colonel had sent them. Ven Bruin had informed him of his decision that morning. With his replacement dead, he would have to endure a while longer. The colonel had pointed out that he was short of warrior acolytes. 'You will find no finer candidates than among this very regiment,' he had stated without conceit.

The three new recruits introduced themselves by their service numbers. Ven Bruin had requested experienced soldiers, but not too experienced. He didn't want them ready to die just yet. He briefed the trio on their duties, which basically amounted to keeping him alive. He suspected they would see less action than they would have liked.

Ven Bruin would remain embedded with the Death Korps of Krieg. His duties therefore were likely to be light, as he would have few heretics to hunt down and expose. At his age, that suited him well. At the same time, he would serve a useful purpose. He also needed that. He needed not to have time to dwell on his regrets.

More importantly, he told himself, *the Krieg need someone too. Someone who sees them for who they are, and understands their value to the Emperor. Someone to keep others – even other members of the ordo – from asking too many questions.*

Someone to keep their secrets...

Sergeant Renick did little but sleep for a week and a half.

She had missed the memorial service, to her chagrin. She was transferred from the troop ship to a void station's medicae ward and then, some three days later, to another ship's sickbay, another antiseptic-smelling bed with scratchy sheets.

Her greatest fear had come to pass. Such were her regiment's losses that it had been officially disbanded. The Cadian 432nd was no more, its proud history counting for nothing. Its remnants had been absorbed into the Cadian 179th. 'You know,' a fellow patient had told her with forced cheer, 'officially, Hive Arathron counts as a victory.' Regardless, she would bear the shame of that defeat for the rest of her service.

She would still serve, of course. The orks may have immolated themselves on one small planet, but the wider Octarius War continued to be fought.

Renick didn't know where she was going, nor how long the journey would take, but she intended to be fighting fit by its end. Her foot, given proper attention, was healing nicely. The burns she had suffered from the black rain were more stubborn – every time her dressings were changed, they suppurated anew – but they wouldn't slow her down.

She was more concerned with the sick feeling growing in her stomach. *It's just a reaction to everything I've been through,* she told herself. She played it down when asked how she was feeling. She held down as much food as she could and concealed her dizzy spells.

She made it to the briefing hall. She was introduced to her new squad, the old one having been split up. She struggled to commit their names to memory. She felt she should say something to them, to inspire them. 'Wherever they send us, I pray there will be orks there,' was what she settled on. 'We have a score to even.'

She wondered what they thought when they looked at her.

They were entering orbit around another world. The 179th's commanding officer outlined their mission to them. Though among new faces, Renick felt she was back in familiar surroundings. They were being deployed to an agri world upon which a heretical cult had arisen. The cultists had captured a space port, blocking vital food exports to hundreds of Imperial planets. They were also broadcasting an astropathic signal to the tyranid fleet. They invited the xenos to come to their world and absorb them into their swarm.

Renick was disgusted. Were there not monsters enough polluting the galaxy without her own kind, human beings, giving in to weakness? It felt like a distraction from her true purpose. In the end, though, her duty was the same. She was to cleanse a world of the Emperor's enemies. Slaughter the unlike. Preserve the Imperial cordon. Hold the line.

Her drop-ship had to put down in a field, its retrorockets torching enough wheat to feed a city for a week. It was a rough landing, which turned her stomach over and forced her to stifle a retch. She dismissed her new squadmates' concerns. 'We have a job to do.'

The air outside was cool and fresh, which made her feel more hopeful. She could see the silver space port dome to the north, just a few miles away, and more ships descending from the sky behind it.

Within minutes, her company was on the march towards that dome. Their artillery units pulled ahead of them and exercised their guns. The Cadians' Leman Russ tanks didn't pack the firepower of the Krieg Demolishers but they had greater range, and the space port, in comparison to Arathron, was only lightly fortified. Muzzles flashed in its long windows and bullets pinged off armour-plated hulls, but as shells punched through the space port's walls, its defenders abandoned their posts. They lacked the bloody-mindedness of orks.

Almost before she knew it, Renick was among the soldiers pouring into the space port from all directions. She glimpsed a flurry of tattered black robes as the cultists scattered before them in howling, gnashing terror. Some attempted to surrender, dropping to their knees with hands clasped in supplication. They were gunned down without pause.

'Fire upon the enemy at will,' Renick bellowed. 'With the Emperor's grace, we'll have this pathetic insurgency mopped up by sunset!' It was good to be reminded of how her world's shock troops had earned their name.

The port was of utilitarian construction, bare rockcrete walls and harsh angles. Renick glimpsed the flutter of a cloak near the top of a half-enclosed square staircase. She led her squad up it, taking three steps at a time. She was halfway up before an unpleasant memory struck her. She remembered taking her previous squad into unknown territory, a desperate battle in a cobbled courtyard. *But the Emperor was with us that time…*

As Renick threw herself around the last tight corner, her legs gave way without warning. She scraped her hands and knees on the hard, rockcrete steps and swallowed bile. Embarrassed, she pushed herself back up as the world spun around her. 'Lost my damn footing,' she muttered to the troopers pressing up behind her. She resumed her ascent with an awkward, lurching gait, keeping one hand on the stair rail for support.

She emerged into a stone-flagged concourse. Running footsteps echoed about her. She dived behind the cover of a square rockcrete pillar as las-beams chipped at its corners. The rest of her squad was pinned down at the top of the stairs, and it looked like no others had found their way up here yet. 'In the name of the Emperor, lay down your weapons and step into the open!' she demanded.

'Spit on your Emperor!' a hoarse voice jeered back at her.

'Your Emperor and all the meat He ever spawned will submit to the Star Gods' majesty,' another hissed.

The cultists were taking advantage of the pillars too. Renick couldn't get a shot at any of them. Gunfire and screams drifted up from the level below. Her trigger finger itched. She voxed her comrades behind her. 'Give me covering fire on three, two, one…'

She dived for the pillar to her right. A renewed flurry of las-beams cracked above her head. She made it to her goal, short of breath but elated, and from her new vantage point saw a pair of lurking black-robed figures and shot them.

She also now had some idea of the remaining cultists' locations. 'I'd say there's roughly a dozen up here,' she voxed. 'Two less now.' *A frag grenade rolled along the concourse should smoke them out,* she thought. As her fingers closed around one, she saw something that froze her in horror.

A bundle of brown tape clung to the pillar by her head. She made out the outline of a smooth, round shape beneath it. *An explosive charge.* Now that she looked, she saw similar packages attached to the pillars around her. 'Stay back. They've mined this floor.' *And I've walked into another trap,* she thought. *At least this time I am alone.*

But hers was not the only life in peril. If this level collapsed, many of those fighting below would be crushed. There wasn't time to warn them. As soon as the cultists were sure they were facing defeat – and that could only be a matter of seconds away – they would trigger their bombs. Unless somebody stopped them; and only one woman could.

She switched her lasgun to full-auto. Her stomach bubbled up again, but a new cold resolve fortified her and she fought the feeling down. *My days were numbered, anyway.* She had been denying the truth to herself for long enough. *For why else would the Emperor send me here, but so that my death might mean something?*

One life, already ebbing away, for potentially hundreds of others...

She spoke into her comm-bead: 'Follow my lead.'

'Sergeant Renick?'

No. No more words, she thought.

Sergeant Renick swallowed hard. She took a breath. She broke cover. She ran full pelt towards the enemy, lasgun blazing as she swept it back and forth in an arc. The cultists were staggered by her sheer audacity. At least two fell before the others recovered their wits enough to strike back, and when they did, most of their shots went wild, as they expected her to try to dodge them.

Most of their shots; not all. A bullet dented her left pauldron, feeling like a punch to her shoulder. Another nicked her right forearm where it was unprotected, but adrenaline numbed her to the pain.

Her mind flashed back to the courtyard again, to a Krieg horseman charging a bike-riding ork. *Courageous,* she had said, while wondering if she really meant *reckless.* Was there such a difference in the end? *Fearless,* thought Renick, with hindsight. To have courage was to act in the face of fear – and was a Cadian trait in which they justly took pride – but the Krieg appeared to have no fear at all. She thought she understood that now; now she had nothing to lose, nothing that mattered. She felt she had nothing left to fear.

Ahead of her she saw a hunchbacked figure with a hooked nose and straggly hair, enrobed in black, of course. A leer froze on the cultist's lips and his rheumy eyes widened as he realised she wasn't going to fall, that she was going to reach him. Her eyes in turn were fixed upon his upraised hand, his fingers closed around a hammer-shaped device that had to be a detonator. A thumb with a long, gnarled nail curled towards the trigger button...

The old man felt like dry bones in a sack as Renick slammed

into him, her weight bearing him to the ground. Still, he fought as if possessed. *Perhaps he is…* She tried to keep him pinned down with her knees, gripping his skeletal wrist with both hands. She drove his knuckles into the rockcrete repeatedly until his fingers spasmed.

The detonator skittered away from him. She trampled over his scrawny, writhing body in her desperate effort to reach it. She caught the cultist's nose with her knee and felt it break. She threw herself on top of the detonator, protecting it. An instant later, two bodies landed on her back. She gasped as knife blades were plunged between her ribs. She tried to throw her attackers off her, but her strength was fading fast. It was up to her squad now – her new, untested squad, but they were Cadian and she knew they wouldn't fail her.

They had rushed up behind their distracted foes, slaying most of them in seconds. Two of the four troopers had fallen in the process. She didn't know if they were dead or only wounded. One of the cultists atop her was dragged away; the other slumped across her with a las-burn through her neck. Renick clutched the detonator to her stomach as her life's blood ebbed away, pooling dark red around her.

A trooper crouched beside her, voxing for medical assistance. She wanted to tell him, *'Tend to the others instead. I can't be saved.'* She couldn't move her mouth to form the words. She thought she might have felt afraid, but she felt proud. *My life must have been worth something,* she said to herself, *if I was allowed to exchange it for so many others.* For hadn't that been her life's purpose, after all?

The Krieg had it right all along, thought Sergeant Renick. *They saw it more clearly than any of the rest of us did. In life, war. In death, peace. In life, shame. In death…*

* * *

The Krieg colonel sat in his Aquila lander's command throne.

His pilot was performing his usual preflight checks. Any second now, he would be asked to brace himself for launch. In the meantime, for once, he was left alone with his thoughts. Those thoughts, as always, were his own, but it's likely that they drifted back to his most recent battle, on the plain to the east of Arathron.

The colonel's hand drifted to his greatcoat's inside pocket. He teased out a small obsidian box, wrapped in a purple ribbon. He untied the ribbon with an almost reverent gentleness. He eased back the box's lid. Inside it, nestled in a layer of purple velvet, were fragments of old, yellowed bone.

The colonel had acquired them on his first combat mission, back when he had been a rookie Korpsman. Back when he could never have imagined living this long, let alone rising to his present rank. They had been lodged beneath a duckboard in a stinking, muddy trench wreathed with poisonous green gas. He didn't know whose bones they had been, which made them ideal for his purpose.

A lot of his people carried such ossuaries with them. This could have been construed as a small gesture of defiance, or even as idolatry. At worst, someone could have called it blasphemy. At best, it signified that, even at the heart of their regimented civilisation, there remained a kernel of sentiment. As an officer, the colonel didn't believe he should encourage such a practice. As a man, he found comfort in it.

He closed the box, retied its ribbon. He held it to his heart, let it rise and fall with his chest as he breathed deeply. 'We do not forget,' the colonel muttered to himself.

The Krieg 43rd was also swiftly pressed back into service.

Another ship had crashed upon another Imperial world. Another infestation from the stars. This time it was an Eclipse cruiser of the aeldari, embroiling themselves in – and adding to – Octarius' woes for obscure reasons of their own.

The escort's last communication, intercepted by a listening post, had been garbled and brief. Some threat had been exposed aboard, likely tyranid in nature. It was not known if that threat had yet been neutralised.

The ship had come down in a barren, mountainous region, a thousand miles from the closest hive city. No distance at all to a tyranid swarm. Nothing had yet stirred within it, so far as could be discerned. The Krieg's orders were to surround the ship and destroy anything emerging from it whether tyranid, eldar or some unholy hybrid of the two.

It was a highly risky plan. The worst-case scenario was a tyranid swarm engorged upon a complement of potentially thousands of aeldari. No single Astra Militarum regiment could hope to withstand such a force. The Krieg, therefore, were not to approach the ship. They were not to 'poke the nest', as one lord general put it. It was hoped that a force of Raven Guard or Salamanders could be spared to assist them, if either could be disengaged from their own vital missions, deeper into the system… one day soon…

Death Korpsmen ringed the silent carcass of the aeldari cruiser. They thrust their entrenching tools into the cold, hard earth. It appeared to trouble none of them, whether new recruit or veteran, that the odds were stacked against them. They had been expected to fail before. If death was their ultimate goal, then what did it matter if it happened here or on the next battlefield, or on the one after that? As long as they died well and for a purpose; as long as they atoned.

It wasn't long before the silence broke.

Huge, winged, feculent horrors ran the gauntlet of the Krieg's Earthshakers, swooping upon their trenches. They slashed at their human prey with claws, tore at them with their teeth. Their putrid flesh rippled and reshaped itself into every imaginable type of weapon. Extruded bio-cannons spat out parasitic organisms that burrowed through flak armour and consumed their victims from the inside out. The air became thick with excreted, choking spores, but this hazard impeded the masked Korspmen not in the slightest.

They met their attackers, the sworn foes of their Emperor, with the full strength of their arms, every weapon in their arsenal and to the last breaths in their bodies. Never once did they hesitate, nor question their manifest duty, and many members of the Death Korps of Krieg died noble deaths that day.

But more, many more of them, lived.

'Now you know the whole story.'

Ven Bruin sat back in his throne. He pushed back the brim of his black capotain hat and massaged his tired eyes. On the table before him, the eye of a pict-recorder glowed, the only witness to the inquisitor's confession.

He would leave the recording with his personal effects. Upon his death and not before, his acolytes would ensure that it reached the right people in the Ordo Hereticus. *Not much longer now...* He had not felt strong in many years.

He had lost count of the evenings he had sat here, transfixed by that light, searching for the words to express his most deeply buried thoughts. The words, the right words, were important. He hadn't found them yet.

'I saved a world,' he said aloud.

'*We* saved a world,' he corrected himself, 'for I lacked the strength to make that decision alone. All the same, a world was saved. A world that, though not without its problems – as has every other world – continues to thrive in the service of the Emperor.

'And many would say I forfeited my soul in the process...

'But was it not a price worth paying? Though the loss of one soul may indeed be cause for grief, might it not be outweighed by the billions – in due time, the billions upon billions – potentially saved? By the good and faithful deeds of the many who would otherwise have died or never have been born?

'And in time might that single soul not even be redeemed?'

Ven Bruin leaned forward, staring earnestly into the light. 'I put that question to you, for the Emperor knows I have pondered it long enough myself. A question, I believe, that cuts to the heart of who we are and what we believe. A question embodied by none more than the famed Death Korps of Krieg.

'Many years ago, a man of Krieg – a faithful and dutiful man – faced a similar dilemma to my own. He was braver than I, for his sacrifice was greater and yet he made his choice alone, and to this day his name is revered by his descendants. The Krieg follow Colonel Jurten's example in all things. When faced with the same choice he had made...'

He drew in a deep breath, held it captive for a while, then let it go.

'In how many battles, on how many worlds, have the Death Korps been engaged?' he mused. 'How many heretics, mutants and xenos have they slain? How many people live in the Emperor's light today because of them? The Krieg seek atonement, but for what? For the sins of their ancestors, they say. For the Chairman and his council and those misguided apostates led astray by them. But what of their hero, their saviour? What of Jurten? And what, for that matter, of themselves?'

Ven Bruin took a longer pause there. He poured himself a glass of amasec, took a fortifying gulp from it. He had waited so long before speaking of any of this. *Perhaps too long.* The only man who knew his secret, the Krieg colonel who had facilitated his mission into Arathron, had been killed in action three months later. He had been replaced by four more since, or was it more? It was hard to tell one from another.

He shifted his position in his seat. 'I have served with the Krieg, lived with them, thirteen years, and still I feel I hardly know them. I have never heard one talk about his... origins. I expect you know as much about the subject as I do, which is no more than noted by Inquisitor Larreth a millennium ago. A long time ago, to be sure...'

Interrogator Ferran's face appeared to his mind's eye, furrowed in its habitual frown. Ven Bruin had trained him, nurtured him, but failed to make him understand.

'And perhaps it is time to revisit the matter,' he conceded. 'It may be past time. That is your prerogative, of course – and perhaps, when presented with fresh information, the High Lords' conclusion may be somewhat different this time. But I ask you, urge you to consider, what would be gained from such an inquisition?

'At best the Krieg would accept your judgement upon them, that you know the Emperor's will better than their saviour did, and they'd march to the gallows willingly. At worst, you would ignite a war that may last generations. In either case, a priceless resource would be lost to us. When it often seems as if our foes will always outnumber us, replenishing their forces more quickly than we had imagined possible, then...'

He chose not to follow that train of thought.

'Consider this instead,' Ven Bruin suggested. 'That the Krieg are well aware of their world's... shall we say, unconventional practices, and it is one more source of shame to them. It is part of the reason why they place so little value on their lives. They consider their unworthy souls a fair exchange for the salvation of so many others. The Krieg, one might say, take our sins upon themselves…' He thought of a lone masked soldier, standing stiffly in the centre of a subterranean chamber. '…so the rest of us, if we are very fortunate, if the Emperor wills it, may keep our hands clean.

'My conclusion is the same as that reached by Inquisitor Larreth. Though centuries have passed since her investigation, I believe that nothing much has changed. I believe – though it goes against everything I once knew, everything our ordo stands for – that some secrets should be kept from even our eyes.

'Colonel Jurten was a soldier of the Emperor. His faith was what defined him. And he fashioned his people in his image. The Death Korps of Krieg is what the Imperium itself created. One might say they are its inevitable product, and its purest manifestation. And we need them. There are questions, therefore, that should never be asked of them, answers we should never hear – lest they reveal something we don't wish to see about ourselves.

'I have come to believe that our entire philosophy hangs by that slender thread.'

Ven Bruin couldn't sleep.

The pict-recorder lurked on the table outside his bedchamber. The words he had spoken into it, the words that would comprise his legacy, whirled about his mind. Tomorrow, he would likely erase them and begin afresh. He always did.

He found himself throwing back his sheets, swinging his bare feet onto the cold floor, walking out into the adjoining room. Reaching for the device. At first he thought he would watch his own report back, perhaps take notes on how it might be improved.

Instead, he opened the back of the recorder and prised out its memory crystal.

He slotted another into place, a copy of a recording held in his ordo's deepest vault. *A partial copy...* He traced the runes on the recorder's control panel, and light flared from its innards again. This time it coalesced into the shape of a tall, stern-looking, white-haired woman. She was clad in ancient power armour, embossed with purity seals.

Although she wasn't really there, just a translucent image, still he felt Inquisitor Larreth's judging glare across the gulf of centuries.

He caressed the control runes again. The image of Larreth jumped and flickered as he searched for a quote from her to give him inspiration. He wanted to hear about her visit to Krieg again, but he knew that section of her report was the most heavily censored. He settled upon her account of her first meeting with Krieg's people.

'*The planet was dead,*' the image of Larreth intoned. '*Every reading confirmed it. How could it be, then, that a ship had just–*'

Ven Bruin skipped forward.

'*–detected no deformities in the Krieg men's postures. Still, something about them–*' Skip. '*–graver reason to hide their faces from us. Might they have been afraid, I suggested, that we would–*' Skip.

'*"What is your name?" I asked him.*' He allowed the recording to run on.

'*The Krieg colonel cocked his head a little. He looked as if he didn't understand the question. That only made me more determined that, this time, I would brook no evasion from him. I fixed him with a glare. I hoped my eyes would make an impression upon him, though I could not see into his. And finally, he gave me his answer – with hindsight, perhaps the only answer I ought to have expected.*

'*"My name," the Krieg colonel told me slowly, as if he had only just worked it out himself, "is Jurten."*'

949.M40

THE RISE

The planet wasn't dead. Not quite. Not yet.

It just happened that it had been cremated. And buried.

Its pockmarked surface was dusted grey with ash. It was littered with barbed wire coils, spent casings and the corroded carcasses of once proud tanks and weapons platforms. The detritus of centuries of strife. The ash also swirled around dry bones, stripped of their clothing, left to rot where they had fallen.

The sky was as grey as the land. The skeletons of hive cities jutted from every horizon, ashes drifting round their crumbled spires too. The only sources of water were black and frozen solid. Krieg was held in the pitiless grip of a winter that had lasted half a millennium and showed no sign of abating. A nuclear winter. And yet...

And yet, from somewhere upon that blasted wasteland, there came a defiant, booming sound. A percussion beat of guns. They battered at the walls of one of the broken hives. They kept up their onslaught for several minutes, while the echoes of their thunder took several more to die down.

In the meantime, there was a stirring in the trenches that criss-crossed the grey planet like old, knotted scars. Hundreds of small, dark, faceless figures came bubbling up out of their dugouts. They spread out, clutching weapons to their chests, as they advanced at speed in almost supernatural silence. Behind the city walls, barely glimpsed figures shifted, and a hail of gunfire met the faceless soldiers. Though scores of them were cut down in seconds, the rest ploughed on through the storm.

They poured through gaps in the walls. They wrenched the defending gunners away from their cannons and set about them with guns and knives. Reinforcements were hiding in the ruined outskirts, however, waiting to spring an ambush. They moved to outflank their attackers, and a melee ensued in which both sides fought with savage precision. Neither gave the other any quarter – though both wore the same uniform of dark fatigues, heavy greatcoats, spiked helmets and dark-eyed rebreather masks.

The skirmish ended suddenly, on some imperceptible cue. Attackers and defenders stepped away from each other and lowered their weapons. The fallen but still living on both sides were given medical assistance, some by the very soldiers that had inflicted their wounds upon them. The dead were relieved of any reusable equipment.

A small group of older men with braided shoulders emerged from the trenches and must have issued more imperceptible orders, because both factions of Korpsmen formed up in front of the hive together, standing stiffly to attention.

An officer addressed them, giving feedback on their efforts. They could have been stronger, faster, more resilient, he told them. They could have tried harder. Overall, though, they had performed within expectations; and although some had died, the important thing was that none of them had broken. They had passed the test.

As the officer spoke, there came an unexpected distraction. He heard a screaming engine behind him and turned to see the grey sky split by a blazing contrail. His eyes lingered on it, never having seen such a sight before. Nor had the Krieg Korpsmen – few of whom had seen the sky at all before today – but they knew better than to raise their heads to look.

'We are privileged today,' the officer told them, 'to witness the writing of a fresh page in our history. The God-Emperor of Mankind has heard our humble plea and despatched His servants to inspect all we have built here. That shuttle is taking our commanding officer to greet them. Should we pass this test, should we be judged worthy, then you will be among the first soldiers in five hundred years – over fifty generations – to fly from this benighted world, to fight and to die in His service.'

If the Korpsmen were heartened by that prospect, if they dreaded it, it didn't show. It must have been a peculiar notion for them, having spent their short lives so far under artificial light. Still, one environment was likely little different from another to those so insulated from it; and, after all, they had been bred to serve a single purpose, and there were no enemies left here for them to subdue.

'The traitors are finally vanquished, the Emperor be praised.'

Krieg's civil war had ended four months ago, when the last traitors holding out beneath Hive Auros had been cremated in their bunker.

'We have excised their cancer from Krieg's heart. That is only the beginning.'

The vox-hailer voice had provided the soundtrack of their lives. Its words forever echoed in their ears. They knew it better than they knew their own mothers' voices, if they remembered those at all. The voice was reputed to belong to Colonel Jurten himself, addressing them across the ages. Having given Krieg a future, he had pre-recorded speeches for all the days he had known were yet to come.

'Krieg is saved,' these Korpsmen had repeatedly been told, 'but now it is time to look beyond our skies again. There are other worlds out there in the grips of the heretic, the mutant, the xenos scum, and each must face a purging of its own.

'There are also worlds – there must also be worlds – still resisting that corruption, holding the line against it. Worlds that have taken up arms in the Emperor's name. They have probably forgotten that Krieg once fought alongside them. If they recall our name at all, it is likely as one tainted by weakness and failure.

'The time has come to change that, for Krieg to fight for the Emperor once more. We have already won a great victory for Him – in a war that the finest of His generals considered unwinnable. We have shown that with toil and faith and sacrifice, anything can be achieved. Now, we shall take that message to the rest of the galaxy. The time has come to make up for our lost years, for the actions of our treacherous brethren.

'We have won the battle for our world,' was the message that the voice returned to more than any other and these Korpsmen had never thought to question it, venerating the speaker above all others but for one. 'Now, we fight for our very souls.'

The shuttle had flown out of sight, swallowed by the grey smoke clouds.

'We'll run the combat exercise again,' the senior officer decreed, 'this time with the roles of the two factions reversed. Then, should our Imperial visitors look down on us from their mighty voidships, should their augurs reach this far, they will see an army of disciplined, committed warriors. They'll see that we are ready.'

The Korpsmen fell out, their boot heels stamping up ash clouds in perfect unison.

Half returned to the outskirts of the hive, while the others tramped back to the trenches. They checked their weapons, from the grand but ancient heavy cannons in their emplacements to the lasguns that had only recently rolled off the factory lines but were already scuffed and dull with use. They loaded shells and slapped new power packs into their breeches. They checked the readings on their rebreather units and ensured that their hoses were tightly secured. And they waited.

They waited for an order from their officers, who had returned to their dugouts behind the lines. It came, as had the last one, over a short-range vox-channel, and barely had the words been spoken when the Death Korps of Krieg sprang into action.

The Earthshaker cannons boomed again, though there was little of the hive walls left to chip away at. They targeted their fire at the barking guns behind them and, within minutes, at short range, had knocked half of them out. Then came the second order – to advance – and, once again, masked soldiers teemed across the wasteland.

Again there was fighting in the ruins, and again, many of the combatants were slain.

'Some of you will die more quickly than others,' their guiding voice had told them. *'Some will never set eyes upon the enemy. This is not a matter for regret. None of you – none of us – will live to see our final victory, but every life expended makes us stronger. Each sacrifice counts. Our lives are worth no more than the Emperor chooses to make of them.*

'In life, we all have much to be ashamed of. Atonement is achievable through death.'

And so they fought.

They fought for all they were worth, as their leaders had instructed, as they always had and always would, for what else would they do? They fought because they believed they had nothing to lose. They had nothing to live for and everything to die for. They fought – and the sounds of their pitched battle rang out across the grey wastes of their ravaged, irradiated world, for no one else to hear.

A world that had not known peace in five hundred years and never would again.

A world whose very name meant *war*.

ABOUT THE AUTHOR

Steve Lyons' work in the Warhammer 40,000 universe includes the novellas *Iron Resolve*, *Engines of War* and *Angron's Monolith*, the Imperial Guard novels *Death World*, *Ice Guard* and *Dead Men Walking*, and the audio dramas *Waiting Death* and *The Madness Within*. He has also written numerous short stories and is currently working on more tales from the grim darkness of the far future.

YOUR
NEXT READ

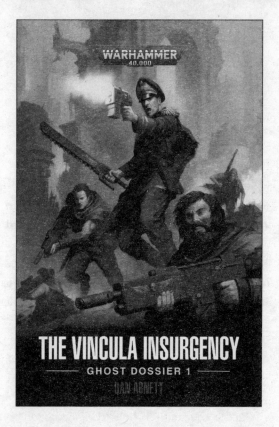

THE VINCULA INSURGENCY: GHOST DOSSIER 1
by Dan Abnett

Ibram Gaunt and the freshly formed Ghosts of Tanith find themselves attempting to establish permanent peace in the ruined border town of Vincula. But something stalks them through the shadowed streets, threatening to test the newly founded regiment.

An Extract from
The Vincula Insurgency
by Dan Abnett

The question isn't how he died. A close-focus anti-personnel mine, Militarum issue, had been rigged under the seat, arming via a pressure pad when he sat down. And then he got up to leave.

The question isn't who killed him. Insurgents have been targeting Imperial infrastructure and staff for nine weeks.

The question is, how did they get in?

Ibram Gaunt stands at the window and looks down. The street, Clavis Street, a main thoroughfare, is twelve storeys below. There is no ledge, no hand-hold, no toe-hold. Nests of razor wire clump every buttress, at every floor, around upturned crowns of spikes.

It's hot. The city smells of hot plastek and burning fuel. There's a breeze from the east that brings the noise of traffic and worship-horns, but it's as dry as leather.

Gaunt stands a moment longer, hands behind his back. He makes like he's observing, but he's seen all he needs to see. An unscaleable wall. An absence of answers. But he stands, gets some air on his face, dry as it is. Gets it in his lungs, imagines it's borne from some cooler place in the hills, not sandpapered by heat and smoke.

There's an awful, hacking gurgle coming from the room at his back. Shrapnel, maybe spalled casing from the device, maybe bone shards from the victim, has punctured the room's climate system. Pipes have ruptured. It's still running, but it's drowning in its own coolant. Blue fluid drools down the wall from the grille. The air gusting from the vents is no longer cold, and it stinks of ammonia. He wants to turn it off, because it sounds like a wet death rattle, but he knows how unbearable it's going to get without the unit.

One moment longer with the open air, at a window stripped of glass by overpressure.

'Do we have a name?' he asks.

'Talaxin,' someone says. 'Intendant, third grade. Payroll and, uhm–'

Someone checks their notes.

Gaunt turns. The office is generally the way this Talaxin must have seen it when he arrived that afternoon. Shelves, files, two charts pinned up. The front of the desk is marvellously intact, but it has no back, and there's no chair.

'Payroll?' Gaunt says.

The Administratum aide, whose name Gaunt has not been told, is still checking his data-slate.

'Payroll and provisioning,' the aide replies. 'Materiel requisition, answering to Intendant Fallastrine and Provision-slash-Audit.'

Gaunt nods, as though this means something. Militarum and Administratum speak different languages.

'Security check on all other offices,' Gaunt says.

'That's been instructed, sir,' says the aide.

'But is it being done?' Gaunt asks.

The aide's data-slate doesn't tell him that, so he nods and steps out to check. The office air is filmed with motionless smoke. There's a halo of cooked blood, black as baked treacle, coating the remains of the desk, across the floor, up the walls and the bookcases, across the ceiling. A few ceiling tiles, scorched, have started to dip. Gaunt looks at the Tanith corpsman at the door. Chayker has brought a body bag. There's nothing to put in it.

Gaunt takes another look out of the window. Twilight's falling. Far below, an impossible climb below, he can see figures on the street, lit by the headlamps of Militarum trucks and carriers.

The climate unit chugs, splutters and dies, aspirating its own coolant. The sudden lack of noise is oppressive. Nothing remains except the muted wash of city noise, and the hum of the flies. Breathless heat comes instantly. Gaunt feels the sweat break on his back before he's even out of the room.

Trooper Raglon follows him down the stairs.

'That's what? Six?' Gaunt asks.

'Eight, sir,' Raglon replies, consulting his slate. It's not a slim steel tablet like the aide's. It's Militarum issue, sturdy, with a vulcanised cover for field-wear. It's slow, perhaps defective. Or perhaps Raglon is. He hasn't got the hang of it yet.

'I thought it was six,' says Gaunt. They're taking the stairs because the building's elevators have been locked down during the sweep. Red emergency lighting has come up, thanks to tumblers shaken by the blast. Raglon's trying to walk and work.

'Six in the last twelve days,' says Gaunt.

'Oh, yes,' says Raglon. 'Yes, six, in that period. Two others, but at the back end of last month.'

Gaunt pauses, turns, takes the slate from Raglon. He taps the surface quickly, closing data blocks.

'Clear the sub-panels,' he says. He's been using slates since the start of his career. 'See? This and this? They auto-archive and you can recall them with that icon. If you clear them, there's more cogitation power available for the work at hand.' He hands it back.

'Thank you, sir,' says Raglon. He hadn't noticed the icon. No one's even told him about the icon. The colonel-commissar's had him working as adjutant for three weeks, since Kosdorf. Raglon hopes it's not going to last. He's a vox-trooper. He's got the patch for it on his sleeve. He did basic on casters and comm-ops, not this kind of duty.

It should have been Cluggan.

'So, six,' says Gaunt. He starts walking again, taking the stairs at a pace. 'Eight total. That's since securement. All minor, low-tier Administratum.'

'Yes, sir,' says Raglon. 'Except one. One was a local tithe collector seconded to the occupation council.' Raglon remembers that. He doesn't have time to check it. But he's pretty sure.

'Litus B.R.U. had security responsibility for this building,' says Gaunt. More a statement than a question.

'Yes, sir. Do you want to revise that?'

'I want to talk to their C.O., certainly. I want the sentries quizzed. I want a review of procedure, and a look at any security feed. Set me up with a meeting, their C.O.'

Raglon pauses, concentrating on the slate.

Gaunt stops, and looks back at him. 'You can schedule it via the Militarum message annex,' he says.

'Yep,' says Raglon, opening a sub-panel in error.

Gaunt bristles very slightly.

'I'll just send a runner, Rafflan,' he says, and starts walking again.

'Raglon, sir,' says Raglon.

'What?'

'It's Raglon, sir.'

Gaunt thinks about it, nods.

'Right,' he says. He's generally good with names. Raglon, Rafflan. Both vox-troopers. Easily done.

Raglon hesitates for a second, then follows. It's not the first time. It's as if they all look alike. All Tanith. All lasmen, interchangeable. Gaunt remembers Cluggan well enough, because he mentions him from time to time, but that's no good to anyone because Cluggan died at Voltis. It's a name Gaunt should erase. More cogitation power available for the work at hand. Feels like they've got to be dead before they're remembered.